DON'T CRY,
TAI LAKE

DON'T CRY, TAI LAKE

QIU XIAOLONG

MINOTAUR BOOKS ❧ NEW YORK

DON'T CRY, TAI LAKE. Copyright © 2012 by Qiu Xiaolong. All rights reserved. Printed in the United States of America. For information, address St. Martin's Press, 175 Fifth Avenue, New York, N.Y. 10010.

www.minotaurbooks.com

Library of Congress Cataloging-in-Publication Data

Qiu, Xiaolong, 1953–
    Don't cry, Tai Lake : an Inspector Chen novel / Qiu Xiaolong.—1st ed.
        p. cm.
    ISBN 978-0-312-55064-6 (hardcover)
    ISBN 978-1-4299-7354-0 (e-book)
    1. Chen, Inspector (Fictitious character)—Fiction.   2. Police—China—Shanghai—Fiction.   3. Shanghai (China)—Fiction.   I. Title.
    PS3553.H537D66 2012
    813'.6—dc23

                                                                    2012005486

First Edition: May 2012

10 9 8 7 6 5 4 3 2 1

For the polluted lakes and rivers in China

ACKNOWLEDGMENTS

IN 1988, I FINISHED a Chinese poem, "Don't Cry, Jade River," as the title piece of a collection that was to come out the following year. In 1989, I reviewed the galley in the United States, but what happened in Beijing that tragic summer made the publication in China impossible, including an introduction written by my friend Xu Guoliang, to whom I want to express my thanks and apologies again. The galley, after twenty years, finally made its way into the English poem in *Don't Cry, Tai Lake,* except for the former being fictional, and the latter, real and far more disastrous.

As always, I want to thank my editor, Keith Kahla, for his extraordinary work, and I also want to thank my copy editor, Margit Longbrake, who gave birth to her daughter, Jane Ray Longbrake McKeown, just upon starting her copyediting work, which she completed beautifully in *yuezi* (the first month of motherhood).

DON'T CRY,
TAI LAKE

ONE

CHIEF INSPECTOR CHEN CAO of the Shanghai Police Bureau found himself standing in front of the gate to the Wuxi Cadre Recreation Center.

His vacation in the city of Wuxi was totally unexpected. Earlier that Sunday morning, Chen was in Zhenjiang, attending an intensive political seminar for emerging Party officials training for "new responsibilities," when he got a phone call from Comrade Secretary Zhao, the former second secretary of the Central Party Discipline Committee. Though retired, Zhao remained one of the most influential figures in Beijing. Zhao was too busy to take a vacation arranged for him at the center in Wuxi, so he offered it to Chen instead.

Chen was in no position to decline such a well-meant offer, coming from the Forbidden City. So he immediately left the seminar at the Zhenjiang Party School, took a long-distance bus to Wuxi station, and then a taxi to the center.

He had heard a lot about the center, which was located in a scenic area of the city. It was something like a combination of a resort and a sanatorium, known for its special service to high-ranking cadres. There were strict regulations about the Party cadre rank required for admission, and Chen was nowhere close to that rank. Chen knew an exception was being made because of Zhao. Qiao Liangxing, the director of the center, was not around when Chen arrived. A front desk receptionist greeted Chen and led him to a white European-style villa, with tall marble columns in front, enclosed by an iron fence with gilded spikes and a shining stainless-steel gate. The villa stood alone on a tree-shaded hill, separate from other buildings. The receptionist showed Chen all due respect, as if the villa being allocated to him determined his status rather than the other way round. Without any other specific instructions from Qiao, however, all she could do was check Chen in with a detailed introduction to the center and its location: Yuantouzhu, or Turtle Head Park.

"Our center gets its name from a huge rock projecting over the Tai Lake, like a turtle tossing its head above the water. The park was founded in 1918 and covers an area of five hundred hectares. It is a scenic peninsula on the northwest shore of the lake, surrounded by green hills and clear water; it is considered the best resort area in Wuxi. As for the center, at the south end of the peninsula, it was built in the early fifties for high-ranking cadres."

While listening to her introduction, Chen reflected on the way China took for granted the assumption that the Communist Party cadres, having conquered the country, deserved to enjoy all sorts of luxurious treatment.

"Last but not the least, people staying here can easily walk into the park, but the tourists in the park may only look at the center through the gate. So enjoy your vacation here," the receptionist concluded, smiling, leaving the key as well as a park pass on a mahogany table in the hall before she left, closing the door carefully after her.

Chen moved to the front window. Looking out, he saw part of a curving driveway lined with shrubs and evergreen, and then further down the wooded hill, another driveway for someone else's villa. To the other side, there were rows of multistory buildings, with identically shaped balconies aligned like matchboxes, as those in a large new hotel. He didn't have a panoramic view of the center, but his villa was undoubtedly one reserved for top Party cadres.

It was a nice, large building consisting of nine rooms in all. He had no idea what to do with all those rooms as he walked upstairs and downstairs, examining one after another. He finally put his small suitcase in the master bedroom on the first floor, which commanded a fantastic lake view. Adjacent to the bedroom was a spacious living room, featuring a marble fireplace with a copper screen in an exquisite pattern, a black leather sectional sofa, and an LCD TV. One side of the room was a wall of tall windows overlooking Tai Lake.

Also on the first floor was a study with custom-made book shelves, some books, and a desk with a brand new laptop on it. The windows in the study were large, but looked out on the driveway and the hill beyond it.

Chen went back to the living room and started to pace about, stepping on and off an apricot Persian rug. His footsteps echoed through the entire building. Finally he decided to take a bath. He grabbed a cup and a bottle of Perrier from a silver tray on a corner table and settled himself in the master bathroom, which also had a scenic view.

Soaking in the tub, he had the luxurious feeling of becoming one with the lake, as he watched the tiny bubbles rising in his glass of Perrier.

Outside, a rock frog was croaking intermittently, and there was the murmur of an unseen cascade. Looking out, Chen discovered that the lambent melody was actually coming from a tiny speaker hidden in a rock under the window.

Of late, Chen often felt worn out. With one "special case" after another on his hands, he hadn't been able to take a break for months. A vacation could at least take his mind temporarily off his responsibilities and obligations.

Besides, there was nothing really important being handled by his Special Case Squad at the moment, and if something should come up, Wuxi was only an hour's trip from Shanghai by train. If need be, he could easily hurry back. In the meantime, though, his longtime partner, Detective Yu Guangming, should be able to take care of things there.

But it didn't take long before the chief inspector felt a slight suggestion—as if it was rising up from the still water in the tub—of loneliness, which was only magnified by the enormous size of the empty building.

The bubbles in the French water were gone, so he got out of the tub, put on his clothes, stuffed the paperback he brought with him into his pants pocket, and went out for a walk.

The center was connected, as the receptionist had said, to the park by a back entrance. Through the fence he saw tourists pointing and posing with cameras. He was not keen on becoming a tourist just yet, so he headed in the other direction, along a quiet, small road.

He had probably come in along the same route earlier, but sitting in the back of a taxi, he hadn't been able to see much. There wasn't anyone in the area, with the exception of an occasional car driving by at high speed. The road was fairly narrow. On one side, there was a wire fence stretching along like a wall, and a bushy, unkempt slope beyond it that stretched over to a wider road in the distance. On the other side, hills were rolling and rising upward here and there, interspersed with tourist attraction signs.

Ahead the road merged into a tiny square with bus stop shelters, a tea stall with bowls spread out on a makeshift table with a couple of benches, and a pavilionlike kiosk with a roof that was held up by vermillion posts, which sold all sorts of souvenirs. A group of people were getting off a gray bus, most of them carrying maps in their hands. The square couldn't be far from the park.

He felt anonymous, yet contentedly so. He strolled about, taking out his own tourist map of Wuxi, which he had bought earlier at the bus station.

He hadn't visited Wuxi for years. As a child, he and his parents had taken a day trip, riding from one tourist stop to another. Cutting across the square, he noted that it appeared quite different from what he remembered.

He was soon lost, in spite of the map. Like Shanghai, Wuxi had been changing dramatically in recent years. There were quite a few new street names that were unavailable or unrecognizable from his outdated map.

But he wasn't worried. If he couldn't find his way back, he could always hail a taxi. He liked walking—even more so as he slipped into the role of a tourist, a sort of different identity. Perhaps he was still not over having been pushed into becoming a cop when he graduated college years ago.

After passing a street corner convenience store with a twenty-four-hour-business sign, he ventured into a side street, and then into another one—a shabbier, somber, cobble-covered, and yet quaint one—which was almost deserted. This street seemed to fit into his memory of the city. Toward the end of it, he slowed down at the sight of a dilapidated eatery. It had a red wooden door and white walls, with a couple of rough tables and benches outside and several more inside, and an orange paper pinwheel spinning in the rustic window. Outside, there was a colorful row of wooden and plastic basins with fish swimming in some and rice paddy eels in others. Eels were usually placed in a basin without water, Chen reflected.

Perhaps because it was past lunchtime, or perhaps because of the location, Chen was the only one lingering there, except for a white cat with a black patch on its forehead, dozing by the worn-out threshold.

Chen decided to sit at a table outside, with a bamboo container holding a bunch of disposable chopsticks like flowers. It was a warm day for May, and he had walked quite a distance. Wiping the sweat from his forehead, he was grateful for a fresh breeze coming fitfully along the street.

An old man came shuffling out of the kitchen in the rear, carrying a dog-eared menu. Most likely he was the owner, chef, and waiter here.

"Anything particular you would like, sir?"

"Just a couple of small dishes—any local specialties, I mean," he said, not really hungry. "And a beer."

"Three whites are the local specialties," the old man said. "The white water fish may be too large for one person. And I wouldn't recommend the white shrimp—it's not that fresh today."

Chen remembered, from his Wuxi trip with his parents, his father raving about the "three whites"—white shrimp and white water fish were two of them, but he couldn't recall what the third white was. Another local specialty he liked was the Wuxi soup buns, sweet with a lot of minced ginger. At the end of that long-ago trip, his mother carried home a bamboo basket of soup buns. He still remembered that, but couldn't recall the third "white." Perhaps he really was a "helpless gourmet," as his friends called him, he thought with a touch of self-irony.

"Whatever you recommend, then."

"How about Wuxi ribs and sliced lotus roots filled with sticky rice?"

"Great."

"And a local beer—Tai Lake Beer?"

"Fine," Chen said. The lake was known for its clear water, which could mean a superior beer.

It took the old man only a minute to return to the table with a bottle of beer and a tiny dish of salted peanuts.

"The appetizer is on the house. Enjoy. So, are you a tourist here?"

Chen raised the map in his hand, nodding.

"Staying at Kailun?"

Kailun might be a hotel nearby, but Chen didn't know anything about it. "No, at the Wuxi Cadre Recreation Center. Not far from here."

"Oh," the old man said, turning back toward the kitchen. "You're a young man for that place."

The old man was understandably surprised: the center was only for high-ranking cadres, most of whom were old, while Chen looked only thirtyish.

Though the vacation had come as a surprise to Chen himself, he didn't say anything in response, but simply took out his book and put it on the table. Instead of reading it, however, he started sipping his beer.

Life could be more absurd than fiction. In college, he had majored in English, but upon graduation he was state-assigned to a job in the Shanghai Police Bureau, where, to the puzzlement of others as well as himself, he had been rising steadily through the ranks. At the Zhenjiang Party School, some predicted that Chen had a most promising official career ahead of him, that he was capable of moving much further than his current job as chief inspector.

But here, he was quite content to be a nameless tourist on vacation, with a bottle of beer and a mystery novel. Su Shi, one of his favorite Song dynasty poets, had once declared it regrettable to "have no self to claim," but at the moment, at least, Chen did not find it so.

The old man was bringing the dishes Chen had ordered.

"Thank you," Chen said, looking up. "How is business?"

"Not too good. People are telling stories, but it's really the same everywhere."

What stories? Chen wondered. Presumably about the poor quality of the food. That wasn't uncommon for a tourist city, where customers seldom go to a restaurant a second time, stories or not. But the ribs were delicious, done nicely with plenty of mixed sauce, rich in color and taste. The sliced lotus root, too, proved to be crisp, fresh, yet surprisingly compatible with the sweet sticky rice filling.

It was a rare privilege to be the only customer in a place, he thought, crunching another slice of the pinkish lotus root. Soon, he had a second beer, without having opened the book yet, and his mind began wandering.

So many days, where have you been—/like a traveling cloud/that forgets to come back/unaware of the spring drawing to an end?

Shaking his head, he pulled himself out of the unexpected wave of self-pity, and took out his cell phone. He dialed Detective Yu back in Shanghai.

"Sorry, Yu, that I didn't come back to Shanghai before leaving on vacation. Zhengjiang was simply closer to Wuxi."

7

"Don't worry about it, Chief. There are nothing but small cases here, and none of them special, either. There's nothing for our Special Case Squad."

"Was there any reaction to my extended absence in the bureau?"

"With your vacation having been arranged by Comrade Secretary Zhao, what could Party Secretary Li say?"

Party Secretary Li had become increasingly wary of Chen, whom he was beginning to see as a threat to Li's position as the top Party official in the bureau. Li was headed to retirement, but—if things worked out his way—not that soon.

"Keep me posted, Yu. Call me anytime you like. I don't think there is anything for me to do here."

"Are you so sure?"

Chen knew the reason for his partner's skepticism. Chen had had vacations before—unplanned, unexplained vacations—that turned out to be nothing more than a pretext for an investigation. What's more, Chen had once investigated a highly sensitive case under Zhao's supervision.

"Zhao didn't mention anything to me," Chen said. "Remember the anticorruption case? He promised me a vacation then, and I think that's what this is about."

"That's good, boss. Enjoy your vacation. I won't bother you unless it's an emergency," Yu said, then added, "Oh, you know what? You have a fan in Wuxi. I met a recent graduate from the Police Academy in a meeting two or three months ago. Sergeant Huang Kang. He bugged me for stories about you."

"Really!"

"He'll never forgive me if I don't tell him that you are vacationing in Wuxi."

"Let me enjoy myself in peace for a couple of days first. Once Huang knows, he, as well as others, may come over, bringing with them cases they want to discuss. My vacation would become anything but a quiet one," Chen said. "But what's his number? I'll call him later, and say that you insisted on it."

Chen copied the number into his notebook. There was no hurry. He would wait until a day or two before the end of his vacation to call.

Chen put away his cell phone and turned his attention to the book he'd brought with him. It was a novel with an interesting title: *An Unsuitable Job for a Woman,* and a Guangxi publisher had been pushing him to translate it. Mysteries had begun to sell well, and the contract they were offering for the translation wasn't bad. However, in comparison to the occasional business translations that he did for his Big Buck businessmen acquaintances, it was nothing.

Chen had read only two or three pages when he noticed someone approaching the eatery. Looking up, he glimpsed a young, slender woman, who glanced in his direction, dipping her head like a shy lotus flower in a cool breeze.

She appeared to be in her mid-twenties. She was wearing a black fitted blazer, a white blouse, jeans, and black pumps, and she carried a satchel slung over her shoulder. She moved to the other outside table. She had a bottle of water in her hand, ignoring the proprietor's sign objecting to customers bringing in their own drinks. Instead of calling for a menu, she shouted, "I'm here, Uncle Wang."

"One minute," the old man said, sticking his head out. "Do you have to work this weekend, Shanshan?"

"I'm just checking a new test at the office, but it's getting more complicated. Don't worry. At most it will be a couple of hours in the afternoon."

Apparently she was no stranger here. The old man, surnamed Wang, was probably not a relative, or she would not have prefixed Wang with Uncle.

The old man shuffled out with a steaming plastic container, which must have been microwave-warmed. She had probably left her lunch here earlier in the day, and it might have been a common arrangement. In the course of the economic reform, state-run companies had been shutting down their employee canteens as a money-losing business practice. So she probably had to find a way of eating somewhere else.

She opened the plastic container and inside, on top of white rice, lay an omelet with lots of chopped green onion. She pulled a pair of bamboo chopsticks out of her satchel.

"The green onion is fresh from my own garden," Uncle Wang said with a toothless grin. "I picked it this morning. Totally organic."

Organic—an interesting word to say here, Chen thought as he sipped his beer in silence.

"That's so thoughtful of you, Uncle Wang."

Uncle Wang went back into the kitchen. The two of them were left alone.

She started eating in a leisurely manner, adding a small spoon of hot sauce to the rice. She pulled a crumpled newspaper out of her jean pocket and began reading. A frown started to form in her delicate eyebrows. Chen caught himself studying her with interest.

She was attractive, her oval face framed by long black hair and animated with a youthful glow. Her mouth subtly curved under her delicate nose, and there was a wistful look in her clear, large eyes.

The characters printed on the satchel said: Wuxi Number One Chemical Company. Perhaps she worked there.

Occasionally, Chen liked to consider himself a detached aesthetic, like the persona in those lines by Bian Zhilin: *You are looking at the scene,/and the scene watcher is looking at you.* It was an ingenious way to describe one's scene-eclipsing beauty. Bian was a contemporary poet he had studied in college, but was something of a Prufrock in real life. Chen considered himself different from that. Still, there was nothing improper, he reassured himself, in a poet watching in detachment. Not to mention that, as a detective, he was in a natural position to observe.

Chen laughed at himself. A worn-out cop on his first day of vacation couldn't automatically switch back into being a vigorous poet.

He was in no hurry to leave. Having finished the ribs and lotus root, however, he thought it might not appear proper for him to sit too long with nothing left on the table. So he rose and went over to the rice paddy eels squirming in the plastic basin close to her table. As he squatted down, examining, touching the slippery eels with a finger, he couldn't help taking in her shapely ankle flashing in the background above the somber water in the basin.

"Are the eels good?" he asked loudly, still squatting, turning over his shoulder to direct his voice toward the kitchen.

The young woman unexpectedly leaned over, whispering to him, her hair nearly touching his face. "Ask him why he keeps the eels in water."

Chen took her suggestion.

"Why do you keep the rice paddy eels in water?" he called toward the kitchen.

"Oh, don't worry. It's for the benefit of our customers," Uncle Wang said, emerging from the kitchen. "Nowadays people feed eels hormones and whatnot. So I keep them in water for a day after they're caught, to wash out any remaining drugs."

But could drugs really be washed out of their systems that easily? Chen doubted it, and his appetite for eels was instantly lost.

"Well, give me a portion of stinking tofu," Chen said. "And a lot of red pepper sauce."

Presumably, stinking tofu was a safe bet. Chen looked up only to see the young woman shaking her head with a sly smile.

He restrained himself from asking her to explain. It wouldn't be so easy to talk across the table with the old man going in and out of the kitchen. There was something intriguing about her. She knew the proprietor well, yet she didn't hesitate to speak against the food here.

Soon, Uncle Wang placed a platter of golden fried tofu on the table along with a saucer of red pepper sauce.

"The local tofu," he said simply, heading back the kitchen.

"The tofu is hot. Would you like to join me?" Chen turned to the young woman, raising the chopsticks in a gesture of invitation.

"Sure," she said, standing up, still holding the water bottle in her hand. "But I have to say no to your stinking tofu."

"Don't worry," he said, signaling the bench opposite and pulling out another pair of chopsticks for her. "Some people can't stand the smell, I know, but once you try it, you may not want to stop. How about a beer?"

"No thanks," she said. "The local farmers use chemicals to make that tofu, though perhaps it's a common practice now. But what about the water they use to make it—and to make the beer? You should take a look at the lake. It is so polluted, it's undrinkable."

"Unimaginable!" he said.

"According to Nietzsche: God is dead. What does that mean? It means that people are capable of doing anything. There is nothing that is unimaginable."

"Oh, you're reading Nietzsche," he said, impressed.

"What are you reading?"

"A mystery novel. By the way, my name is Chen Cao. It's nice to meet you," he said, then added with a touch of exaggeration, in spite of himself, "As in the old proverb, it's more beneficial to listen to your talk for one day than to read for ten years."

"I'm simply talking shop. My name is Shanshan. Where are you from?"

"Shanghai," he said, wondering what kind of work she did.

"So you're on vacation here. A hard-working intellectual, reading English in a Wuxi eatery," she said teasingly. "Are you an English teacher?"

"Well, what else can I do?" he said, reluctant to reveal that he was a cop. Teaching was a career he had, in his college days, imagined for himself. And he felt an urge, at least for a while, to not be a cop. Or not be treated as a cop. Police work had become a bigger and bigger part of his identity, whether he liked it or not. So it was tantalizing to imagine a different self, one that wasn't a chief inspector—like a snail that didn't carry its shell.

"Schoolteachers earn quite a lot, especially with the demand for private tutoring," she said, casting a glance at the dishes on the table.

He knew what she was driving at. Chinese parents spared no expense for their children's education, since that education could make a huge difference in an increasingly competitive society. Detective Yu and his wife Peiqin, for instance, spent the bulk of their income on private lessons for their son. A schoolteacher could make a small fortune by giving private lessons after hours, sometimes squeezing ten students or more into a small living room.

"No, not me. Instead, I'm debating whether or not to translate this book for a small sum."

"A mystery," she said, glancing at the book cover in English.

"Occasionally, I write poems too," he responded impulsively. "But there is no audience for poetry today."

"I used to like poetry too—in middle school," she commented. "In a polluted age like ours, poetry is too much of a luxury, like a breath of pure air or a drop of clear water. Poetry can't make anything happen except in one's self-indulgent imagination."

"No, I don't—"

Chen's response was interrupted by the shrill ringing of a cell phone in her satchel.

Taking out a pink phone and putting it to her ear, she listened for a moment. Then she stood up, her face quickly bleaching of color in the afternoon light.

"Something wrong?" he said.

"No, it was just a nasty message," she said, turning off the phone.

"What was the message?"

"'Say what you're supposed to say, or you'll pay a terrible price.'"

"Oh, maybe it was a prank call. I get those calls too," he said. *But usually nothing that specific,* he didn't add.

Her brows knitted again. She seemed to know the call was more than a practical joke. She looked at her watch.

"I've got to go back to work," she said. "It's nice to have met you, Mr. Chen. I hope you will enjoy a wonderful vacation here."

"You have a good weekend—"

He thought about asking for her phone number, but she was already walking away, her long hair swaying across her back.

It was probably just as well. It was only a chance meeting, like two nameless clouds crossing each other in the sky, then continuing on with their respective journeys. That was probably not a metaphor of his invention, but he couldn't recall where he'd read it, Chen mused as he watched her walk.

She turned before crossing the street and said, waving her hand lightly, "Bye," as if to apologize for her abrupt exit.

"Another beer?" Uncle Wang said, coming back to the table. He noticed the platter had hardly been touched. "I can refry the tofu for you."

"No, thanks. Just a beer," Chen said. "Do you know her well?"

"I know her parents well, to be exact. She was assigned a job here upon graduation. She is alone in Wuxi, so she comes here for lunch. I just warm up the food she that brings by in the morning."

"What kind of work does she do?"

"She's an engineer. Something to do with environment. She works hard, even on weekends. She left rather suddenly. What did you two talk about?"

"She got a phone call and she left. A nasty prank call."

"There are some people who don't like her."

If that was the case, then, the phone message could be a warning, not a practical joke. Still, who was he to worry about it? He hardly knew her.

He finished his second beer and was ready to leave. He decided to curb his cop's curiosity. After all, he was on vacation.

TWO

THE NEXT MORNING, CHEN woke with a start. He thought he heard first a knock on the door, then heard the doorknob turning. Still disoriented, he sat up in bed, thinking that he must have been dreaming.

"Room service."

A young attendant came in bearing a sweet smile and a silver tray of coffee, toast, jam, and eggs. She had clear features, a slender figure, and a willowy waist. She might have been specially selected to appeal to high-ranking cadres.

He got out of bed and tried to find some change for a tip in the pocket of his pants draped over a chair, but she had already left the tray on the nightstand and had withdrawn light-footedly.

The coffee tasted strong and refreshing. This was like staying in a five-star hotel, except that it was even more sumptuous. A whole villa to himself. He sipped at his first cup of coffee in bed, looking out the window at an expanse of lake water shimmering in the morning light.

Then his phone began tinkling, as if rippling up from the dainty coffee cup.

It was Comrade Secretary Zhao in Beijing.

"I know you've been working hard, so enjoy the vacation, Comrade Chief Inspector Chen, and don't worry about things back at the bureau."

"But the vacation was supposed to be for you."

"I'm retired, so I'm practically on vacation every day. You should take it. It's also an opportunity for you to observe—do social research about China's reform. Keep your eyes open to new things and any problems that might arise in the current economic development. You have to prepare yourself for new responsibilities—not necessarily as a policeman, and not just in Shanghai. At the end of your vacation, write a report and turn it in to me."

It was a hint, but a positive one. It was the Party's tradition for a young cadre to do "social research" before being promoted to a higher position.

"But I'm a stranger here. People might not talk to me."

"I'm not looking for anything special. In the report, I mean. Just your impressions and observations. I'll make sure that the people in Wuxi know that I asked you to come."

"Thank you, Comrade Secretary Zhao. I'll keep my eyes open and report to you."

After the call, Chen was vaguely disturbed. Zhao might simply want to see things through his eyes, so to speak, but he might want something more. It wouldn't be a bad idea for Chen to have something like an emperor's sword, however, in case he really wanted to do something while he was in Wuxi. In ancient times, a trusted minister might receive from the emperor a sword, a symbol of supreme empowerment that enabled that minister to do whatever he thought was right and required in the emperor's name.

In the meantime, he was going to enjoy the treatment usually reserved for high-ranking cadres. There was no point looking a gift horse in the mouth. He didn't have any specific plans for this vacation, which might be the very thing to tune himself up—to get his body's yin and yang rebalanced, according to Dr. Ma, an old Chinese-medicine doctor he knew in Shanghai.

Chen once again looked out the window to the lake. He took a deep breath, dimly aware of a tang in the air, which might be characteristic of the lake. The water looked green under the morning sunlight. He thought of a line in a poem entitled "South of River," an area including Wuxi: *When spring comes, the water is bluer than the skies—*

The doorbell rang, interrupting his thoughts. He went to open the door, and saw a gray-haired, stout man standing there, smiling, holding up a bottle of champagne.

"I'm Qiao Liangxin, the director here at the center. I'm so sorry, Comrade Chief Inspector Chen," Qiao said with sincerity. He stepped in and turned on the air conditioning. "I was in a meeting in Hangzhou yesterday, so I didn't know about your arrival—not until I got Comrade Secretary Zhao's message. He called again this morning and said that you've been doing a fantastic job for the Party and that you should have a wonderful vacation. A vacation like the one he himself enjoyed a few years ago. I hurried back, but you were already here. I really apologize."

"You don't have to, Director Qiao," Chen said, seeing no need for Qiao's apology. Qiao's Party rank was higher than Chen's. For that matter, so were the ranks of most, if not all, of the other cadres staying at the center.

"This is the best building in our center. These are premium accommodations reserved for the top leaders from Beijing. The exact same arrangements have been made for you as would be for him."

"I am overwhelmed, Director Qiao."

"If there's anything else you need, let me know. We're going to assign a young nurse to you too."

"No, don't worry about a nurse. I'm just a little overworked, that's all. But I do need to ask you for a favor," Chen said. "Keep my vacation here as quiet as possible. The presence of a chief inspector may make some people uncomfortable."

Chen had conducted several high-level investigations, and this place was crowded with high-ranking cadres. He had no idea what some of them would think; he wasn't that popular in the system.

It was not always easy to be, or not to be, Chief Inspector Chen.

"You make a good point, Chief Inspector Chen," Qiao said. "So I won't call you Chief Inspector in the presence of others. Our old Comrade Secretary mentioned that you have a lot of important work on your hands. Do you have anything special planned during your stay here?"

Apparently, Qiao was having suspicions about the purpose of Chen's visit.

"No, it is just a vacation."

"Wonderful. Let me arrange a welcome lunch for you—a banquet of all the lake delicacies. I'll summon the other executives and some local officials too."

"No, please don't do that, Director Qiao. You have so many things on your plate already." Though not a stranger to lavish meals at the government's expense, Chen shunned the prospect of spending two or three hours at a banquet table, saying things in official language that he didn't want to say, in the company of officials he was in no mood to spend time with. He came up with an excuse. "Besides, I have a lunch appointment today."

"Then another time," Qiao said, moving to the door. "Enjoy your day in Wuxi. There is a lot to see."

After Qiao's visit, Chen felt obliged to leave the villa and head out to his "lunch appointment."

He had planned to go to the park, but he changed his mind when he saw that it was packed with tourists. He could go there another time, preferably in the evening, when it would be less crowded. Instead he made a right turn again, following the same route as the day before.

He noticed weather-beaten tourist attraction signs along the way, but there were no tourists walking there. At a turn in the road, a black limousine sped past him at full speed. He had to quickly flatten himself against the hillside. The road must have been built so that Party officials could enter and leave the center without having to walk through the crowded park.

He cut through the small square and took several unfamiliar turns, but to his surprise, he found himself heading toward Uncle Wang's place again.

It couldn't be because of her, Chen assured himself. The food there was not bad, he thought, trying to rationalize his return to Wang's. Also, there was the quiet, anonymous atmosphere. He was nobody there, and there was nobody else there, either.

As for the possible food contamination she had warned him against, it would probably be the same everywhere.

Uncle Wang didn't seem surprised at his reappearance.

"You're early, Mr. Chen. What would you like today?"

"It's not quite lunchtime yet. Perhaps a pot of green tea first."

"Sure, a cup of tea to start. Whenever you're ready to order, let me know."

Soon, a pot of tea was placed on the table, along with a dish of fried sunflower seeds and a light blue ashtray half full of cigarette butts, presumably the same one as yesterday.

He sat sipping his tea and looking around the street.

Not far away, a family of three was eating brunch out on the street, sitting in a circle consisting of a plastic chair, a wooden stool, and a bamboo recliner, without a table in the center. The little boy was gazing up at a brightly colored kite dangling from a tree while being chided by his mother, who was insistently pushing the bowl up to his mouth. His father was enjoying a leisurely smoke, looking over his shoulder. All of them seemed contented and at peace with their surroundings.

Past the family, there was a middle-aged peddler squatting over a piece of white cloth, on which he exhibited an array of souvenirs and knickknacks. It was a strange place to have chosen. On a side street not frequented by tourists, there would hardly be any customers for his goods. Still, the peddler, dressed neatly in a short-sleeved white shirt, looked contented, like someone relaxing in front of his own house. But then Chen didn't know this area, so his interpretations of these people could well be wrong.

Anyway, they seemed to be ordinary people and ordinary scenes, and they calmed him.

Ready to settle down to work, he took out his notebook. He conceived some lines on the experience of being a non–chief inspector here. For the past few months, he had been writing less and less, with the always-present excuse of his heavy workload.

Where else are we living—/except in our assumed identities/in others' interpretations./So you and I are zoomed, posing/against a walnut tree whispering/in the wind or a butterfly soaring/to the black eye of the sun./Only with ourselves in the proper light,/and the proper position too,/can we be recognized as meaningful,/as a woodpecker has to prove/its existential values/in the echoes of a dead trunk . . .

The lines moved in an unanticipated direction, growing inexplicably melancholy. He slowed down, yet he persisted. It was something worth doing, he told himself.

Uncle Wang came over to add hot water to his purple sand teapot.

It was probably close to the lunch hour, but Chen remained the only customer. It was none of his business, but he thought of the young woman again. Holding the pen, he was bothered by something she had said—about the irrelevance of poetry in today's society. Maybe reflecting on identity was a sort of "luxury" affordable only to a nothing-to-do tourist like himself. People were too busy getting whatever they could in today's society. Who would care about these metaphysical ideas? Besides, it hardly mattered whether being a cop was fulfilling or not. What else could he possibly do?

"Take your time," Uncle Wang said, coming back to the table with a menu. "No hurry."

Having read through the one-page menu describing local freshwater fish, shrimp, lilies, and chestnuts, Chen decided on the white water fish. It was "live, fresh from the lake, recommended," according to a smaller line of print in parentheses. There was no way to add hormones to the lake, he figured.

"Good choice, the fish is medium-size today," Uncle Wang said. "Live."

It was quite an experience seeing the old man prepare the fish outside. It wasn't a large one, but it was still struggling, its silver scales shining and tail thrashing. The old man finished his job in two or three minutes and he threw the fish into a wok full of sizzling oil.

Soon after, the fish was served, still steaming hot, its skin golden and crisp, its appealing white meat tender. It was lying sensually atop a bed of red peppers.

"Not too many people today, Uncle Wang?" Chen asked, raising his chopsticks.

"Well, most of my customers come from the chemical company nearby. The food in their canteen is no good. But this morning something happened at the plant."

"What—you mean Shanshan's company?"

"Yes, several police cars rushed there early in the morning. Someone was murdered, I heard. I didn't think the employees would come out for lunch today."

"Oh . . ." Chen said, putting down the chopsticks. He hastened to remind himself that it was not his business—not here in Wuxi.

He was aiming his chopsticks at the fish again when Shanshan appeared, crossing the street to the eatery.

Uncle Wang greeted her in a loud voice, "Shanshan, you're late today. Your friend has been waiting here a long while."

It was true that Chen had been sitting here for quite a while, but he had not been waiting for her. He chose not to contradict the old man, instead smiling and waving his hand at her. She had to have taken him for a bookish tourist. Why not continue to play the role?

She stopped and nodded at him before turning to Uncle Wang.

"No time for lunch today, Uncle Wang. I have to hurry to the ferry. Leave the lunch in the refrigerator for me, please?"

"But you have to eat something. Let me warm you a couple of steamed buns. You can eat them on the way."

Uncle Wang dashed into the kitchen, leaving the two of them alone. She took a glance at his notebook spread out on the table. A question seemed to start rippling in her large eyes, eyes that were serene, clear like lake water. The metaphor came to mind before he realized it was inappropriate given what he'd heard of the lake water here.

"I thought you might come here for lunch," he said.

"Something happened in the factory. A mess. Now I have to catch a ferry."

She wouldn't talk to an almost stranger about a murder, a reluctance that was quite understandable.

"Well, what do you think of my choice today?" he asked, trying to change the topic. "It's one of the three special whites in Wuxi."

"Not good."

"Really! The white fish came fresh from the lake. It was recommended on the menu."

"You're from Shanghai, so you don't know. Local farmers raise fish in enclosed ponds, and they add drugs to the water to increase production. For instance, antibiotics, lots of them—so the fish won't get sick," she said. "Now let's suppose, instead of being pond-raised, the fish is caught in the lake. You should take a good look at the lake. The water is so polluted that it is totally undrinkable. How could the fish from there be any good?"

He had heard stories of serious environmental problems throughout the country, not just here in Wuxi.

"Is the water really so bad? Not long ago I heard a song about the beautiful water of Tai Lake. You know it."

"Yes, they play it on TV," she said, pausing before she went on. "You're a tourist, so you may not know. Have you seen or heard of the green algae blooms in the lake?"

"No, I haven't been back to Wuxi in years, and I only arrived yesterday. I haven't been able to walk around the lake yet."

22

"The whole lake is covered with a thick, foul-smelling canopy, leaving people without drinking water for the last several days." She raised the bottle of water.

"Have people tried to do anything about it?"

"What's the use? The city government calls the outbreak a 'natural disaster'—due to the warm weather, the bacteria 'exploded' at rates unseen in the past. Whatever reason they may make up, though, you wouldn't believe it if you saw pictures of the factories dumping waste into the lake. The local residents form long lines to buy bottled water, and the neighboring cities shut sluice gates and canal locks to prevent the contamination from spreading. Still, the local officials won't do anything because Wuxi's economic boom has been built on the ever-increasing revenue of the factories around the lake. Economic miracle indeed. The only standard for success in today's China is money, so people are capable of doing anything and everything."

She wasn't just being fastidious about food or jumping on one of the fashionable trends of vegetarian diets or organic food. Instead of simply doing the job she'd been assigned, checking on environmental problems, it seemed that she had made efforts to look into the social and historical causes too.

"Oh, I shouldn't be such a wet blanket," she exclaimed, noticing the fish sitting untouched on the platter.

"From my window at the center, the lake appeared okay. Like in a Tang poem, the spring water ripples bluer than the sky." At least one advantage of an identity as a bookish tourist was that he could quote poetry at length, letting it say what might otherwise be too difficult. Serious, yet not that serious.

"Where are you staying?"

"Wuxi Cadre Recreation Center."

"But that's a place for high-ranking cadres, and you're—you told me you're a schoolteacher."

"Someone gave me his vacation package. A small potato like me couldn't afford to let it go."

"I see," she said, eyeing him up and down. "For free?"

"For free." He wondered whether she believed him. But it was true, and he noted that she was not in a hurry to leave—not yet.

"You're going to the ferry," he said on the spur of the moment. "How about letting me walk you to the ferry? You can tell me more things about the lake."

And something about the murder too, he thought but didn't say.

"I'm not a good guide for a tourist."

"No, perhaps not for a tourist, but what you said about the lake interests me," he said, pointing at his notebook before he closed it. "As I said, occasionally, I write poetry too. The image of the horribly polluted lake may serve as a poignant background, like in 'The Waste Land.'"

She studied him with a sort of mixed expression, and then changed her mind.

"Fine, let's walk there. But I have to warn you, it's not the part of the lake you can see from your window at the center."

"It doesn't have to be," he said. He rose and left some money under the platter on the table. "Let's go."

They were already close to the end of the street when Uncle Wang hurried out of the kitchen, waving his hands, shouting out to them.

"Your white fish, Mr. Chen, and your steamed buns, Shanshan!"

"Don't worry about it. We're going to the lake," he said, waving back at him. "I'll buy something for her on the way."

THREE

THEY WALKED ON WITHOUT immediately beginning to talk. A light breeze stirred the tops of the trees with a rustle like a sigh, which hung in the air before falling back into silence.

Shanshan was surprised, but then not too surprised, by Chen's offer to walk with her to the ferry. Was the man interested in a vacation fling? She was in no mood for it. Still, it would have been impolite for her to refuse, particularly after having spoiled his appetite for the fish.

"Thank you in advance," he said, "for a different, non-tourist introduction to Tai Lake."

"Well, you'll see the lake for yourself. But you seem to have developed a passion for Uncle Wang's place."

"The center is close by. I've got nothing to do there, so I wandered along a trail and ended up at his place this morning." He added, "But I didn't think about the possibility of seeing you there."

Smiling, she chose not to respond. It was unusual for someone staying at the center to visit the same grubby place a second time, just to sit and read for a couple of hours. She didn't think he had really been waiting for her there, but a tourist could be lonely, no matter how fantastic the center might be. She'd never stepped into it, but she'd heard about the luxurious treatment there.

"My parents took me to Wuxi when I was a child," he went on, "but it was many years ago. I barely remember anything except the Wuxi soup buns my mother brought back home—standing all the way in an overcrowded train, carrying a small bamboo basket of them. I'm going to bring a basket back for her, if I can find the old restaurant where she bought them. Indeed, *Who says that the splendor/of a grass blade can prove/to be enough to return/the generous warmth/of the ever-returning spring sunlight?*"

"The city has changed a lot," she said, unexpectedly touched by the way he talked about his mother. What about her own parents? They would be worried sick if they learned what happened at the company. "I hope you find the restaurant you're looking for, but many restaurants and stores sell Wuxi soup buns. You might even find them at the railway station. But I've been here three or four years, so I am not sure. I came here after I was assigned to work at the plant after I graduated from Nanjing University."

"So you majored in environmental protection."

"Yes."

"You're lucky to get a job in the field you studied."

"What about you? You majored in English, I assume."

"Well, yes, but I wanted to write and translate."

There seemed to be a glitch in his voice, she noted, as they turned onto a quieter path that led to the lake.

"But weren't you writing something at the eatery?"

"Oh that, just some random thoughts about the construction and deconstruction of one's identity in others' interpretations."

"That's too abstract for me. Can you give a concrete example?"

"For example, to Uncle Wang, I'm probably nothing but a gourmet customer, ready to indulge in a large platter of fried white fish. It is a convention in Chinese literature to depict a man of letters traveling to enjoy the local delicacies, as in the writings of Yuan Mu, Lu Xun, Yu Pingbo—"

"But you *are* a man of letters, aren't you?" she said. "So in your interpretation, we live only in others' interpretations."

"Well done. You put it succinctly."

Normally, she would have been intrigued by his conversation, but she was disturbed by what had happened at the company. Still, she couldn't help taking another look at him—possibly in his mid-thirties, tall, austerely good-looking, dressed in a beige jacket, white shirt, and khaki pants. Nothing conspicuous, yet with an air of prosperous distinction that fit well with his clothes. Slightly bookish, well read, poetry-quoting in his conversation, and well connected too, considering his stay at the center. But he wasn't one of those upstarts, who wouldn't have revisted Uncle Wang's place.

"By the way, have you received any more phone calls like the one yesterday?" he said abruptly, with genuine concern on his face.

"No, not today," she said. It was strange. She'd been getting the sinister messages for the past two weeks. Every day, around the same time. But not today. Could it have something to do with the death of Liu Deming, the general manager of the chemical company?

The police had questioned her earlier in the morning, focusing on her recent arguments with Liu. Her work as an environmental engineer, she admitted, hadn't been agreeable to Liu. It was also true that Liu had been making things hard for her. But she'd never even thought of murdering him.

A dog's barking in the distance, fierce, persistent, broke her reverie.

No one had accused her of anything yet, but how it would play out, no one knew. She was under a lot of pressure. Not only from the cops, but from her coworkers as well. People were talking and pointing stealthily behind her back, as though she were the prime suspect.

So it wasn't such a bad idea to let Chen accompany her to the ferry. It distracted her, albeit temporarily, and kept her from dwelling too much on those disturbing thoughts. He turned out to be not unpleasant to walk with.

"Oh, something happened at your company today?" Chen asked, as if reading her thoughts.

She didn't want to talk about it, but she responded nonetheless.

"Liu Deming, the general manager of our company, was murdered last night."

"Oh, that's horrible." He added, "Has the murderer been caught?"

"No, there are no suspects or clues so far. He was murdered at home—or, to be exact, at his home office not far from the company office."

"Did he have enemies or people who really hated him?"

"You're talking like a cop, Mr. Chen."

"Sorry, I was just being curious," he said. "You're right. It's not a pleasant topic."

After another turn in the road, they came within view of the lake. Chen pointed at a flat-bottomed sampan and, like a tourist, declared, "Look."

The sampan dangled on a frayed rope tied to a stunted tree at the edge of the water, which looked impenetrable. As they moved closer, however, there seemed to be a swirl of movement down there with a silver glimmer under the surface. He picked up a pebble and flicked it into the water.

"It's so peaceful here," he said. "The air contains a sort of quietness unimaginable in Shanghai."

"The ferry is further to the south. We're taking a different route from the usual tourist path."

"That's great," he said, then changed the subject again. "You said something about the water quality earlier."

"So you'll be able to see for yourself. We are walking there now."

Several minutes later, she slowed down.

"See the green stuff over the water, Mr. Chen?"

"Yes, green algae, but please call me Chen, Shanshan."

"Can you smell it?"

He squatted down, inhaled deeply, and frowned.

"Oh, it's horrible," he said, shaking his head. "The lake used to be a scenic attraction because of its clear water. When I was a kid, even tea made with lake water was better because of it, or so my father told me."

"Would you now make tea with the lake water?"

"No. Now I understand why you carry a bottle of water with you. But how could it have become so heavily polluted?"

"The algae blooms that are ruining Tai Lake, like other Chinese freshwater lakes, are mainly caused by high concentrations of nitrogen and large amounts of phosphorus in the water. In the past few years, industrial emissions have been getting more and more out of control. The result is what you see today."

"Nitrogen is a main ingredient in soap powder and fertilizer, right?"

"Yes, it is also found in many other chemical products and wastes," she said. She pointed to the buildings looming along the far shore of the lake. "Look at them. Paper mills, dyeing factories, chemical companies, and whatnot. In the last twenty years or so, those plants have sprung up like bamboo shoots after the rain. Now they make up more than forty percent of the city's total economic output. Relocating them is out of the question—there are too many of them. The local officials aren't eager to do anything about it."

"How do you explain that, Shanshan?"

"As the old saying goes, when there are too many people involved, the law cannot punish. For the local government, the most important thing is to show off their accomplishments to the Beijing authorities—particularly in terms of the local economy. The city government has pledged an annual revenue increase of ten percent. At what expense the increase is achieved is not their concern. On the contrary, any environmental effort that could reduce the income is unacceptable to them. They're concerned only with how they'll move up as a result of the 'economic success.' All they care about is this particular moment while they are here. They don't care about what might happen in ten years, or even one year after they leave Wuxi. Last year, the former mayor was promoted to a ministerial position in Beijing because he presided over a revenue increase for three years in a row. All the officials know this only too well. And that's not even to mention all the 'red envelopes' that they receive from businesspeople."

"But there must be some government agency in charge of taking care of the situation."

"Sure, there's a city environmental office, but it exists only for appearance's sake. Some of the factories are equipped with wastewater processing facilities, but they generally choose not to operate those facilities. The cost of doing so would wipe out their profits. So they have the facilities for the sake of appearances, but continue to dump waste into the lake in spite of the worsening crisis. From time to time, when the central government in Beijing issues some red-letterheaded documents, the local environmental office may put up a show of checking pollution levels, but it informs those companies beforehand. So before they arrive, the waste treatment facilities start operating, and the sample they take will then be up to the government standard."

Talking, they crossed an old stone bridge in the shape of a crescent moon, which looked to be in bad repair, and skirted along the bank where willow tree limbs hung like a curtain.

"I'm no expert," he said deliberately. "But I've seen green algae in other lakes, I think. Even in the tiny pond in the Old City God's Temple Market in Shanghai. Of course, never anything so serious as here."

"Let me tell you something. The water in Tai Lake contains two hundred times more harmful material than the national standard, and even the Wuxi disease control center can't deny that figure," she said, taking a drink from her bottle. "Of course, there's more than a single cause. In addition to the industrial pollution, sewage treatment measures also lag far behind the social and economic development of the Yangtze River delta. In the early nineties, the annual industrial sewage entering the lake was estimated at 540 million tons, and household sewage at 320 million tons. But nowadays, the total sewage is more than 5.3 billion tons. Only thirty percent of the household sewage is treated before being dumped into the lake."

"Wow, you keep all of those figures in your head?" With an apologetic smile, he asked, "Do you mind if I smoke? I need to digest those figures. This is a serious problem for China."

"Go ahead," she said, noticing that he took out a soft pack of *China*, one of the most expensive brands. Then she realized that she must sound like a research report. "Sorry for the lecture. I forget you're on vacation."

Perhaps it wasn't just a subject that she was passionate about; talking about it also gave her a sense of self-justification. She was unpopular at the company, where people took her as something of a Cassandra figure, and that morning she almost became a murder suspect.

"No, you don't have to apologize. On the contrary, I'm grateful for your conversation—or your lecture, if you want to call it that. It's something I could never have learned from the official publications. It's really shocking."

She couldn't help noting the look of serious attention on his face, bookish yet sincere. She hadn't had an attentive audience like Chen before. Nor one where she didn't have to worry about the consequences of talking openly. He wasn't local, and would probably be gone in a week.

"Your work is truly important, Shanshan," he said in earnest.

"I'm a nobody in the company. No one cares about what I say. If anything, it only marks me as a troublemaker."

"Because of your work?"

"It was naïve of me to take the job so seriously. I was hired for the sake of appearances, which I found out after I started work. All my research was put into a newsletter available only to the company executives. I doubt whether they ever read it, or whether they did anything about it if they did read it. Time and again, I felt obliged to speak out against Liu's business decisions, like shutting down the waste treatment facility or fabricating the reports being sent to the agencies. But what difference did it make?" She smiled a bitter smile. "It's strange that I'm telling you all this."

"There is one line in a Confucian classic, Shanshan. *Some people may never really know each other even if they're together until white-haired, but*

31

some people may be true friends the moment they meet each other, taking down their hats."

"Yes, I remember that line too."

"Now," he said, "do you think the phone message you got was because of your work?"

"That's possible, but I doubt Liu would have gone to the trouble. He could have easily fired me."

A siren sounded not too far away, and Chen looked up. The street they had just turned onto was lined with food stalls and souvenir kiosks. They were close to the ferry.

"Wait a minute," he said and walked over to a stall.

She saw him talking to a man behind the counter at a snack stall under a white-and-red striped umbrella. Chen pointed at something, then came back carrying a large brown paper bag.

"Slices of roast beef and steamed buns. You can't drink only water, Shanshan."

"Thank you, Mr. Chen, but you don't have to do that."

"I promised Uncle Wang. You can break the bun into two and put the beef in between, which is a very popular way to eat them in the northwest. The sauce is also in the bag."

"You're an impossible connoisseur. I'm sorry about spoiling your appetite back at Uncle Wang's place."

"It was for my own good, and I really appreciate it. Here is my cell number," he said, copying his number on a scrap of paper torn from the top of the bag. "I would love to continue our conversation, because, as in the old saying: *to listen to your talk for one day is more beneficial than to read books for ten years.* I hope I can have another chance during my stay here."

"Well, in that old saying, it is '*for one night*' rather than '*for one day*,'" she said teasingly, amused by his pedantic way of saying things. "Bye."

She found herself walking, light-footedly, in an improved mood as she turned to the plank that led to the ferry boat, flashing over her shoulder a smile at him who was still standing there watching her.

FOUR

THE FERRY BOAT DISAPPEARED into the mist-enveloped distance.

Chen turned away and started strolling back to the center, whistling, when his cell phone vibrated. It was a text message from her: "Now you have my number too, Shanshan."

That's good, he thought with a smile. Her text showed an enthusiasm for new technology that was perhaps characteristic of one of her age. It had taken him a couple of days to learn how to write and send a Chinese text message properly. He'd persisted because he had no choice. It was necessary for his work. But he didn't enjoy doing it. However, a lot of young people seemed to be text-messaging all the time.

He couldn't help looking back in the direction of the ferry again, and when he did so, he was struck with a feeling of being watched. Someone else was looking in his direction, raising a cell phone as if to take a picture, but then turning away abruptly when he became aware of Chen's attention. It might be a coincidence, but there was something about the man. He was middle-aged, medium-built, wearing a short-sleeved white shirt. Chen might have seen him before, though at the moment he couldn't recall where.

But maybe his suspicious nature was getting the better of him. In Wuxi, he was an anonymous tourist on vacation, not a cop investigating a crime. There was no reason to believe someone would be shadowing him here. Chen resumed walking, and after passing several booths, he looked back over his shoulder. The man was no longer in sight.

What he had just learned from Shanshan, he contemplated, might go into his report for Comrade Secretary Zhao. He would have to do some homework first, but he was in no hurry and felt sure it was relevant.

Soon he got lost again. The map he pulled out didn't really help. After wandering for two or three blocks without any real sense of direction, he saw a group of tourists heading to a willow-lined road, their guide holding a tourist group banner. They were talking, gesticulating, pointing at a roadside sign that indicated the way to the park, through which, he guessed, he could cut back to the center.

He followed them to the front gate of the park, where a large billboard declared that an entrance ticket cost thirty yuan. He showed his center pass and got in for free. Another advantage available only to high-ranking cadres.

The park was alive with tourists, most of them from nearby cities. He was pretty sure some were from Shanghai for he heard a young couple speaking in the unmistakable Shanghai accent. The woman was four or five months pregnant and beaming contentedly, clutching in her hand a pair of tiny earthen babies in colorful costumes—wares that were a specialty of Wuxi.

Near the lake, he noticed a crowd waiting to board several large cruise ships. One of the ships looked so modern and luxurious, shining silver in the sunlight, it was as if it were sailing out of a Hollywood movie.

To the west, not far from the dock, several tourists were waiting their turn to take their pictures in front of an enormous rock, the flat surface of which bore four bold Chinese characters in red paint: *Preg-*

nant with Wu Yue. Wu Yue referred to the lake area. It was originally a phrase praising the lake's expanse, but it had long since become a popular background for tourist photos because of a folk belief that the rock was auspicious for young couples eager to start a family.

Passing by a bronze statue of a turtle, the theme of the park, he caught sight of a teahouse built in the traditional architecture style—white walls, vermilion pillars, lattice windows, and a large Chinese character for *tea* embroidered on an oblong yellow silk pennant that was streaming in the breeze. Crowds of people were sitting at outside tables, drinking tea, playing poker and chess, and relaxing in sight of the surface of the lake, which was dotted with so many white sails that they looked like clouds.

It was a fantastic scene. However, for the locals, who had seen it hundreds of times, it might seem merely a place for tea-drinking.

Chen chose a bamboo table with a tree-framed view of the lake shimmering in the sunlight. The water didn't look as dark-colored as it did near the ferry, in Shanshan's company.

A waitress came over and set down a bamboo-covered thermos bottle and a cup containing a pinch of tea leaves.

"Before-Rain tea, it's the newest pick of the year and the best tea leaves in the house," she said, pouring a cup for him.

The tea looked tenderly green. He didn't pick up the cup immediately. Instead he slowly tapped a finger on the table, thinking about what Shanshan had said about the water. He picked up a newspaper from a rack near the table, but when he saw a picture on the front page of local leaders speaking at an economic conference, he put it back down.

Shanshan's words had more than impressed him. For many years, environmental protection had been practically irrelevant to the Chinese people. Under Mao's rule, they were famished, literally starving to death, particularly during the so-called Three Years of Natural Disaster in the late fifties and early sixties, and then again during the Cultural Revolution. People's top priority had been survival, and that meant feeding themselves with whatever was available. Then under Deng's rule, China began to catch up to the rest of the world for the first time in many years; as Deng put it, "Development is the one and only truth." So environmental protection still didn't move to the top of the nation's agenda.

It was little wonder that she had had a hard time with her work at the chemical company, or that she had been receiving threatening calls because of it. He wondered whether he should contact the local police. He had her phone number, and they might be able to trace the ominous call. Besides, now there had been a murder at her company.

He pulled out his cell phone and dialed Sergeant Huang of the Wuxi Police Bureau.

"Oh, you should have told me you were coming, Chief Inspector Chen," Huang exclaimed, not trying to conceal the excitement in his voice. "I could have met you at the railway station."

"Well, you are the first one I've contacted here. My vacation was an unexpected development to me as well."

"I'm so flattered—I mean, for you to call me first. I'm really glad that you chose to vacation in Wuxi."

"I got a call from Comrade Secretary Zhao, the retired head of the Central Party Discipline Committee. He was too busy to take a vacation that had been arranged for him, and he wanted me to come here in his place. So here I am, enjoying a cup of Before-Rain tea at Yuan-touzhu."

"That's fantastic, Chief Inspector Chen. I've heard so much about you—and about your connection to Beijing. You worked on a highly sensitive anticorruption case directly under Comrade Secretary Zhao. What a case that was. I've studied it several times. I'm a loyal fan of yours. I not only followed your extraordinary police work, but I've read all your translations too. It would be a dream come true to meet you."

"I would like to talk to you as well."

"Really? I'm nearby right now," Huang said. "Can I come over?"

"Of course, come and join me for a cup of tea. I'm at the teahouse in the park, close to the bronze turtle statue." Chen added, "Oh, and not a single word to your colleagues about my vacation here."

"Not a single word to anyone, I promise, Chief Inspector Chen. I'm on my way."

In less than twenty minutes, Huang appeared, hurrying over to Chen's table in big strides, wiping his forehead with the back of his hand. He was a dapper, spirited young man with a broad forehead and penetrating eyes. He grinned at the sight of Chen.

"I spotted you from a distance, Chief Inspector Chen," Huang said. "I've seen your picture in the newspaper."

Chen had another tea set brought to the table and poured a cup for the young cop. Chen then lost no time in bringing the conversation around to the murder of Liu Deming.

To Chen's pleasant surprise, Huang turned out to be one of the officers working on that very case. He had been at the chemical company discussing the case with his colleagues when he got Chen's call.

"You've heard about it? Of course you have," Huang said, his face flushed with anticipation. "You're not really on vacation here, are you?"

Chen kept sipping at his tea without immediately contradicting him. To the local police, his vacation couldn't help but be suspicious, even before he expressed interest in the murder. He was known for covert investigations in several highly sensitive cases.

"Well, I thought it would be great to come here, and relax for a week or so, with nothing to do. But in just one day, I've already found it kind of boring. I'm not complaining, but maybe I have a cop's lot cut out for me, as both Detective Yu and his wife Peiqin have said before. Then I happened to hear about the case," Chen said. "I'm not going to try to investigate: it's not my territory, and I know better. I simply want to kill some time."

"Sherlock Holmes must have something to do. I totally understand, Chief. Can I just call you Chief, Chief Inspector Chen?"

Whether Huang believed him or not, the young local cop was eager to model himself on those fictional detectives he admired. So he provided a quite detailed introduction to the case, focusing on what he considered strange and suspicious.

The Wuxi Number One Chemical Company's being the largest in

Wuxi and Liu's being a representative of the People's Congress of Zhejiang Province combined to make the murder the top priority for the Wuxi Police Bureau. A special team had been formed for the investigation; Huang was the youngest member of the team.

They had started by building a file on Liu Deming. Liu had worked at the company for over twenty years. When he took over the top position of the state-run company several years ago, it was on the brink of bankruptcy. He managed to lead the company out of the financial woods, then make it profitable, and then to successfully expand. Capable and ambitious, Liu had established himself as an important figure in the city—a "red banner" in the economic development of the region.

In recent years, however, Liu had been involved in some controversies. For one thing, the company was in the process of going public, turning into something between state-owned and privately-owned—a new experiment in China's economic reform. It was the first company attempting to do this in Wuxi, and Liu himself stood to become the largest shareholder, with millions of shares in his own name. He was going to be a capitalist Big Buck, so to speak, though still a Party member and general manager of the company.

No less controversial was the pollution that was the result of his increasing production and maximizing profit by dumping tons and tons of untreated wastewater into the lake. It was an open secret, and his company wasn't the only one to dump industrial waste wherever it liked. With the deteriorating water quality of the lake, however, local people had begun to complain. The Wuxi Number One Chemical Company was the largest plant by the lake, so it was an easy target. The city authorities had tried to exercise a sort of damage control, hushing up the protest, but with limited success.

On the night of the murder, Liu had been working at his home office—an apartment about five minutes' walk away from the plant—not at his home, which was about five miles away. It wasn't uncommon for the busy boss to spend the night at his home office when he was overwhelmed with work. The last several weeks had been a hectic period for

the company, with lots of things going on, in particular all the preparations and paperwork for the forthcoming IPO. Not just Liu but
several other executives and their secretaries had come in to work on
that Sunday. Liu was last seen walking by himself, entering the apartment complex around seven P.M.

The next morning, his secretary, Mi, didn't see him show up at work.
She called his home, home office, and cell phone, with no response at
any of them. So thinking that he might have overslept, she walked over
to his home office. Liu sometimes had trouble falling asleep, especially
when working late, so he took sleeping pills. She saw his shoes outside the door—he always changed into slippers in the apartment. When
no one came to open the door after she knocked for several minutes, she
called the police.

Liu was found dead in his home office, killed by a fatal blow to the
back of his head. The wound appeared to have been inflicted with a
heavy blunt object, which was confirmed in the preliminary autopsy
report. The cause of death was massive skull fracture with acute cere-
bral hemorrhage, but there was hardly any blood at the scene. There
was no bruising or abrasions on his body. There was no tissue, blood,
or skin under his nails.

The time of death was established to be between 9:30 P.M. and
10:30 P.M. the previous night. The crime scene people found no sign of
forced entry, nor of any struggle. There was no murder weapon or fingerprints found—except for one on the mirror in the bathroom, left
by his secretary, Mi. That didn't mean anything, though, since Mi
sometimes worked there as well.

There didn't appear to be anything valuable missing from his
apartment, either. Both Mi and his wife checked and confirmed this.

The police suspected that the murderer was no stranger to Liu. The
home office was in an expensive, well-guarded apartment complex.
According to his neighbors, Liu didn't stay there often, and he barely
mixed with them. Occasionally, he was there with Mi, working late into
the night with the door shut tightly. As far as the security guard could
recall, however, Liu was alone that evening, and no stranger came to

visit him later. Non-residents had to check in with security and leave the name of the resident they were visiting.

The local cops had also interviewed a number of people close to Liu. There were hardly any promising leads there, either.

Mi maintained that Liu hadn't mentioned expecting a visitor that evening. Mrs. Liu reported that Liu had called earlier in the day and told her that he was going to work on some important documents and wouldn't be coming home. After speaking to him, she went to Shanghai in the late afternoon and didn't return until the next day. Fu Hao, the associate general manager of the company, now the acting general manager, said that Liu had been so busy of late that they'd hardly talked during the day.

At the end of his briefing, Huang took a sip of the lukewarm tea and leaned over across the table.

"You're no outsider, Chief. There's something about this case. Not only was a special team formed, but that the governmental authorities—not just at the city level—have been paying a lot of attention to the investigation. We've gotten several phone calls from the city government. I've heard that even Internal Security is looking into it, working sort of parallel investigation."

"Internal Security," Chen repeated. "Have they done anything?"

"For one thing, Liu's phone records were snatched away before we could examine them."

"That's something. You're very perceptive, Huang."

"But I haven't met with any of them—face to face, I mean. So I'm not sure how involved they are."

"Yes, find out for me," Chen said before he realized that he had unwittingly slipped back into his familiar role, talking as if he were in charge of the case and Huang his subordinate. While he hadn't yet decided whether he would attempt to do anything about the investigation, it wouldn't hurt, he thought, for him to take a look. "I've heard about the company. About its success at the expense of the environment, with the lake water and food around here being badly contaminated. "

That enquiry, suggested by his talk with Shanshan, could also be seen as being in line with Comrade Secretary Zhao's instructions. It was time for Chen to start paying attention to the problem. Still, he thought he had better not ask too many questions at this stage, or he could raise unnecessary alarm.

"Well, it is said that some people are getting sick by drinking the water or eating the fish, but nothing is really proven," Huang said, scratching his head. "I don't think it's something relevant to the murder. There are many factories like Liu's here. Wuxi has been developing rapidly, and as Comrade Deng Xiaoping put it, 'Development is the one and only truth.'"

It wasn't up to Chief Inspector Chen, coming from Shanghai, to debate economic development in Wuxi. And he wasn't an environmental expert like Shanshan.

"Oh, another thing, Huang," he said, on the spur of the moment. "Someone I know here has been getting threatening calls. Can you check on it for me?"

"What's his name and number?"

"Her name is Shanshan, and here is her number." He copied her number onto a scrap of paper and handed it to Huang.

"Shanshan?"

Chen thought he caught a fleeting hint of surprise in Huang's expression. "Do you know her?"

"No, I don't. You know her well?" Huang asked.

"No, I met her yesterday."

"I'll check it out for you, Chief," Huang said, glancing at his watch as he stood up. "I think I have to go back to the team. It's almost five."

"Thank you so much, Huang. Call me when you learn anything new." He added, almost as an afterthought, "Send me some information about the case."

He watched Huang's retreating figure disappear into the crowd, which began to thin out with the approaching dusk. Chen remained sitting there, brooding, and staring into his empty cup of tea.

After several minutes, he looked up at the bronze turtle statue, which must have overheard—if endowed with supernatural powers as in those folk tales—just another tale of human tragedy. But the brown turtle remained squatting, meditating, impervious to human suffering. What kind of a man was Liu? Chen hadn't even seen a picture of him, but Liu might have come here himself, sitting, sipping at his own tea, and staring at the turtle statue.

Chen swept his gaze over to the tilted eave of a multistory wooden tower silhouetted against the evening spreading in the distance. The time-and-weather-worn tower suddenly appeared melancholy. He was struck with a sense of déjà vu—possibly from recollecting more lines by Su Shi, his favorite poet from the Song dynasty.

It is nothing but a dream, / for the past, for the present. / Whoever wakes out of the dream? / There is only a never-ending cycle / of old joy, and new grief. / Someday, someone else, / in view of the tower at night, / may sigh deeply for me.

FIVE

THE CENTER WAS A nice place, after all.

Chen took a walk around early Tuesday morning and began to get a better sense of the layout. The location spoke volumes for the center. Originally a huge lakeside area of the park, it had been converted into the Cadre Recreation Center for the benefit of veteran cadres, so they could enjoy the lake in peace and quiet without having to mix with the noisy tourist crowd.

There were several others like him walking around at a leisurely pace. Every one of them must have led a quite different life somewhere else, in a provincial town or in a large city, each powerful and privileged in their respective ways. In the blue-and-white-striped pajamas of the center, however, they appeared anonymous for the moment.

Even here, though, there was a sort of recognizable hierarchy. In the two gray multistory buildings near the entrance, the rooms were probably like those in a hotel; though still quite nice, each of them boasting a small balcony, they were probably not for very high-ranking cadres. In contrast, there was another building close to the center of the complex, and the size of the balconies indicated much larger rooms inside. Looking up, Chen saw a white-haired man step out onto a balcony on the third floor, stretch, and nod at him. Chen nodded back and moved on.

Soon, he saw a teahouse built in the traditional architectural style. It was much like the one he had seen in the park, but it stood embosomed in green foliage on the top of a raised plateau, adjacent to a modern-style building. From the distance, he could see several elderly people sitting outside by the white stone balustrade, drinking tea, talking, and cracking watermelon seeds.

It might be a good place, he reflected, for him to sit and study the initial report Sergeant Huang had faxed him that morning. The chief inspector was still debating as to whether he should get actively involved in the investigation.

He was surprised at the sight of a waterproof escalator stretching up the hill, leading directly to the teahouse. It wasn't so much the technology of the escalator that surprised him but the fact that it was installed on the slope in the first place. Anyone who couldn't walk up the flight of stone steps nearby could easily use the elevator inside the building next to it.

He turned away and walked to the clinic attached to the center instead. According to the brochure, the clinic provided convenient medical checkups for high-ranking cadres. Chen didn't think there was anything wrong with him, but since he was there, he decided to see a doctor of traditional Chinese medicine.

Chen's experience at the clinic proved to be quite different from that at a Shanghai hospital, where he usually had to wait a long time, standing in line, going through a lot of paperwork. Here, the nurses were practically waiting on him, not to mention that there was so much advanced equipment—all imported here for those high-ranking cadres.

The doctor felt Chen's pulse, examined his tongue, took his blood pressure, and gave his diagnosis in a jumble of professional jargon spoken in a strong Anhui accent:

"You have worked too hard, burning up the yin in your system. Consequently both the qi and blood are at a low ebb, and the yang is insubstantially high. Quite a lot is out of balance, but nothing is precisely wrong, just a little of everything." He dashed off a prescription and added thoughtfully, "You're still single, aren't you?"

Chen thought he knew what the doctor was driving at. According to traditional Chinese medical theory, people achieve the yin-yang balance through marriage. For a man of his age, continuous celibacy wouldn't be healthy. The old doctor in Wuxi could be an ideal ally, Chen thought with a sense of amusement, for his mother in Shanghai, who worried and complained about his failure to settle down.

The prescription specified that the medicine be brewed fresh every day and then taken while still hot. The pharmacist at the clinic said that it was no problem to fill the prescription; Director Qiao had given specific instructions to provide whatever Chen needed.

Leaving the clinic, Chen continued walking instead of going back to his villa. He wasn't entirely comfortable getting special treatment under the assumption that he was a high-ranking cadre. He'd noticed that some of the old people were looking at him with curiosity. It wasn't likely that they recognized him. Still, at his age, he was quite conspicuous in this place.

Cutting across a small clearing with hardly any people around, he found himself walking up a flight of stone steps. He ended up at the back of the center, where he discovered a trail that wound down the hill. He followed the path, which was dotted with nameless flowers, and after a couple of turns it took him to a wire fence that separated the center from the lake, with a deserted road between the two.

He perched on a rock close to the foot of the hill and pulled out the fax. There didn't seem to be anything really new or different from what Huang had already told him. After reading it a couple of times, he pondered what he could possibly do while still staying in the background. He didn't think it would be a good idea for him to visit the crime scene or to interview any possible suspects. Still, something like an informal talk with people not being targeted by the local police might not be a problem. Perhaps a visit to Mrs. Liu. He didn't see anything exactly suspicious about her. He was just a little bit curious about her decision to travel to Shanghai right after learning that her husband wouldn't be back home that night. At the very least, she'd be able to tell him something about Liu.

Of course, another possible source of information would be Shanshan. For that interview, he'd better not reveal that he was a cop. He took out his cell phone, yet didn't dial it. Deep down, he felt uneasy about not telling her he was a chief inspector, but he reassured himself that he was doing it for a good reason. And he wondered if the threating calls she had been getting had anything to do with the case.

He underlined several lines in the fax. There were some other points possibly worth looking into further. The timing of the murder, for one, and he scribbled a couple of words in the margin of the fax, though he was not sure about it.

Then to his surprise, he felt rather tired, and he rubbed his eyes. It was still quite early in the day. He couldn't tell if the doctor's diagnosis had had a psychosomatic effect on him.

He looked up, shaking his head. A little further to the north, he noticed a fence door had been left unlatched, which was probably unnoticeable from outside. Someone could have stepped out, having forgotten to lock the door behind them. He stood up to peer about, believing he must be close to the tourist area called Frost-Covered Goshawk Islet on his map.

As he started making his way back, a quietness unexpectedly enveloped him. He thought of several Tang dynasty lines: *Only the sound / of a tiny pine nut / is heard dropping here / in the secluded hills . . . / There, a solitary one, / you must lie awake, thinking.*

He tried to ridicule himself out of the mood. The Tang poem was about a night scene in the hills. Besides, who could be the "solitary one"?

Shortly after he got back to his villa, a young nurse appeared with freshly brewed medicine in a small thermos bottle.

"You'd better drink it quickly," she said with a sweet smile. "A hot fresh dose could make a huge difference. There will be another dose delivered here in the afternoon."

Afterward, he was rinsing the bitter herbal taste out of his mouth when a phone call came in from Director Qiao.

"You have to have lunch with us today, Chief Inspector Chen."

"You don't have to do that, Director Qiao. You've already done so much for me."

"But we'd like to consult with you over lunch."

"About what?"

"The center has been funded by the state up to now, but we're considering possible reforms. Unlike hospitals, we don't have our own way of making money. So we are thinking about opening part of the center to the public. Of course, service to Party cadres like yourself will remain our top priority. Our clinic and its location, however, may prove an attractive alternative to tourists, especially for those from Shanghai. They can stay here, just like staying in a nice, quiet hotel, and at the same time, enjoy a convenient and comfortable physical checkup. Now, you're from Shanghai, where you are a celebrity. So you would be the very man to bring this message back to Shanghai."

There might be something to this logic, Chen thought. The center was huge but far from fully occupied. Watching from his window, he had seen buildings with a considerable number of unlit windows at night. In recent years, state-run institutions like hospitals had resorted to charging their patients ever-increasing fees and getting "red envelopes" from them too, but the center was not in a position to do the same. They had to get by with the limited funds they received from the state.

But it was none of his business. Nor was Chief Inspector Chen here in Wuxi for business consultation. Still, Director Qiao seemed sincere in his approach, and Chen could not politely refuse.

He agreed to a late lunch, with the bitter taste of the herbal medicine lingering on his tongue.

There was still more than an hour before the lunch, so he sat himself in front of the laptop in the study and fumbled for an Internet connection. In spite of the instruction sheet beside the computer, he couldn't get it to connect. It was an imported laptop loaded with Chinese software. At least he could try to write something. So he hunched down over the keyboard, though nothing came to mind for several minutes.

He took the laptop into the living room and sat where he could see the lake view outside the tall window. Then he thought of the unfinished poem he had started the day before—about one's identity in others' interpretations. The image of Shanshan walking along the lake shore with him started to intrude. What kind of man could he have been in her interpretation or imagination?

The phone on the table rang. He picked it up, heard the operator saying something indistinctly, and then Uncle Wang's voice rushing over it in agitation.

"I know you're vacationing at the center, Mr. Chen, but I had to call you. Shanshan is in trouble."

"Oh—how?"

"This morning she came by, as usual, to put her lunch in my refrigerator, but before she stepped in, a couple of fierce-looking strangers appeared out of nowhere, intercepted her, and walked her into a car waiting outside. Afterward, I tried to call her at work. Someone there told me to keep quiet, that she's been detained for interrogation."

"Really! Do you know why?"

"She had some sort of an argument with Liu, her boss. That's about all I know. Now that Liu's dead, people must suspect her."

"Just because of an argument about work? That's outrageous. Do they have any evidence?"

"I have no idea. But Shanshan's incapable of doing anything like this. I know her, Mr. Chen. I've known her since she was a child. "

"I'll look into it, Uncle Wang. Don't worry. In the meantime, if you think of anything else, call me. Here is my cell number—" He paused, changing his mind, "No. I'll come over and see you. Don't move."

He must have sounded like a cop, he thought, placing the phone back in the cradle. And it was true that he was preparing to act like a cop, though only the day before, he had reassured Sergeant Huang that the murder wasn't his case and that he was just curious, only someone bored while on vacation.

His change in attitude was because of her. That much the chief inspector would admit to himself.

He left a short message for Director Qiao at the center office, apologizing for being unable to meet for lunch, then hurried out.

The road was just as attractive as before, but he was in no mood to look around like a tourist this time. It only took him about ten minutes to reach the eatery.

"She's in trouble, I know," Uncle Wang kept repeating. "I knew this was going to happen long ago. She stood in their way."

"In whose way?"

"She was responsible for environmental protection, a job that made her 'a nail in the eye' to the people in power. It wouldn't have been that bad if she didn't take her job seriously. But she did. It wasn't just Liu, but also those associated with him, who made things difficult for her. She told me about it. That's one of the reasons she comes here for lunch. They don't even let her eat a meal in peace there."

Again Chen thought back to the ominous phone calls she'd been receiving. But could the pressure, no matter how unbearable, been enough to drive a young, spirited girl like Shanshan to murder?

"You have to help her, Mr. Chen. She's a nice girl. She thinks so highly of you too."

Apparently, Uncle Wang had read too much into the thing between them. But had she said something about him to Uncle Wang after they parted at the ferry?

Other than the pressure at work, however, the old man was unable to tell him anything new or helpful. So what was Chief Inspector Chen going to do?

Under normal circumstances, he could try to contact the local police, who might have no objection, though an understandable reluctance, to his looking into the case. Wuxi being so close to Shanghai, there might be occasion for them to help each other, and Chen's own rising status as one trusted in Beijing might be useful to the Wuxi police.

With Internal Security lurking in the background, however, it could be a different story.

He grabbed his cell phone and dialed Sergeant Huang.

"I need to talk to you, Huang."

"Oh yes, Chief. Where?"

"Well," he said, aware that Uncle Wang was watching him closely. It wouldn't do to talk in the presence of the old man. Looking up, he saw a barbershop across the road, one sporting a conventional pole with a helix of red, blue, and white stripes spinning. "Come to a barbershop on Wuyou Road, south of the Bus 1 terminal. I'll meet you there."

He took his leave of Uncle Wang and walked across to the barbershop, which had the refined name of WuYu Hair Salon.

A young girl in a backless slip came trotting out, "Welcome, boss. My name is Green Jade."

It was a mistake, he realized immediately, seeing her nipples imprinted on the thin material as she took his hand and practically dragged him in. A large number of so-called hair salons nowadays were simply a cover for sexual services. Having seen many of them in Shanghai, he should have known better

He saw several other girls in the salon. One of them wore a red silk *dudo* bodice embroidered with a pair of mandarin ducks, and another simply had nothing on but a black lacy bra. They all looked at him curiously. He didn't look like a regular customer at such a place, he guessed.

Green Jade led him to an inner room dimly lit with a solitary fluorescent light and started running down the available services the moment he sunk down into a leather recliner. "We provide all kinds of services, boss. Thai-style massage, foot washing, Japanese-style massage, oil back rubbing, oil body rubbing, hair washing . . . Whatever you want, you just name it."

"I just want to have my hair cut."

"No, we don't cut hair, we only wash hair. Leisurely hair wash, luxurious, luscious. It'll bring a relaxation to your every nerve, I guarantee it."

"Go ahead," he said resignedly. It was too late for him to back out. Huang must already be on his way.

The leather recliner designed for hair washing allowed him to practically lie on his back, with his head reaching out under the water. Green Jade spared no time applying shampoo to his hair, rubbing and massaging his scalp, pressing his temples with her fingers. She might have had some profession training, he mused as she stood, bending over him, her breasts almost bouncing out of her slip.

In the fluorescent light he noticed there was a deep-red rash on her bare arms and shoulders.

"Oh, you're having allergy attack, are you?" he exclaimed with an involuntary shudder.

"Don't worry. Many people are having the same problem here. For some, it's much worse. It's all because of the lake water, you know. There is so much industrial waste being dumped into it."

It was further confirmation of the disastrous pollution problem, for which people were paying a terrible price.

"Let me rub your shoulders too, boss. They're so tense. You must have worked hard. Relax," she said, her hands beginning to work on him.

Before he could say anything, however, her fingers began brushing his groin.

"Let me rub your little brother too."

"What are you talking about?"

"You'll really enjoy it, and you can take pity on me at the same time. For washing your hair, I make only ten yuan, but for rubbing your little brother, I make sixty."

He was going to protest as her hand started reaching for his belt, when Huang burst into the room. Without seeing Chen, whose hair was covered in lather and whose face was partially obscured by a towel, Huang started shouting for him.

"Chief Inspector Chen!"

The salon was thrown into consternation and all the girls were flabbergasted. Green Jade was transfixed at the sight of Huang in his police uniform, raising her two hands high as if in surrender.

"I'm here. Don't worry, Sergeant Huang," Chen said, rubbing his hair with a towel. "Let's leave."

He paid in accordance to the price listed on the menu on the wall. Green Jade kept thanking him, her face flushed, her hair disheveled. It was not as expensive as he had anticipated, but then perhaps the price charged was due to the presence of Sergeant Huang.

As they left the salon, Chen saw that Huang had come in a local police car.

Uncle Wang was serving a customer at an outside table, and there was no other place outside for them to sit and talk, so Chen followed Huang into the car and lost no time in asking about Shanshan.

"Your people have detained Shanshan, haven't you?"

"You're right on top of the latest developments, Chief," Huang said, offering him a cigarette. "There's a new focus in the investigation—on the people who had a grudge against Liu. She's been detained because of her arguments with Liu. According to Mi, Liu had said something about firing her. So Shanshan has a possible motive. She was also heard threatening Liu about a week or so before his death in his office—saying that he would pay a terrible price. At least a couple of people in the company heard it."

"I have reason to believe she was arguing with Liu about work, and she was warning him about the consequences of the industrial pollution. I strongly suspect she made no threat to Liu personally. So, who heard her make the threat?"

"Mi, and Zhou Qiang, the sales manager, who called her a bitchy busybody. It is true that some people in the company don't like her."

"What about her alibi?"

"She doesn't have one. She said she was alone in her dorm room that evening, watching TV and reading, and she then went to bed around ten."

"Most of the people in the dorm would have given you a similar answer. A considerable number of them are single, and Wuxi is not a city with a lot of entertainment at night."

"Wuxi is not Shanghai, I know," Huang said. "But the murderer is someone who was not a stranger to Liu. As we suspected from the very beginning, it's someone who knew where Liu was spending the night."

"But others in the company also know about Liu's home office. It's no secret. As you mentioned yesterday, Mi, the secretary, knew Liu's whereabouts better than anybody else. And Mrs. Liu too."

"That's true."

"It would make more sense for Liu to have told the people close to him about his plans for the night. With the rancor between Shanshan and Liu, how could she have possibly known where he would be?"

"How—I don't have an answer to that."

"Besides, with the problems between the two, it's beyond me why Liu would have let her in, and then let her strike a fatal blow without struggling—even if she had paid him an unexpected visit that evening." Chen paused before going on, "No, I don't think she should be detained without any evidence or witnesses."

"I see your point, Chief. As your friend, she may have told you things we don't know."

"Whether she's my friend or not makes no difference. In fact, as I told you, I met her just two days ago," he said, wondering whether Huang would take his word for it. "As cops, we have to tell ourselves what we can do, and what we can't."

"I couldn't agree more. You're a man of principle. I would not have detained her, but I'm the youngest one on the team; they wouldn't listen to me. Not to mention that Internal Security is in the background, and they backed the decision."

That was probably true, Chen thought, but he still hoped Huang would try to get her released. "There is something strange about this case, Huang. To begin with, the timing of the murder. It happened just as the IPO for the company is coming up, and in the midst of the persisting controversy about its dumping of industrial waste," Chen said deliberately. "I'm stuck here on a vacation that has been pushed on me, as I've told you, and I really have nothing to do at the center. I think we can look into this case together—you and I."

"You mean we can work on a case together? That would be absolutely fantastic, Chief Inspector Chen—to investigate under your supervision. I've dreamed of it for a long, long time."

"No, it's not my case. Nor is it the time for me to make a move out in the open. I'm not a cop while I'm in Wuxi. We have to make sure of that." Chen added, with touch of self-irony, "I know you like Sherlock Holmes stories. Remember how he occasionally stays in the background and lets the police do the job?"

"Yes, he does that in several stories, Chief Inspector Chen."

"None of your colleagues should know about my working with you."

"Whatever you prefer."

"But for me to work on a case, whether in the background or in the foreground, there are things I do, and things I don't do."

"I understand."

"For one thing, I don't want to crack a case by detaining and interrogating people without justification."

"You mean—" Huang left the sentence unfinished with an edge of hesitation in his voice.

Chen knew why the young cop was hesitant, so he decided to give him another push.

"Honestly, I was surprised when I was told to come here on a vacation I don't need. But Comrade Secretary Zhao must have his reasons."

It was no more than the truth, but to the young cop, it hinted that Chen had been sent here for something highly confidential; something Chen himself had wondered about.

"I happened to know Shanshan," Chen went on after a dramatic pause, "because of something said by Comrade Secretary Zhao. He read an article by her—something about environmental protection. So he wanted me to do some research on new problems in China's economic reform," Chen said. He thought it wasn't too much of a fabrication. "I'm about to write a report on sustainable economic development, development that is not at the expense of the environment. It's not at all my field, but I couldn't say no to him."

"No wonder you came to know her so quickly," Huang said with an awestruck look on his face. "I really appreciate your trust in me, Chief Inspector Chen. I understand it's highly confidential. I'll do my best."

"Give me what additional information you may have about the case. In particular, has the final autopsy report come out yet?"

"Yes, I'll get you a copy too."

"Don't mention Zhao or me to anybody," Chen added in a hurry, reaching for the car door handle. "It's a very delicate situation, but you're capable of judging how to deal with it."

"Sure, I'll follow your instructions."

"Then we'll get to work, Sergeant Huang," he said. "I'll discuss the first step we're going to take soon, but in the meantime, I'm going to write a report about it for Beijing."

SIX

ON WEDNESDAY MORNING, CHEN called Shanshan.

"I tried to get hold of you yesterday, Shanshan. I called you several times, but without success."

"Something happened at the company. It turned out to be a false alarm," she said. "But they didn't let me go until the evening."

"What!" he said, acting surprised.

Sergeant Huang had informed him that she'd been released the previous evening. How Huang had managed it, Chen didn't ask, but Huang mentioned that Internal Security had shifted its attention to somebody surnamed Jiang, who had been feuding with Liu. In other words, Jiang was a more likely suspect. Still, Chen had become increasingly interested in the case, whether or not Shanshan was out of the woods.

For one thing, Internal Security wouldn't have intervened in a simple homicide case, even though Liu was an important man in Wuxi.

"I'm glad that it was nothing but a false alarm. But I think you need to take a break, Shanshan."

"What is false or not false, I don't know. And I am taking the day off."

"That's good," he went on. "How about an excursion around the lake today?"

"We walked along the lake the day before yesterday, didn't we, Mr. Chen?"

"Well, had we but world enough, and time—"

"What are you talking about?"

"Just a line from a poem by Andrew Marvell," he said. "My vacation here is only for a week or so, you know. Since you've taken the day off, why not?"

"You're really persuasive."

"Good. We'll do something to relieve shock."

"Relieve shock?"

"Something fun, so your mind won't dwell on the unpleasant experience. Tell you what: I haven't yet taken a boat trip here. So let us go, you and I, drifting in a gondola."

"What a poetic tourist." But she then said, unexpectedly, "Where shall we meet?"

"How about under the bronze turtle statue in the park? I'll be waiting for you there."

Soon, he found himself standing under the bronze turtle statue, leaning against the gnarled back of an old tree trunk. It was such a scenic park. The sun hung above the tilted eaves of an ancient lakeside pavilion, gilding the water with its reflections. A line of white ducks patrolled the bank nearby. He felt he could spend the day there—in her company.

His gaze shifted toward the dock, which was as crowded and noisy as the day before. A large boat was chugging out. A young couple leaned against the white rail on the top deck, sharing one ice cream cone, beaming blissfully, as if nibbling at the world in their hands.

He then saw Shanshan coming through a gourd-shaped stone gate, tripping across the meadow dappled in the shadow of a boxwood tree, and carrying a nylon string bag of bottled water. She was dressed for the occasion, wearing a lightweight maroon trench coat over a white strapless dress and white high heels.

She was dressed for his company, he observed. Confucius says, *A woman makes herself beautiful for the man who appreciates her.* It wasn't necessarily antifeminist, depending on the viewer's perspective.

"It can be windy on the lake," she said, explaining her trench coat. Her smile was radiant. She shook hands with him, and her fingers felt wonderfully soft.

Across the lake, a water bird took flight, swirling and soaring away into the distance. They started walking along the lake. It took them quite a while to find a boat they liked. Most tourists preferred the large, comfortable, modern-looking passenger ships or power boats, which were less expensive, costing only about ten yuan per person. But Chen had something different in mind.

They finally settled on a mid-sized sampan with a tung-oiled canvas awning, under which there were a couple of settees covered with indigo homespun, and a small bamboo table in between. It wasn't quite as antique-looking as he'd hoped, but it was cozy.

There was cabin room for four, but there wasn't another customer waiting at the moment. Chen offered to hire the sampan for the two of them and pay the difference. The sampan man agreed readily. He was a jolly one, in his fifties, with a weather-beaten face as rugged as in an oil painting, yet with a shrewd light in his eyes. He pulled out, standing on the stern and speaking with a loud voice:

"You're a lucky man, sir, with such a beautiful girlfriend sitting beside you. Indeed, a romantic spring day in the same boat with her is worth every penny you're paying."

Chen smiled without commenting. He seated himself opposite Shanshan. She looked at him, her hands on the table. Her eye glinted with something hard to identify, yet appealingly enigmatic. In classical Chinese literature, there was a stock phrase describing "autumn waves" rippling in a beauty's eye. She was still so young that the waves in her eyes were spring rather than autumn. There was a red paper cutting stuck to the cabin wall behind her, he noted. The cutting, though slightly torn, was a recognizable pattern of fish and flower, symbolic of passionate love and fruitful marriage.

The sampan moved further out, swinging a little from time to time, riding in a channel marked on both sides by poles stuck upright in the water.

She took off her trench coat, her white shoulders flashing against the somber background. Picking up a cup from the table, she poured some water from the bottle she carried with her.

"You're so careful."

"You can't be too careful these days."

"That sounds like a line I read long ago."

"Again? You're so into poetry," she said with a teasing smile that illuminated her vivacious face. "Are you always such an impossible romantic as a tourist?"

"I don't know, but as a tourist, I've always wanted to spend a day on the lake," he acknowledged. "And there's a more pressing reason, of course—I wanted to be with you."

His words just now sounded like an echo of something he'd read long ago, though it could have been prose and not a poem. He found it easy to slip into the role she'd assigned him.

"Shall we go to the Three Celestial Islets?" the sampan man said. "With all the Taoist temples, pavilions, pagodas, jade and crystal towers there, it is filled with really heavenly scenes."

"The Three Celestial Islets is a tourist attraction next to the park," she said. "According to one interpretation, the islets look like a turtle from across the water. It's always packed with tourists."

"No, I'm not the typical tourist," Chen said. "I can't help but think of some lines from Su Shi: *Only it could be chilly there, / in the jade and crystal towers. / Incomparable to dancing here / in the human world.*"

"You're absolutely right," the sampan man said. "My boat is dancing at your command."

"What are you thinking now?" Shanshan said.

"Well, some other lines come to mind: *Water flows in the rippling / of her eyes. / Hills rise in the knitting of her brows. / Where is a traveler going* to visit?/ *The enchanting landscape/of her eyes and brows.* That's not my poem, but one by Wang Guan, a Tang dynasty poet. For him, spring and beauty are one, that's why the poem ends like this: *When you catch up with spring,/south of the river, make sure/to stay with her.* So I'm staying here with you."

"You are overwhelming me," she said with a light, wistful smile. It was no longer fashionable to quote poetry in today's society, but it didn't seem to irritate her.

"What a poet you are!" the sampan man cut in, having overheard their conversation. "Would you like to hear a couple of sampan songs?"

"Sampan songs?"

"Yes, a time-honored convention here," the sampan man responded with a broad grin. "Remember the love songs in the stories about Tang Bohu?"

Tang was a legendary romantic scholar and painter in the Ming dynasty. There was a singing boatman in those stories, Chen recalled.

The sampan man began to sing in his deep voice with a strong Wu accent, a song celebrating the eternal theme of love:

Red peach blossoms blaze
all over the hills,
with the spring water
of the river flowing around.

The flower color will easily fade,
my lord, like your passion,
while the water runs on,
never-ending, like my feelings.

To his surprise, Chen recognized the song as one composed by Liu Yuxie, another well-known Tang dynasty poet. It was a sort of boat melody for lovers in ancient times.

"Well done," Shanshan said, clapping her hands.

"Bravo!" Chen said. "I'll add ten yuan to the fee."

The sampan man's eyes, Chen noticed, seemed to be anchored on Shanshan. Perhaps he was singing to her, reminded of his own younger days. She must have been aware of it too. She smiled good-naturedly at Chen as she patted his hand across the table.

The sampan kept gliding on, the sampan man still singing, declaring passion unchanged from time immemorial.

The willow shoots green,
the river water smooth,
she hears him singing
across the waves.

It shines in the east,
it rains in the west.
It is said not to be fine,
but fine to me.

Chen was amazed. It was another boat song by the same Tang dynasty poet, and the second stanza contained a clever pun that was both about and not about the weather.

In the distance, there were a couple of rowboats, some sharp-nosed, some blunt. One of them seemed to be checking nets in the waves, just the way it was done in the Tang era. However, factories also loomed along the lakeshore, with their smokestacks pouring out smoke against the brownish hills. Not far away, several water birds were seen scavenging among washed-up dead fish.

"One more," Shanshan said to the sampan driver.

The Qing River meanders
against myriads of willow shoots.
The scene remains unchanged
as two decades ago . . .

The same old wooden bridge,
where I parted with her,
brings no news, alas,
for today.

The last song astonished Chen with its abrupt sad ending. He looked up to see the willows lined along a curving stretch of the bank, just as in the poem.

Where would he be in two decades? Would he remember this day in the boat? he wondered.

"We also provide a special boat meal," the sampan man said, wiping sweat off his forehead with his hand. "Fish and shrimp, all fresh and live, straight out of the water. I'll throw in the net right now, if you like."

"That would be interesting," Chen said. He had read about boat meals—where a fresh catch was prepared there and then, cooked on a tiny stove, and served in the cabin.

But then he caught a glance from Shanshan. She didn't say anything, perhaps reluctant to be a wet blanket again, but he knew her reservations about the contaminated lake. There was no point discussing it, however, in the presence of the sampan driver.

"Well, we're not that hungry," he said. "Not now, thank you."

"Thank you," she echoed.

"That's fine. You have my boat for the whole day. No rush on the meal," the sampan man said in good spirits, stealing another look at her. "Now, I happen to know a boat meal story."

"Yes, tell us the story," she said.

"This story is the supposed origin of the well-known dish called Emperor Qianlong's Live Carp. This specialty is available in some fancy restaurants, served on a willow-patterned platter with the carp's eyes still turning."

"Really!" Chen said, also intrigued.

"According to the story, Emperor Qianlong, of the Qing dynasty, was exceptionally fond of traveling incognito. During a trip south of the river, disguised as a merchant, he was caught in a storm at night. When he finally boarded a sampan, he was cold and hungry as a drenched wolf. Now sheltered, he paid some silver for a meal. The boat girl was young and capable, dressed in a blue homespun tunic and shorts, bare-legged and barefoot, all alone in the sampan. She pulled out an urn of Maiden Red—"

"That's the name of some Shaoxin rice wine, right?" Shanshan inquired, now in higher spirits too.

"Yes, it's traditional for people to bury an urn of rice wine underground when a daughter is born. It would then be unearthed on important occasions years later—for instance, when she gets married. Anyway, back to the story. That urn of Maiden Red must have been stored for years. It tasted so mellow that he drained several cups without taking a break. Soon he was beginning to forget he was an emperor. The boat girl took pity on him, still looking as wet as a chicken drowning in a pond. She fried for him a live carp she'd just caught from the river. The fish turned out to be too large for the small wok in the boat, so she had to fry it with its head and tail sticking out of the sizzling oil. She served the fish hot and fresh on a willow-pattern platter. The fish tasted extraordinarily fresh and tender, with its eyes still goggling once or twice in the dark—"

"Yes, I've heard of this dish," Chen said. "I've had it at a Beijing restaurant, but never heard the story about it."

"Oh, the story is not finished yet. Now comes the climax." The sampan man paused dramatically. "Qianlong must have had too many cups of rice wine. Raising his chopsticks, he swayed and attacked the fish savagely, but of all a sudden he saw the fish turn into the girl, who was writhing, bleeding and thrashing under him as he fell to sucking her small toe as if it was a dainty ball of carp cheek's meat . . . Afterward, it became a special palace dish."

"What a bizarre story about a fantastic special dish," Shanshan said. Turning to Chen, she added unexpectedly, "A connoisseur like you should not miss an experience like a boat meal. Go ahead and order whatever you'd like. But after such a story, no fish for me."

"Don't bother fishing for anything from the lake," Chen said to the boatman. "A simple boat meal will do."

"Yes sir, a simple boat meal," he said. The sampan man must have caught their earlier hesitation, for he continued, "but I have something special today—white shrimp."

"One of the three special whites of the lake?"

"No, I didn't catch the white shrimp here. I got it from Ningbo, and it's still quite fresh. I live on the lake, so I know better."

If anything, it confirmed Shanshan's statements about the toxic lake food. "Well?" Chen said, looking up at her.

"Most locals would indeed know better," she whispered, leaning over the table. "He is probably telling the truth."

It turned out to be a boat meal different from any he had read about or imagined. It was simple, sure enough. A hot pot over a small burner of liquid gas, with frozen tofu, cabbage, and sliced beef, in addition to the white shrimp. The sampan driver pulled it all out of a cooler. They put the food into the boiling water, dipped it in the special sauce, and then enjoyed it.

It was a unique experience, with the hot pot sizzling between them, their chopsticks crossing each other in the cramped space. The white shrimp, almost transparent in the hot pot, tasted surprisingly fresh. Shanshan didn't eat much, though, touching only tofu and cabbage. She picked up a shrimp by mistake, but she peeled it with her slender fingers and put it onto his saucer, seemingly apologetic for her fastidiousness.

Perhaps she was not ideal company for a gourmet like him, he thought, amused at himself. But what's the big deal? It was good for a change. After all, he would only be here for a week.

Around them, a thin mist seemed to be congealing, and the air grew slightly damp. It was probably going to rain.

He made an effort to bring the conversation around to a topic not appropriate for a tourist. "I went to Uncle Wang's place yesterday. Don't worry. I remembered what you told me, so I didn't order any lake fish there."

"I know. Uncle Wang told me that you made phone calls for me."

"Don't mention it. I was worried about you, so I tried to find out what was going on."

"I really appreciate it, Chen. But for a tourist, you're very resourceful."

"I'm nobody, Shanshan. I know nothing about police procedure, but I do know that it's wrong to treat you like that. Like the old proverb says, if one sees something not right, one must draw out his sword to intervene," he improvised, casting himself in an archetypal role from classical Chinese literature. He added, with a self-deprecating shrug, "Alas, I have no sword in my hand."

"Well, it's getting warm here," she said, her eyes alert, her brows lightly arched. "Shall we move to the bow?"

Chen became aware of the boatman standing out on the stern, capable of overhearing their conversation.

"Good idea."

They climbed out to the bow, where they enjoyed a better view of the lake and the hills in the distance. With no chair or bench there, they had to seat themselves on the deck, which, though a little wet, bothered neither of them.

She sat cross-legged in a lotus position, but soon shifted. Leaning back against the outside post of the cabin, she stretched out her long legs and slipped off her shoes. She tilted her face to the light and blossomed into a smile. The wind was ruffling her shoulder-length hair, as though adding to the temptation.

Again, he tried to convince himself he didn't have to be a chief inspector at the moment. He could simply be a man in the company of a woman he cared for.

A bass sprang out of the algae close to the boat and snapped at something hardly visible in the misty air. The silver scales flashed against the dirty green mess, and the fish plunged back into the water, twisting and swimming away.

"Thank you, Shanshan. I've been enjoying the boat trip—every minute of it," he said, feeling that the moment was fleeting. But considering her possible involvement in a murder, he had to slow down, he told himself. At least until he could really check it out.

"Uncle Wang told me a little," he said, "but I don't have a clear picture of what happened at your company."

"I don't know what Uncle Wang said," she said, "but he hardly knows anything. What do you want to know?"

"Tell me what's been going on at the company of late, as much as possible."

"Why?"

"For one thing, I've been translating mysteries, so I'm naturally interested in a murder case. I may also be able to help a little," he said, taking her hand on an impulse, "through some connections here."

She didn't take hers away, but she didn't meet his gaze, looking instead at the green mass that stretched out, almost touching the horizon in the afternoon light.

"I don't know where to start, Chen."

"For starters, how about the IPO plan for the company? I think you mentioned it. Why should the company go public? I mean, what's the reason behind it, given that it's a state-run company? Or what's the connection to the issue of environmental protection?"

"I'm no expert on the latest reforms on the ownership system in China," she started slowly. "For my parents' generation, there was nothing but state-run companies. Then things began to change with the economic reforms launched by Comrade Deng Xiaoping, and non-state-run companies came to the fore. An increasing number of state-run companies have been falling apart in recent years. They can barely survive in today's market. So some people proposed a reform in the ownership system. It's based on the theory that a company can't succeed unless someone owns it. In other words, with socialism and communism gone to the dogs, everything has to depend on a capitalist interest. So entrepreneurs simply took over a bunch of state-run companies, buying them at an incredible bargain."

"Yes, a lot of deals like that were made under the table, I've heard," Chen said. "It has resulted in a huge loss of state property."

"However, the situation for our company is different. The ownership system is to be changed, but it is not being purchased by an outside entrepreneur. Rather, the company will become a public one, owned by shareholders. As a consequence, Liu, the company's general manager, could end up owning millions of shares. He would have been able to buy them at a huge discount—an 'inside price'—or simply get shares for free through all sorts of tricks—say, setting five cents per share as the inside price for executives like himself, when each share will be immediately worth twenty or thirty yuan once it goes on the market. What's more, Liu was in a position to purchase shares without paying a single penny from his own pocket. It would have been easy for him to get the money by mortgaging the chemical company."

"It's called *catching a white wolf with your bare hands*. I read about it somewhere."

"You're not that bookish, are you?" she said, nodding. "In Western countries, it's a matter of course for the owner to have the largest number of shares, since he started the company. But people like Liu simply happen to be in a position that enables them to turn state property into their personal property, all in the name of economic reform."

"Yes, these Communist Party officials turn into billionaires, but at the same time they remain Party officials," he said, looking up at her. "You've made a thorough study of the issue, Shanshan. It's as if you were teaching a course."

"It's because the IPO plan is somehow related to the pollution problem. That's why I've been paying attention to the so-called reform. A successful IPO depends on having an impressive balance sheet, so for the last half year, Liu has been dumping industrial waste into the lake like never before. It was a business decision designed to drastically reduce production costs. For his own personal gain, the world itself can go to hell. He was already in his mid-fifties, getting nearer to retirement, so he had to rush the process."

Shanshan's lecture testified to something he'd sensed in her. She wasn't merely a "flower vase," a pretty but naïve girl. Things in China were complicated. The reform was, as Deng Xiaoping had said, like wading across the river by stepping on one stone after another. But which stone was next, no one could tell. For instance, the changes in the ownership system were confusing to most people, and some simply didn't bother to understand.

Shanshan didn't have to worry about these things, which weren't in her field. But apparently she did, studying all the factors that were behind the current environmental problems.

The pending IPO could actually be another one of the new problems that Comrade Secretary Zhao wanted Chen to pay attention to.

"Thank you for enlightening me. I've finally got some idea of what is going on with the IPO," Chen said. "Do you think Liu's death could be connected to it?"

"That I don't know."

"Another question. You told me that Liu died at his apartment—or, rather, his home office. Can you tell me something about that place?"

"It's close. Only a five-minute walk from the company. It's just another privilege provided to the Party officials. The apartment was assigned him in recognition of his hard work, and it's in addition to the two-story house he bought with the company housing subsidy. But many people work hard at the factory, and they didn't get an apartment. Some of them still don't have even a single room."

"He stayed there all by himself?"

"What do you mean?" she asked, then added without waiting for his answer, "Mi, his 'little secretary,' was there with him, of course."

"Did he go there a lot?"

"Perhaps the only one who could really say is his little secretary."

"Yes, she would be there to help him with his work, right?"

"And help with his bed too."

"Oh that!"

He should have guessed. Nowadays a big boss, whether at a private or a state-run company, had to have a "little secretary"—a young girl who accompanied him in the bedroom as well as in the office. It was a sign of his status and, of course, more than that.

"A little secretary. I see. Do people know about the relationship between Mi and Liu?"

"Are you from Mars, Chen? That's how she became his secretary in the first place. What are her qualifications? She had barely graduated from middle school when she was hired. It's an open secret, but people don't want to talk about it."

"In other words, Mi would know not only about Liu's whereabouts that night, but a lot more."

"As far as I know, if Liu was there for some business reason, she would be the one to make the plans and preparations. If it wasn't for business, she would be the one to make the bed."

This was quite different from Sergeant Huang's version, according to which Mi didn't know anything about Liu's plans that evening and instead had worked late at the office, a fact that had been corroborated by a colleague.

"That's right," he said, aware that it wasn't easy not to talk like a cop. "But that evening, it could have been something he didn't want her to know about."

"That's possible. Who can really tell what's happening between a man and a woman?"

"He must have paid her a lot."

"At the company, her pay was appropriate to her position as a secretary. To give the devil his due, Liu at least tried to keep up appearances."

"Well, whatever he was worth, it could have eventually been all hers. For her, it would have been only a matter of time."

"She might not have been so sure about that. If a little secretary doesn't turn into a Mrs. in a year or two, then a little secretary she'll remain. The boss may have all kinds of reasons to do or not to do something. How much Liu gave her in private was, of course, another story."

"That's a very good point," he said. "But what about Mrs. Liu? She knew about Liu's evening plans, right?"

"I don't know, but she knew about the little secretary Liu kept there—"

The sampan swayed and she lurched forward, her hand touching his shoulder for support.

"Now tell me about your argument with Liu. It was about a week before his death, I heard."

"You've heard a lot, Chen. We argued several times. For Liu, profit was more important than everything else. That's what had made him— and not just as a general manager but as a much-propagandized representative of China's economic reform. It probably would have to be a top priority to keep up production at whatever cost for anyone in his position. But I had to do my job as an environmental engineer."

"You did the right thing."

"But that day, about a week ago, he snapped and started shouting at me in his office. People must have heard our argument." She added softly, after a pause, "I don't want to speak ill of him now that he's dead."

A short silence ensued. Another fish jumped out and fell back in, splashing. The boat was probably in the middle of the lake.

"That's the Wuxi Number One Chemical Company," she said abruptly, pointing to their left. "Over there, I can show you something in the water."

"Move over there," Chen called, rising to give the order to the sampan man.

"There?" The sampan man looked puzzled. It was far from any scenic sights, and no tourist would be interested going there. But the sampan went there as instructed.

"Let's stop here for a while," Shanshan said to the sampan man. Turning to Chen, she said, "Take a close look at the water here."

Already Chen could see a difference in the color of the water close to the chemical company. But it was more than that. An immense expanse of the water was covered in something like a heavy blackish-green shroud. It was substantial, almost solid, and stretched far into

70

the distance. He hadn't seen anything like that in the Huangpu River in Shanghai or, for that matter, in any other river.

"Do you see something over there that looks like a dam, Chen?"

"Yes, what's that for?"

"This horrible green mess might be permissible here since no visitors come around, but it wouldn't be allowable near the park, and definitely not near the center. So the dam is designed to keep tourists like you from seeing this."

She spoke less reservedly today than she had before, about the problems and about the people responsible for them. After the detention she had suffered, Chen reflected, that was understandable.

He knew that her history with the company might make her not such a reliable source for the investigation, though he chose not to believe that.

"What you see here is not the worst of it," she went on. "A couple of miles up, it is even worse."

"I just read an article in the newspaper which claimed that green algae might be a longstanding problem for the lake."

"How can you believe what's written in those Party newspapers? They would never trace back the ecological disaster to industrial pollution. In the past, you might see a small green patch here or there in the lake, and occasionally the water would be too rich with nutrients because of the weather, but it didn't affect the quality of the water for the whole lake. Nothing like this."

She was speaking fervently, as if to justify her work. There was no need for it, certainly not for him. He knew she was doing the right thing. So he tried to say something to lighten the moment.

"I'm no expert," he said, "but the water reminds me of a Tang dynasty poem about the south: *the spring water ripples bluer than the skies, reclining/against a painted barge,/I fall asleep, listening to the rain.* The lake water turns green, more or less naturally, with the arrival of spring. In a way, you might call that poetic."

"You really think so?"

Then she did something totally unexpected. She shifted to the side of the boat and put her feet into the water.

He didn't know why she suddenly chose to dangle her feet here, her white ankles flashing above the darksome, smelly water. He leaned over, her long black hair straying across his cheek. Watching, he wondered whether he should do the same, and he bent over to undo his shoelaces. But she was already pulling her feet out of the water. They were covered with a layer of green grime, as if painted: wet, slimy, and sticky.

"Would you call that poetic?"

"You didn't have to do that, Shanshan."

He grabbed one of her feet and tried to find a handkerchief. He ended up wiping the algae off with a small packet of paper napkins, which turned out not to be an easy job. His hands quickly got smeared too.

He couldn't claim it was poetic for him, but even so, it was almost surreal, yet touching. Her bare soles yielding in his hands, her soft toes flexing against his clumsy fingers, she seemed inexplicably vulnerable. He had known her for only a couple of days, with his identity as a chief inspector unrevealed to her.

But she had proved her point. And she had done so in a way he had never read about in classical poetry.

"Let's go back," he said to the sampan man.

"Where?"

"To the Wuxi Cadre Recreation Center."

"Wow!" the sampan man said, with a puzzled expression on his face when he noticed the grime on her feet and on Chen's hands.

"You want to go back?" She, too, looked up at him in surprise.

"I am no expert like you, Shanshan. But I don't think exposure to the chemicals will do you any good. You have to wash off your feet with clean water."

"I appreciate your offer, but you don't have to worry," she said, shaking her head.

He also shook his head, resolutely.

They remained sitting like that for a long while, not speaking, her feet still in his hands.

The sampan man began to exert himself, looking over his shoulder from time to time.

The center's fence at the foot of the hill came into view.

"Pull over," Chen said, "we want to get off here."

"Here?" the sampan man repeated, not seeing a dock or an entrance.

Chen had him row the sampan over to something like a landing near the concealed door in the fence.

"I know a shortcut. We can get in through there," he said and paid the sampan man generously. "It's for the full day, as we agreed, plus fifty for the boat meal and a tip for the boat songs. Is that enough?"

"More than enough, sir. Thank you so much. But you're from the center, so it's little wonder. Sorry that I was so blind as not to recognize Mount Tai."

It was an old proverb, often used to describe one's failure to recognize people of high status or importance.

Chen helped Shanshan to the shore and carried her shoes, which she didn't immediately put back on. The ground was gritty against her bare soles, and she leaned slightly against his shoulder for a minute. He pointed at the villa glittering in the afternoon sunlight.

"That's where I am staying."

"Oh, that looks like a villa."

"Yes, let's go there. You can wash your feet and we can have a drink."

"No, not today," she said, looking down at her feet. "What a sight I would be for your high-cadre center."

"In classical Chinese literature, there is an expression about 'walking lotus flowers,' which refers to a beauty walking barefoot. So what's wrong with that?"

"You're being sarcastic again," she said. "No, definitely not. I don't want to make a mess of your room."

"As it is, it's already a mess."

"Well, some other day. I'll keep your invitation in mind and take a rain check."

"Yes, do keep it in mind. When you come, if you come through the main entrance, make a right turn at the first crossing, and you'll see the white villa. It's a freestanding one. Number 3A. You can't miss it. At night, you can see its green-shaded windows against the shimmering expanse of the lake."

"I wish I could say something similar about my room, my dorm room. It's number 3B, but that's the only resemblance. It's as small as a piece of tofu and no one in the center would care to see it."

"Why not?" he said. "I'll take a rain check."

They arrived at the fence door and she took the shoes from his hands, yet still didn't put them on.

"Thanks for everything, Chen."

"Thank you, Shanshan."

Standing at the door, he watched her walk barefoot along the road, turn as she took out her cell phone and shut it off, and then hasten away.

SEVEN

THERE'S NOTHING TOO SURPRISING about Chief Inspector Chen, Sergeant Huang recalled Detective Yu saying. Waiting under a tall tree near the back exit of the park, Huang contemplated that statement.

He couldn't help taking another look at the entrance to the center, which still seemed mysterious, almost forbidden, to a local like Huang.

He had been surprised by Chen's request for help for Shanshan. Was it all because of something mentioned by Comrade Secretary Zhao? It was said that the romantic chief inspector had a way with women, and he had only been in Wuxi for two or three days. There was no telling what Chen was really up to, what with his connections in Beijing. He could have been dispatched here for something highly secretive. In that case, Shanshan might be involved in a way far beyond what a low-level cop like Huang could fathom.

She had been released, but Internal Security, while shifting their focus to Jiang, made a point of keeping her on their radar. And new information about the situation between her and Liu only rendered the situation even more murky. Was Chen aware of her connection to Jiang? Huang decided not to say anything about it until he learned more.

Chen had called about an hour ago, saying that he had some time and that he wanted to meet with Huang. It was already two in the afternoon, and Huang wished Chen would have called earlier. Huang had to come up with a last-minute excuse to get away from the special team.

He saw Chen striding out of the center. It was a rare opportunity, Huang hastened to reassure himself, to work with this legendary chief inspector.

"You're on time, Chief," Huang said, stepping out to meet him. "What are we going to do today?"

"I'd like to interview Mrs. Liu. For that, I need your help. I don't have any official authority here, and I don't think she would talk to me unless you are with me."

By doing this, Chen was stepping out of the background. It wasn't exactly a surprise move, that of targeting Mrs. Liu. The local police had also looked into it, but several factors had made it difficult for them to press. She had no motive, she had a solid abili, and Liu had had his little secretary for years. Then the scenario pushed by Internal Security regarding Jiang blocked any further efforts in that direction by Huang and his colleagues.

It was a step that Huang welcomed for another reason. No one would notice such a move by the two of them. Both Internal Security and his team were no longer paying any attention to Mrs. Liu.

"Let's go then," Huang said. "Shall we take a taxi? It would be about half an hour's walk."

"If you don't mind, let's walk. We can talk along the way."

"Good idea."

At Huang's suggestion, they took a shortcut through the park, moving along the bank outlined in weeping willow shoots and blooming peach blossoms, with a variety of boats sailing on the lake in the background.

It began drizzling. Several birds twittered in the shining wet foliage.

"It's a beautiful lake," Huang said.

"Yes, it is, but alas, so terribly polluted. *The rain falling in the river,/weeds overspreading everywhere,/six dynasties gone like a dream—/the birds keep twittering for nothing./Uncaring, the willows lined/along the City of Tai cover/the ten-mile-long bank, as/before, in the green mist.* I would only have to change a couple of words in the last line—*against the green algae.*"

It was just like the idiosyncratic chief inspector that Huang had heard about to quote poetry in the middle of an investigation, but great detectives could afford to be eccentric—Sherlock Holmes, for example.

"Anything new, Huang? I mean, in your investigation."

"Nothing new for our team, but inspired by our conversation last time, I made some inquiries on my own."

"Yes?"

"Your discussion about the timing of the murder really made me think. So I started researching things in the company of late. One of them being, of course, the coming IPO. Once Wuxi Number One Chemical Company establishes itself as a publicly traded company, it'll enjoy huge amounts of capital pouring in from the stock market, which will further consolidate its domineering position in the industry. This could be a serious threat to its rivals."

"So you think it could have been an attempt to derail Liu's IPO plan?"

"It's possible, isn't it?"

"It's possible, but there're other ways to do that, easier and perhaps more effective ways too," Chen said. "It's a direction worth exploring, but let me say up front, that one problem with your theory is that it's difficult to pinpoint a particular rival. With fierce competition in the marketplace, a successful company could have a lot of competitors, and not necessarily just in Wuxi. Besides, a rival may or may not benefit from Liu's death. It's still a state-run company, and there will be a smooth transition after someone is appointed to succeed Liu. It will still go public, eventually. The murder may have put it off for a time, but won't kill it. "

"That's true," Huang said, nodding.

"Keep digging," Chen said encouragingly as they walked out of the park. "But tell me about Mrs. Liu. How has your team covered her?"

"Zhou Liang, a senior member of our team, interviewed her. According to her, she was in Shanghai, playing mahjong with three others that night. Zhou checked it out and her alibi is solid."

"She went all the way to Shanghai for a mahjong game?"

"For mahjong, you have to have longtime partners. And it's quite common for people to play all night long. She was originally from Shanghai. It takes only an hour to go back and forth by train and she goes almost every weekend."

"Every weekend. Interesting," Chen said. "So she knew Liu wouldn't be coming back home that night, and she left for Shanghai for a mah-jong game. What a couple!"

"Well, about two or three years ago, there were some stories about family problems. But their relationship turned out to be okay. They purchased a mansion in both their names. And she apparently has a large bank account for her personal expenses."

"What about the home office and Mi, the little secretary?"

"About the home office, the apartment was assigned to him through the state housing plan because of his position. No one would decline such an apartment that they didn't have to pay a penny for. Since they have already had the large house, it was called a home office more or less as a means of justification. As for the little secretary, I've heard rumors about her. But a young, pretty girl can easily be the target of gossip, and it's difficult to tell how much of it is real. Mrs. Liu must have known about her for a long time. There's a popular saying about the newly rich and successful: 'The red flags stream all around outside the wall, but the red flag also stands tall, erect inside the wall.' "

"What does it mean, Huang?"

"A Big Buck may have mistresses, secretaries, concubines, and whatnot, but he doesn't necessarily divorce his wife, nor does it mean he has trouble at home. Home is a safe harbor for him. Besides, the Lius were said to really dote on their son. He's graduating from college soon. Last summer, he was an intern here at the company, and, an indulgent mother, Mrs. Liu came over frequently, bringing home-cooked dishes."

Chen listened attentively without comment. They turned in to a noisy, shopper-thronged thoroughfare, which led to a small quiet street. There, a young recycler in rags rode a junk-laden tricycle with a disproportionately huge sign describing all the recycled items. He rode down the street, his tricycle crammed with indescribable stuff, moving at leisure, as if strolling through his own courtyard. Passing, he looked back at them and grinned.

"The other factor we have to take into consideration," Huang resumed, "is how the coming IPO would affect her. The way things were going, it would probably be only a matter of months before it was complete. Liu stood to rake in tons of money and, as his wife, she did too. She had no compelling reason to do anything at this particular moment."

"That's a good point," Chen said.

The street changed again, this time into a promenade paved in colored stones, where they saw a road sign pointing to another park.

"Oh, Li Park," Chen said, pointing to a colorful billboard with a representation on it of a beauty in ancient costume sitting in a boat. "The Li Lake is a tributary of the Tai Lake, right?"

"Yes, but some locals consider it a different lake."

"It's also the lake where, after a decisive battle between the Wu and Yue in the Spring and Autumn Warring Period, Fan Li and Xi Shi spent their idyllic days in a boat, living happily ever after. I read about it in a brochure at the center. However, it's nothing but a story meant to attract nostalgic tourists."

The idiosyncratic chief inspector could be impossible, Huang thought, talking about a legendary beauty from more than two thousand years ago while on the way to interview a possible suspect. Huang had been to Li Park many times, looking at a number of paintings and poems about Xisi, but he never cared whether the ancient story was true or not.

"We're close," Huang said. "Their home is just behind Li Park."

Sure enough, they soon came to a villa complex. It was a high-end area, where the new construction bordered the lake, yet boasted of convenient access to downtown. That morning, to Huang, it didn't seem that far from Liu's office, particularly not with a company car at his disposal.

Liu's house was a three-story building located in a cul-de-sac of the complex, with a large yard in the back and a three-car garage at the side. There was a car parked in the driveway. It wasn't a company car, Huang noted.

"It's larger than the villa at the center," Chen commented, walking up the stone steps.

"The center was built in the early fifties," Huang said, as he pressed the doorbell, not sure about Chen's point.

The woman who answered the door appeared to be in her early fifties. She was slender and quite nice-looking for her age, her hair slightly streaked with silver. She was wearing an elegant silk house robe and soft-heeled slippers, and beside her were several pairs of slippers spread out on a wool mat inside the door.

"Mrs. Liu, I'm Sergeant Huang of the Wuxi Police Bureau," he said, showing his badge, "and this is a colleague of mine."

"My name is Chen," Chen introduced himself. "Shall we remove our shoes, Mrs. Liu?"

"I don't think the police have to do that," she said indifferently.

"Of course we want to do that," Chen said, bending to untie his shoelace. "It's such a magnificent house."

She led them to an immense living room with tall windows overlooking a well-maintained meadow and flowerbeds in the back. There appeared to be something of a small pond in the distance, but Huang couldn't see clearly. She motioned them to a beige sectional sofa and offered them tea, before she perched herself on a leather chair opposite them.

"Your people have come here before, officers. So what else do you want with me?"

"First, I want to express my sincere condolences," Chen said. "General Manager Liu did a great job for the Party, for the people, and for the company. We will do our best to bring him justice, Mrs. Liu. At the present, however, our investigation has made little progress, so I would like to talk with you. Anything you can tell may be valuable to us—about him, about his work, or about the people close to him."

"Liu was busy, working like crazy all the time. When he made it home at night, more often than not, he was beat. He had no energy left to talk to me about things that were happening at the company, or about the people working for him."

"Well, what about that evening? Did he tell you that he was going to meet someone at his home office?"

"No, he didn't. He didn't discuss his work with me, as I've told you."

"Did you notice anything unusual about him before that evening?"

"He was getting busier all the time. Other than that, no, nothing."

"A different question: was he sleeping badly of late?"

"What do you mean?"

"Did he have trouble falling asleep and, as a result, was he taking sleeping pills?"

Chen must have read through the autopsy report closely, Huang observed without making a comment, but that's something confirmed by Liu's colleagues.

"Occasionally, I think, but he was a healthy man for his age."

"So you knew that he wouldn't be coming back that evening, didn't you?"

"Yes, I did. He mentioned that he had to work on something important in the office that evening."

"So he always told you his schedule, Mrs. Liu?"

"It really depended on his work. If it wasn't too late, he'd try to come back home and he wouldn't call. But I never knew." She added wistfully, "When he first got his home office, he would always call with his plans for the evening. But then he got so busy, he didn't—not every time."

"You go back to Shanghai frequently—practically every weekend, I've heard."

"Not every weekend."

"But when you heard that Liu wouldn't be coming home for the night, you left for Shanghai that afternoon. Was that Saturday or Sunday?"

"Sunday—" She looked a bit uneasy. "I got back to Wuxi Sunday afternoon, but I was disappointed with his ever-busy work arrangement, so I went back to Shanghai again the same day."

"In other words, you made two trips to Shanghai that last weekend."

"I didn't like the idea of being all alone in this big house."

"So you weren't worried?" Huang cut in. "Leaving such a successful Big Buck all alone, if you know what I mean."

"He was a family man. Our son is graduating from Beijing University this year where he is a literature major, but Liu arranged an internship for him at the company last year, and talked to me about his plan to get him a good position there."

"He was a really good father," Chen said, echoing her implied meaning.

The conversation seemed to be leading nowhere. She spoke cautiously, defending her late husband's image. As a result, she gave up very little. Huang thought that Chen exchanged a glance with him.

"So, the evening of last Saturday, you were with some friends in Shanghai, weren't you?"

"Yes, I was there with several friends."

"Where were you the next morning?"

"I was at a church in Shanghai, also with a friend."

"Which one?"

"Moore Memorial Church. Why are you asking?"

"Oh, the one at the intersection of Xizang and Hankou Road. I know it. I've been reading a book about the Protestant influence on the development of capitalism."

Mrs. Liu looked confounded. So did Huang.

"Well, our church is Methodist."

"Last Sunday evening, what were you doing?"

"I was also with my friends. I've told your colleagues about them."

"Who else do you think might know about his schedule that evening?" Chen went on, unruffled.

"How would I know?"

"For instance, perhaps people who worked for him at the office?"

"What about Mi, the secretary?" Huang chipped in, picking up the cue from Chen.

"I don't want to talk about her," Mrs. Liu said, the lines hardening on her brow.

Chen didn't push, waiting patiently, letting a silence build up in the living room.

"You should have talked to her," she finally said.

"Oh, by the way," Huang said, "Mi was named office chief today. That's quite a promotion for her."

"She's a shameless slut, I'm telling you," Mrs. Liu snapped. "She has only a middle school education. How could she possibly be qualified to be the head of the office staff?"

"Well, she's been Liu's confidential secretary for a long time," Chen said. "He, too, must have trusted her."

"She was nothing to him. She cares for nothing but money, he told me. How could she have been promoted so quickly? The whole world is turned upside down!"

It would have been hard for her to say anything more explicit. After all, it was Liu who made her a secretary in the first place. It was little wonder that Mrs. Liu got so upset with her being promoted so shortly after Liu's death. It might be nothing but a gesture, however, on the part of Fu, the new general manager. Perhaps he was appeasing Liu's staff, before he started building his own power base.

Huang's cell phone rang, and he checked the number. It was the head of his team, and the call was marked urgent. He had to pick up. So he excused himself and left the living room. He hurried out of the house, closing the front door, but leaving it unlocked. It wouldn't do for him to talk in Mrs. Liu's presence.

The call was a long one about the latest developments in the investigation. Another move had been initiated under pressure from Internal Security. Huang frowned, listening, and said little in response.

When he made his way back to the living room, Chen was still conversing with Mrs. Liu. Huang had no idea what the two had talked about during his absence, but she looked cantankerous.

Presently, Chen rose and said that he had to leave. Huang echoed this without further ado.

She showed them the door curtly and banged it closed behind them.

They walked in silence for several minutes, each lost in his own thoughts. Chen had learned little from the talk with Mrs. Liu, Huang supposed, and that wasn't too surprising. After all, what would be her motive to reveal anything?

"How about a drink in Li Park?" Huang said, wiping sweat from his face. It was a warm day.

"Yes," Chen said. "We need to eat too. It's quite late. Let's find a good place in the park."

That was another characteristic of the enigmatic chief inspector Huang had heard about. Chen was an impossible epicurean with an unfailing appetite even in the midst of a homicide investigation. Still, Huang suspected that Chen wanted to discuss something with him. It was quite late in the afternoon, so there wouldn't be too many tourists in the park.

They entered the park and instead of heading to an antique-style restaurant tucked behind a verdant bamboo groove close to the entrance, Chen chose a shabby food stall near the foot of a barren hill. He ordered two lunch boxes with Wuxi-style ribs on top of white rice for both of them.

Holding the boxes, they sat on an isolated wooden bench against the hill. There were no other seats nearby, and no other people around. They didn't have to worry about people overhearing them.

"Excellent choice, Chief."

"In my childhood, it wasn't common for people to go to a park. There was the bus fare and the entrance fee, you know, let alone the cost of a meal there. One day, my mother took me to Xijiao Park and bought me a lunch box. It was the best meal I'd ever had, and it remained so in my memory for several years. Of course, things were different in those years. I'll buy you a Wuxi rib dinner at the conclusion of our investigation," Chen said, chopsticking into his mouth a small piece of the juicy sweet and sour rib. "What do you think of Mrs. Liu?"

"You've touched on something we've overlooked. She actually went to Shanghai on Saturday, and then back again on Sunday. That's strange. Do you think—"

"It would be too conspicuous for it to be something premeditated," Chen said slowly. "By the way, that was a long phone call you got there, Huang."

"Yes, it was from our team leader. About Jiang."

"Jiang—the new person on Internal Security's radar?"

"Yes, that's him. He was officially detained this afternoon. They seem to have gathered new evidence against him."

"What have they got?"

"According to Internal Security, he was blackmailing Liu. When Liu tried to bring in the authorities, he murdered Liu."

"Oh, really? Tell me about Jiang. Whatever details you may have. "

"I don't know much about him. Jiang was an entrepreneur here in Wuxi before he became an environmental activist several years ago. Because of his business background, he knows about the pollution problems firsthand. So he started to speak out about them. Those he publicly named as polluters of the lake became infamous in Wuxi. Then he started to blackmail others with the information he had. They were forced to buy his silence, so to speak. He must have gotten hold of something about Liu's company."

"Do they have any evidence?"

"Not much so far, but that's their theory. Jiang blackmailed Liu for a large sum. Any public exposure of the pollution caused by the chemical company at this juncture could jeopardize the IPO plan."

"So they have nothing but a theory?"

"Well, one local factory has a record of paying Jiang a specific sum, under the guise of hiring him as an environmental consultant. The agreement is a bit ambiguous. It could have been compensation for his help with environmental protection, but it could also be money meant to silence him."

"But in that case, why should he have murdered Liu?" Chen said, shaking his head. "On the contrary, it is usually the person being blackmailed who has the motive to murder."

"Sometime before the murder, the two were heard arguing in Liu's office. According to Internal Security, Jiang threatened Liu with information about the chemical company, and Liu fought back by counter-threatening to report him to the police for blackmail. The local authorities could have easily locked Jiang up, so that's why he murdered Liu."

"What did Jiang say?"

"Of course he denies everything."

"Well, we can't rule out such a scenario, but it's only one scenario and it's not supported by evidence."

"That's about all I can tell you," Huang said, shrugging his shoulders.

But was there something else behind it? Huang thought he could read the question in Chen's eyes.

"Can you find me some more information about Jiang?"

"I'll do my best, Chief. By the way, I've heard that Shanshan knows Jiang."

"Not surprising. They're both dedicated to environmental protection, it seems."

Once again, Huang decided to wait until he found out more before saying anything else.

They finished their box lunches, and Chen got up to throw the empty boxes into the trash bin. Huang took a look at his watch. His team members might start wondering about his long absence.

"One more question, Chief," he said, taking the paper napkin Chen handed him. "What kind of a book are you reading?"

"Which book?"

"The one you mentioned to Mrs. Liu. Something about the relation between religion and capitalism."

"Oh, it's a book by Max Weber. I happened to find a copy in the library of the center."

"But why did you bring up the topic?"

"I wanted to find out whether she's a regular at that church. She hasn't read the book, but at least she knew that Moore is a Methodist church." Chen added pensively, "But there's also a question that I've been thinking about. Why are people capable of doing anything just for the sake of money? A partial answer might be the collapse of the ethical system. Chinese people used to believe in Confucianism, and then in Maoism, but what now? Our newspapers are full of 'new honors and new shames' in this new materialistic age. But who believes in them anymore?"

This might well turn into a lengthy philosophical discussion, which was another characteristic of the inscrutable inspector. Huang had heard about this quirk of Chen's, but he had no idea how to respond. So instead he excused himself on the grounds of having to hurry back to work. No one knew about his collaboration with Chen, so it wouldn't be a good idea for him to be away for too long.

EIGHT

AS THE NIGHT TURNED toward the morning, Chen had a weird dream. He saw himself waking up in the morning as a television weatherman, who shut off an alarm clock and went to work. The nightmare repeated itself over and over: the language of a weather forecast, him speaking in the inevitable tone and manner, before the cameras, morning after morning . . .

Finally, he awoke for real and in confusion, reached out to the alarm clock on the nightstand. He then lay back on bed, trying to figure out what the dream signified, before he remembered that it was a scene from an American movie, *Groundhog Day*, that he'd seen a couple of years ago. But why such a dream would come to him this morning, he had no clue.

Getting out of bed, he walked to the living room and pushed open the window. The lake was enveloped in a morning mist, with a soft, flutelike sound floating over from the opaque mass. What could it be? He listened for two or three minutes without catching the note again.

He then moved to the adjoining breakfast room and sat down at the glass-topped breakfast table that he had been using as a desk. He didn't like the view from the study, though the desk in there was larger. He started reading the new material Huang had faxed over the previous night, making notes for himself.

Around seven thirty, a young attendant delivered breakfast. Placing the tray on the table, along with the morning's *Wuxi Daily*, she withdrew without uttering a single word, lest she break his concentration.

He sipped at the black coffee, which he hoped would help clear his head, taking in the pleasant smell of the fresh-baked goods in the room. He left the croissants and fruit cup untouched, to eat later, during a break, along with a second cup of coffee. It was a sort of routine that he had set up here, a working pattern during his vacation.

Like the weatherman in the movie, he had been playing a role too much, and now it was beginning to play him, in the ever-recurring pattern from the dream, a dream from which he'd had such a hard time waking up.

He was playing a role at the center, that of a hardworking Party cadre, the same role that everybody else here was playing.

Sergeant Huang had agreed to play Dr. Watson to Chen's Sherlock Holmes, though Huang had been going out of his way to do much more than that.

The latest information from the young cop highlighted the noose that was being tightened around Jiang's neck by Internal Security. They had gathered a bunch of new statements from local businessmen, who had sworn that Jiang had blackmailed them with threats that he would expose their problems.

But Chen didn't give their statements too much credit. They could have sworn to any wild story suggested by Internal Security. Jiang being a threat to their business practice, they would naturally cooperate, seizing upon it as a god-sent opportunity to get rid of him. It was difficult to rule out the blackmail scenario, but there didn't seem to be anything firsthand for the police to work with, for instance, a recording of Jiang's conversations with those businesspeople.

When he finally put down the folder, Chen tried to shift his mental focus by recreating on a piece of paper the crime scene scenario being pushed by Internal Security. But a number of details didn't fit. Supposing Liu and Jiang were having a face-to-face negotiation, and a fight broke out. If so, there should have been some signs of struggle at the scene. Liu would have fought back instead of waiting passively for the fatal blow. And the fatal strike would have come from the front, rather than from behind. Then there was the lack of fingerprints too. The criminal could have wiped them up, but if it had been unpremeditated, it was more likely that the killer would have fled without cleaning up.

Moreover, the amount of the blackmail, even if it was a large amount, wouldn't have presented a real problem for Liu. He didn't even have to take it out of his own pocket, it could have been written off as a consulting fee, as the other companies mentioned in the folder had done.

Also, if Liu had chosen to confront Jiang that way, he would have been ignoring the potential consequences—particularly the possible impact on the IPO plan. Jiang could have done something desperate, which would have resulted in a disastrous situation for the both of them, as in the proverb, where the fish dies struggling to get free of the net and the net breaks as the result of the fish's struggles.

Chen lit a cigarette and drained the coffee in one gulp before he stood up and began to pace about the room.

Now, supposing a different man, for a different reason, had come to visit Liu that night. That could explain a lot of things that didn't make sense in the blackmail scenario.

Chen gazed at the smoke rings spiraling up—indeed, a lot of things . . .

The young attendant reappeared carrying the tiny thermos bottle of herbal medicine. She glanced at the breakfast tray, which had hardly been touched except for the coffee.

"The breakfast wasn't good?"

"It's very good. I'll eat it a bit later."

"It's better to take the medicine after you eat."

"Yes, I know that," he said and motioned her to leave the medicine on the table.

He pulled out another cigarette, but changed his mind and put it back into the box before absentmindedly moving over to the French window in the back.

Out the window, on the cedar deck, he saw a tung-oiled paper umbrella unfolded against the railings, red-pointed like a gigantic breast, trembling slightly in the wind. *Everything is imaginable, but not necessarily innocent.* The night before, he had gone for his customary walk in a light drizzle, and left the umbrella out on the deck after he returned.

He sat down in the antique dark wood chair by the window and stretched his feet onto the windowsill. In postmodern theory, it could be said that the sight of the shapely chair arms took him, he thought with a touch of amusement. Indeed, many would be contented to just sit here—

But the morning wasn't going to be a quiet, contemplative one for him. His cell phone rang, sounding like the alarm clock in the dream. He glanced at the number on the screen. It was Sergeant Huang.

"Liu's rival had a solid alibi too."

"Who?"

"Zhang Tonghua, the head of another chemical company in Wuxi, who was Liu's main rival in that line of the business."

"Oh, the man you targeted," Chen said. "Of course, Zhang could have hired a killer to do the job, but then it would have become too much of a wild goose chase."

Chen thought about the puzzling details of the crime scene, details which couldn't be accounted for in a scenario involving a professional killer, either.

"But the timing of it," Huang said, not giving up. "We can't miss the connection between his murder and the IPO plan. Surely it's not a coincidence."

This point had been first made by Chen. Huang had obviously embraced and elaborated upon it and probably saw it as his own by now. Still, it made some sense while nothing else did.

"Oh, about Shanshan's phone record," Huang went on, "I've found something for you."

"Yes?"

"The threatening calls were made from public pay phones. They were by no means a kid's prank calls."

"That's what I suspected."

"What's more," Huang said after a pause, "somebody else is interested in her phone calls. Her calls are being tapped in connection with the investigation into Jiang."

"Oh, that's interesting. Who's bugging her?"

"Internal Security. According to them, she and Jiang know each other well. She could have been involved."

"Have they found anything?"

"Not yet. At least, they haven't said anything to me. But I'll follow up, Chief."

"Thanks for telling me this, Huang," Chen said. "Call me immediately if there's anything new."

After he hung up with Huang, Chen tried to fit the new information into the puzzle. As before, his efforts failed to lead anywhere. So, for the sake of change, he decided to write a report about the environmental issue to Comrade Secretary Zhao. Chief Inspector Chen was a cop, and a busy one, but nonetheless a responsible citizen like Shanshan. It was up to him to write this report, whether it would appeal to the top leaders or not.

He had hardly completed the first paragraph when he found himself slowing down. It was turning out to be much harder than he had anticipated. So far, all he had was a hodgepodge of high-sounding yet empty sentences that didn't prove anything. It wasn't his territory, and he didn't have anything concrete or solid to support his argument. He was quickly losing confidence in his ability to write such a report.

He lit another cigarette and his mind began wandering back to the case. He realized, much to his dismay, that it was only when he was thinking like a cop that he was able to proceed with confidence.

Since when had he become a cop who looked only at his own feet?

True, in case after case, Chief Inspector Chen had been too busy with his job to do anything else, but there's no denying that there were privileges for an emerging Party cadre. He wasn't exactly a high-ranking cadre yet, but he felt a sense of obligation to the system that had treated him well.

Thinking of Shanshan and her arduous uphill battle for the lake, he turned back to the table, opened the laptop and started to type.

> *In a trance of blazing poppies*
> *or in the cooling shade, deeply covered*
> *with moss, you have forgotten*
> *the night we spent on the bridge,*
> *the light in the distance, and the lights*
> *beyond them converging*
> *into music on your retina, while*
> *you conducted with your cigarette*
> *a tone poem of the sleepless lake,*
> *when you no longer belonged*
> *to a place, nor a time, nor yourself.*
> *When another white water bird flies*
> *from the calendar, may you dream*
> *no longer of a pale oyster*
> *clinging to the grim limestone.*
>
> *(Where are you now, as dawn taps*
> *at my window with her rosy fingers,*
> *as the fragrance of coffee and bread*
> *penetrates the wakening mind,*
> *and as the door, like a smile,*
> *welcomes flowers and newspapers?)*

The lines came almost effortlessly, more or less to his own bewilderment. Was he the persona "you" in the first stanza? That's not possible. He had been staying by the lake for only a few days. But a sense of guilt in it was unmistakable. In a symbolist way, perhaps. The second stanza in parentheses probably was the result of his recent experience at the center, but what did it really mean?

Nevertheless, these lines could develop into a long poem and not one about himself, but more about her and the lake, about what's happening in China, and about an unyielding spirit . . .

Then he paused and compelled his thoughts back to the case again, thinking with confidence. There was something else at the crime scene; what, exactly, he couldn't yet tell. So he picked up the list of things in Liu's apartment, a list he had already gone over several times.

This time he came to a stop at one particular item—a lacquer jewelry box with a black pearl necklace, gold earrings, and a green jade bracelet. None of it was of extraordinary value. But it was at his office, not his home. According to Mrs. Liu, she didn't stay there. So why was a jewelry box there? If anything, it only served to confirm Shanshan's account about Mi, the little secretary. But that didn't prove helpful, however, in his effort to connect the dots of possible clues.

Then he pulled out the pictures of the crime scene. He placed them on the floor of the living room, then seated himself in the midst of them. He looked over them one by one. Still, he failed to see anything; all he had was a vague feeling that there was something missing. Perhaps something common in everyday life, but it eluded him for the moment.

He could no longer hide in the background, he concluded. At the very least, he should personally examine the crime scene and talk to some of the people involved. It wouldn't be a big risk. Chief Inspector Chen couldn't help being curious, one could argue, about a murder investigation in Wuxi, the town where he happened to be on vacation.

And he might still keep his movements secret as long as he and Huang proceeded cautiously.

After he took the herbal medicine, fielded a mysterious wrong number phone call, and drank a third cup of lukewarm coffee, he realized that he had spent practically half a day doing nothing in the villa.

He was like one of those high-ranking cadres supposedly recuperating there in lassitude, still wearing pajamas around eleven o'clock.

He felt stupidly useless sitting there.

So he got up to get ready for the rescheduled lunch with Qiao, which he could no longer put off.

The restaurant was in the main building of the center, where the waitresses all wore colorful silk mandarin dresses with high slits, like Qing palace ladies. In the midst of their bowing and greeting, he walked up a flight of steps covered by a red carpet held in place by shining brass clips.

It turned out to be an expensive banquet of "all lake delicacies," just as Qiao had promised, in an elegant private room. Several high-level executives of the center joined in, greeting and toasting the distinguished guest.

"All the lake delicacies are carefully selected. They are not the so-called 'lake special' that you might find in the market," Qiao said reassuringly.

It was quite possible that the meals here were specially prepared for Party officials. Chen had heard about the unique treatment reserved for high cadres—not just for those staying by the lake here.

But what about the ordinary people who lived by the lake?

A huge platter of hilsa herring covered in sliced ginger and scallion was served. The fish was steamed with Jinhua ham and chicken broth, along with some white herb Chen didn't recognize.

"It's not from the lake here," an executive named Ouyang said, the oldest of the group, who was probably going to retire soon. "We simply call it *shi* fish. The chef has to clean and peel off its scales first, but after putting the fish in the bamboo steamer, he will gingerly place the large scales back on the body to prevent the loss of juice and to keep the texture tender."

Shi fish was extremely expensive, costing at least five or six hundred yuan a pound at the market. The way it was prepared was also exceedingly time-consuming.

"Yesterday I walked out along a small road in the opposite direction of the park," Chen said, for once not talking like a gourmand at a banquet. "I happened to pass by a chemical company. People were saying that somebody was murdered there. Have you heard anything, Director Qiao?"

"Yes, I heard about it too. Liu Deming, the general manager of the chemical company, was murdered in his home office," Qiao said. "It is a very successful company, and he was killed right on the eve of a huge IPO too. What a pity! He could have become a billionaire."

"A billionaire, but so what?" Ouyang cut in, shaking his silver-haired head like a dream lost in the light streaming through the windows. "As in the old proverb, rich or poor, people inevitably end up alike in a mound of yellow earth. There's no escaping *kalpa*."

"Or you may say karma, Ouyang," Chen said. "I've heard people are talking about the ecological pollution caused by those lakeside factories."

"No, not karma. I'm not a man of letters, Mr. Chen. I'm too dumb to understand those high-sounding theories about environment. Before the economic reform, however, people here had hardly enough to feed themselves. Many died of starvation during the so-called three years of natural disasters. As Comrade Deng Xiaoping put it well, development comes before everything else. Can you imagine the present-day prosperity of Wuxi without these factories?"

But at what a cost? Chen thought, but didn't say out loud.

"The company donates a large annual sum to our center," Qiao said pensively. "I don't know if the new boss will continue to do that."

Indeed, perspective determined everything, Chen thought. It was little wonder that local officials defended the pattern of the economic development.

Chen had lost his appetite, but he managed to get through the meal, absentmindedly eating, drinking, and saying things as if playing and replaying a CD from a hidden groove of his mind. Afterward, he took leave of his host with some sort of excuse and walked out.

The center was like a miniature park. The pavilions built in the traditional architectural style, alongside Western-style buildings, made for a pleasant mixture of Oriental and Occidental landscape. He followed a cobble-covered path without purpose or direction, walking past a man-made waterfall against grottos of exquisite rocks before he reached the foot of the verdant hill. He ended up near the fence door at the back, though he had come here by a different route last time. As before, no one was there. He sat on a slab of rock, looking out over the shimmering expanse of water.

It's not the lake, but the moment/the lake comes flowing into your eyes . . .

He was thinking of her again, but that afternoon, he started to realize what a battle she had been fighting in her efforts to protect the environment.

Just like those people at the banquet, Liu and the others must have been putting a lot pressure on her.

From the overpass full of sound and fury,
you may see time is like water
covered with all the dirty algae,
empty cans, plastic bottles.
Water has so many delusions,
cunning currents that deceive
with whispering ambitions and vanities.
If you are lost in the revelries
of a solitary green reed in the wind,
the water flows away, leaving you behind.
The lake has so many exits,
once lost, you can never find your way back.
After so many years, you still don't know
how the water flows?

Don't forget what's really important
in a tiny blue test tube.

Virtues are forced upon you
by the tears shaken from the forbidden tree.

The siren, coming from afar,
shouted in terror through the murky mist . . .

He was again surprised by the voice in the lines, apparently one of mighty authority, like Liu and his people, speaking out to Shanshan, though the persona here was also more of a collective one—not necessarily in Wuxi, nor just by Tai Lake. But that voice might work for an ambitious multivoice, multiperspective poem—along with the lines he had dashed off earlier that morning.

With that thought he turned and made his way toward the gate.

NINE

AS BEFORE, HE TOOK the small quaint road and turned to the right, instead of going into the park. Sometimes, walking helped him think, especially along a quiet road.

That afternoon, the road was still quiet, but there was something he hadn't noticed before. At the intersection before the small square, he saw a road sign indicating the direction to the Party School of Zhejiang Province. The school, though not in the park itself, was nonetheless in the same scenic area. A black Mercedes sped along in that direction, honking and kicking up a cloud of dust behind it.

Further along, a tourist attraction sign pointed to a bamboo pavilion partially visible up the hill in the woods. He might have seen an indication of the attraction on the tourist map, something with a poetic name, but that afternoon he was not in a tourist frame of mind.

Soon he arrived at the small square, but he didn't turn in the direction of Uncle Wang's place. He plodded on, thinking once again about the case.

Sergeant Huang alone couldn't help that much, in spite of all the efforts he'd been making. But Chen knew nobody else in the city except for Shanshan, to whom he was still unwilling to reveal that he was a detective. No, a sudden revelation like that would be too dramatic for their relationship. She wouldn't speak as freely to him if she knew he was a cop, of that much he was sure.

He came upon a small pub at the corner of a narrow street. The pub was a simple and shabby one, where customers might have a cup or two with a cheap dish or no dish at all, probably like the old-fashioned tavern in a story by Lu Xun. There were also a couple of rough wooden tables with wooden benches outside.

At one table sat two middle-aged men, hunched with nothing but a bottle of Erguotou between them, drinking determinedly in the middle of the day. Possibly they were two alcoholics already lost in a world of their own, Chen reflected, but he slowed down when he heard something like a drinking game between the two, each saying a sentence of repartee in response to the other, one after the other in quick succession.

"From a fairy tale told to our children long, long ago, the sky was blue—"

"The water was clear—"

"The fish and shrimp were edible—"

"The air was fresh—"

"From a fairy tale told to our children long, long ago . . . now I drink the cup—"

It was almost like the linked verse, a game among classical Chinese poets. The line "From a fairy tale told to our children long, long ago" sounded like a refrain. The participant could repeat it after every four or five lines, perhaps as an excuse to gain a breath. The one who failed to say a parallel line similar in content or in syntax lost the round and had to drink. The only problem with the game was when both of the drinkers wanted to drink. They could purposely lose in order to drink a cup.

Chen had no idea how long the game had been going on. Judging by the half-empty bottle, the two must have been sitting there for quite a while. It wasn't the form of the game but its contents that attracted him. Absurd as those lines might have sounded, they presented satirical, scathing comments on society. Indeed, so many things that had been taken for granted now appeared to be unrealistic and unattainable, as if in a fairy tale.

So he seated himself at a table next to theirs, tapping his finger on the liquor-stained surface, as if beating to the rhythm of the game.

He chose to sit there, however, not just because of the drinking game. The pub was located not far from the chemical company. Into their cups, people sometimes talked with loosened tongues. During another case, some time ago in Shanghai, he happened to obtain a piece of crucial information from a drunkard, an old neighbor he had known for years. Here, in another city, dealing with two strangers, he doubted he could have the same luck. Still, it was worth a try.

Aware of his interest in their game, the two appeared to be growing more energetic and effusive, popping up with proper and prompt responses to one another.

"The court was for justice—"

"The doctor helped the patient—"

"The medicine killed the bacteria—"

"From the fairy tale told to our children long, long ago . . . now I drink the cup—"

A crippled waiter emerged limping out of the kitchen, wiping his hands on an oily gray apron like a discolored map and smiling with a wrinkled face like a dried-up winter melon in the sunlight.

Chen ordered himself a beer, a smoked fish head, and half of a rice-wine-pickled pork tongue. On impulse, he also ordered the white smelt stir-fried with egg. That was one of the celebrated "three whites" here in Wuxi, the one he had not yet tried. Going by the prices on the blackboard menu hanging on the discolored wall, none of them cost more than ten yuan.

The two customers at the neighboring table must have been paying close attention to the discussion between Chen and the waiter. They even halted their game for two or three minutes. At this place, Chen must seem like a Big Buck customer. The moment the waiter limped away with his order, the two started their drinking game again, evidently with even greater gusto.

"An actress did not have to sleep with the director for a role—"

"A child's father did not have to be tested for fatherhood—"

"People did not have to take off their clothes when taking pictures—"

"An idiot could not be a professor—"

"A married man could not keep little sisters—"

"Sex could not be bargained or sold—"

"Embezzlement was not encouraged—"

"Bad guys were punished—"

"Stealing was prohibited—"

"Rats were still in awe of cats—"

"A barbershop only cut hair—"

This time the game went on longer but was also more disorderly, no longer strictly following the parallel structure and without either of them stopping for a cup.

The waiter brought back Chen's order and put it on the table without saying a word, then retreated back into the kitchen.

Raising his cup, Chen noticed that the bottle on the other table was empty and the two were looking at the "feast" on Chen's table. One blinked his eyes obsequiously, and the other raised his thumb in exaggeration. The message was clear: they were waiting for his invitation. Chen couldn't help wondering whether people in their cups were eventually all alike, too addicted to have much self-esteem or dignity left.

He nodded and said, "I happen to have overheard some of your brilliant maxims. Very impressive."

"Thank you, sir. You are one who really appreciates the music," the taller and thinner of the two said, grinning, smacking his lips. "My name is Zhang."

"When the world turns upside down, you cannot but suffer when staying sober," the short and stout one said, with his red pointed nose even redder in excitement. "My name is Li."

Chen raised his cup in a friendly gesture of invitation. Sure enough, they moved over in a hurry, holding their two empty cups.

"I'm from another city and all alone here. As an ancient poet said, *'How to deal with all the worries?/Nothing but the Dukang wine.'*"

"Well said, young man."

Chen pulled out two pairs of chopsticks for them and they didn't wait for a second invitation, attacking the dishes as if they were at home.

"The pork tongue is delicious," Zhang said, pouring beer into his cup, "but the beer tastes like water."

Indeed, their cups were the tiny porcelain cups for liquor. So Chen ordered a bottle of Erguotou, the same as the empty bottle on their table. He also talked to the waiter about a salted yellow croaker pot, which Chen wanted to be sure wasn't from the lake.

"No, just the Erguotou," Li cut in like an old friend. "No more dishes."

Before the waiter came back with the liquor, Li added in a hurried whisper, "You know how salted croaker is made. People spray DDT all over the fish to preserve it longer and cheaper. The other day I saw a fly landing on a salted fish here. Guess what? The fly died instantly. How poisonous!"

"Wow!"

"You're an extraordinary man," Zhang said, pouring himself a cup from the new bottle. "I could tell that with one glance."

"Having listened to your extraordinary wine game, I have a couple of questions for you."

"Go ahead."

"Those comments were deep. But what about 'Fish and shrimp were edible'? Let's not talk about salted croaker. People relish fresh lake delicacies and especially so here."

"Let me tell you something about the fish and shrimp in the lake. You can see how white the smelt looks, can't you?"

"Yes."

"Almost transparent, right?" Zhang said, taking a slow drink from his cup. "Now, let me tell you what. The smelt have long, long been immersed in formalin, so that they look dazzlingly white."

"What? Aren't they naturally white?" Chen said. "The three whites of the lake are widely celebrated."

"In such a dirty, polluted lake, how can the smelt grow to be white and pure? If anything, they are now ghastly green or black, and no matter how long you put them in clean water, they remain discolored. That's where the formalin comes in."

"However contaminated the fish are, people still have to eat," Li said with a dramatic sigh, resolutely chopsticking a smelt into his mouth. "To tell you the truth, I've not tasted it for months, tainted or not. How can a poor, down-and-out man like me afford to pick and choose?"

"Confucius says, *Rites collapsed, music broken*. That's what happens in China today. When Chairman Mao led our country, there was no gap between the rich and the poor. A company boss earned about the same as a janitor. People all had secure jobs that were nonbreakable, like iron bowls."

"You're wrong, Zhang," Li said, putting down his cup. "The gap was there under Mao as well, but you didn't see it, not that easily. Not far away, for instance, is the high-ranking cadre center where Party officials can enjoy all the privileges for free. Could you have ever stepped into it?"

"Yes, this used to be one of the best resorts for high cadres, and they would come here from all over the country. But with the lake now so polluted, they aren't so interested in it anymore."

Was that the reason for Comrade Secretary Zhao's refusal to come here? Possibly. In his position, Zhao could afford to pick and choose. Not so for Chief Inspector Chen. In fact, it was an amazing stroke of luck for him to be chosen to come here. Or was it?

"Wrong again. Do you think those high cadres will have to eat the fish and shrimp from the lake here? No way. Theirs are shipped in specially."

Chen nodded. That was exactly what he had heard earlier at the banquet table in the center.

"What a crying lake! More and more people around here get cancer and other mysterious diseases. My old friend was rushed to the hospital with so much arsenic accumulated in his body that the doctors were all amazed."

"What toxic air people breathe every day! More and more babies are born disfigured. My next-door neighbor had a son who was born looking like a toad, all covered with green hair."

It began to sound like another round of the drinking game, except it was with more horrible, concrete examples. Chen listened without interrupting, or eating, or drinking. He hadn't been hungry and was now even less so, while the other two had kept themselves busy devouring, then discussing, as if anxious to pay him back that way.

"It's all for the sake of profit. But you can't blame those factories alone. What else can people really grasp in their hands? Nothing but money. My grandfather believed in the Nationalists, but Chiang Kai-shek shipped all the gold to Taiwan in 1949. My father believed in the Communists, but Mao's Red Guard beat him into a cripple in 1969. I believed in the reform under Deng for the first few years, but then the state-run company where I had worked all my life went bankrupt overnight."

"Talking about Mao, do you remember the picture of Mao swimming in the Yangtze River?" Zhang said, vehemently poking the eye of the smoked fish head with a chopstick as he changed the topic.

"Yes, I remember it. Mao took that picture before the outbreak of the Cultural Revolution as an evidence of his health," Chen said, glad to comment on something he knew. "It was meant to reassure people that he could still vigorously lead China forward."

"Well, with China's rivers and lakes so polluted now, Mao jumping into the river would be seen as a suicide attempt."

"Eat, drink, and leave Mao alone," Li cut in, with a surly tone. "At least the lake wasn't that bad under Mao. Nor were there so many unscrupulous plants dumping industrial waste into the Tai water. Now it's a country overrun by wolves and jackals."

"Don't be such a sore loser, Li. You lost your job because your factory went bankrupt competing with Liu's. But it's just the way of the brave new world."

"No, that shouldn't be the way. Our plant was run in accordance with the environmental regulations. It was run with conscience, you might say. How much is a pound of conscience worth in today's market? Liu had none at all, but look how much he profited."

"Excuse me," Chen cut in. "I heard that a chemical company head named Liu was recently murdered. Are you talking about him?"

"Yes. Now that's really retribution. Karma." Li poured himself a full cup and screwed the bottle cap on tightly, as if that meant something. But it was of no use because the cap was being unscrewed almost immediately by Zhang.

"Liu's chemical company is damned," Li went on. "Irrecoverably cursed."

"How?"

"A couple of months ago, thousands and thousands of fish died in the water near that company, turning up their white bellies like so many angry eyes staring at the black night. It was all because of the damned poisonous pollution. The Wuxi Number One Chemical Company is one of the biggest enterprises in the city, and it's also the worst polluter. In Buddhism, a life is a life, whether an ant or a fish. For inhuman deeds, there's no escaping retribution. No one escapes."

"You mean Liu's murder."

"Believe it or not, I saw Liu walking by the lake with his little secretary one evening just about one month ago. It wasn't far from here. All of a sudden, she turned into a white fox spirit looming against the dark night. You know how a bewitching fox spirit brings a curse to the man that's with her."

"Liu's little secretary?" Chen said, playing dumb.

"Mi. I think that's her name. What a shameless bitch! She slept her way into that position."

"Come on, I don't buy that story about the fox spirit. That's total bull," Zhang said, noticing Chen's sudden interest as he raised the

106

empty cup high. "But a bitch she is, no question about it. I, too, happened to see something just about a week ago."

"Just about a week ago?" Chen waited, but Zhang didn't go on, staring into the empty cup, as if lost in recollection.

The second bottle of Erguotou was now finished too, Chen noticed. He wondered what kind of a man he appeared to be in Zhang's eyes. Possibly one interested in the "bitch" of a little secretary, for some untold reason. Nevertheless, Chen ordered another bottle.

"So what did you see, Zhang?" Chen resumed when the old waiter placed the new bottle on the table.

"She was walking with another man—a much younger man—arm in arm, billing and cooing and kissing," Zhang said, talking a deliberate long sip from his newly filled cup. "It was under the cover of night. Around midnight, I would say."

"Do you remember what day?"

"I can't remember the exact date, but it was about a week ago," Zhang said, then added, "More than a week ago, I believe."

That was before Liu's murder, Chen calculated, raising his cup only to put it down again.

"That was not too surprising," Zhang went on, shaking his head. "She's still in her early twenties, and Liu was in his mid-fifties. How could he have possibly satisfied her? It would have surprised me if she hadn't been carrying on with a young stud in secret."

"It served Liu right, with his heart smoked in the smell of money like the fish head on your plate."

"No, the dogs ate his heart long, long ago."

"Another question. I'm not a local, but isn't there anyone fighting against the pollution here?" Chen said. "I was at an eatery yesterday. Uncle Wang's, I think. It was not too far away from here. I heard about a young woman engineer who was trying to stand up for environmental protection."

"Oh, she's trouble. True, she may have brought some attention to the problem. But then what? It was no use at all. The chemical company keeps on manufacturing as before, at a great cost to the lake. "

"And she's an impossible bitch too," Li said.

Chen wasn't sure why Li called her a bitch, but he decided not to ask.

"You can't keep your eyes shut all the time. So drown yourself in the cup, and forget all your worries," Zhang said, finishing another cup in a single gulp.

"You should go and see Liu's house. What a magnificent mansion! It's only three or four blocks away, but you can also see the chemical company dorm. Then you'll understand why people want to sell their souls for money."

"Really!" Chen said, his voice rising with a new idea. "Thank you so much for your enlightening talk. But I think I have to leave now. Do you know if there is a cell phone store nearby?"

"Just go straight ahead. Only half a block away. You won't miss it. Tell them Zhang sent you there."

"I will. Again, thank you both so much." He didn't think he could get much more out of the two, so he rose to pay for the meal. It wasn't much, but he didn't want the two of them to go on drinking like that. If they kept getting drunker and louder, they could become a liability.

Before he got to the cell phone store, he came to a halt. He found an envelope—the only paper he had with him—and a pen. Standing against a blossoming dogwood tree, he wrote down a jumble of fragmented lines and images that had come to him unexpectedly.

Terrible headache—
Go drink and forget—
You should see a doctor, man.
What can you see?
In the company production chart,
Does the boss see the curve
of the production rising
or that of the employees falling

with headache, herpes, and sickness?
Look, isn't the pinnacle of the cooling tower
like the nipple of a sterile woman?
Tell me, where are you?
At the hair ribbon of Fortune Goddess,
or at her crutch?

Another bottle of beer pops open,
bubble, bubble, bubble . . .
She pushes away the cup, walking
into the sour drizzle and twelve o'clock.

Who's the one walking beside you?

As before, it could be made into part of a larger whole, but he still didn't have an exact idea of what it would be. Possibly it would be a "spatial form," which was a term he had picked up years earlier, where the form replaced traditional narrative sequence with spatial simultaneity and disjunctive arrangement. Those long-forgotten critical details seemed to be coming back to him all of a sudden. So the stanza about the conversation between two drunkards could also fit in. She, too, finally appeared in the poem. As for the line "Who's the one walking beside you," it might serve as a refrain, like in the drinking game he'd just witnessed. Also, it sounded like an echo, remotely, from a poem he'd read long ago.

He put the envelope away and resumed walking toward the cell phone store.

TEN

IT WAS ONLY AFTER about three or four blocks that he thought he saw the dorm building for the chemical company with its many clotheslines stretching across the outside.

He took a look around. It wasn't yet six o'clock. In the space in front of the building, some people sat outside with their dinner in their hands. A middle-aged woman sat on a bamboo chair, soaking her feet in a plastic basin of herbal liquid. There was also a peddler squatting with his goods spread out on a white sheet under a dogwood tree. There was something eerily familiar about the peddler, Chen noticed, thinking he might have seen him somewhere. It wasn't unimaginable for a peddler to move around in a city of tourists like Wuxi, but this wasn't a tourist area and wasn't a place a peddler would usually choose to set up.

Chen approached a little boy playing with an iron hoop in front of the building and was told that the dorm wasn't only for the chemical company but for several other factories and plants as well.

It was a gray concrete four-story building that might not have been originally designed or intended to be a dorm building. The chemical company must have obtained a housing quota in the years of state housing assignments, but those rooms, instead of being assigned singly, were partitioned and then further partitioned, each into two or three, so that more employees could have something of a temporary shelter. In some cases, it had only space enough for a bed, or worse, for two beds so the space had to be shared by two single employees. Other companies had done the same with the rooms assigned for their employees.

He knew about similar arrangements in Shanghai. Years ago, he'd stayed in such a dorm room himself, albeit only for a short while.

An elderly woman standing near the door in blue-and-white-striped pajamas cast a curious look in his direction as he entered the building.

The old wooden stairs creaked under his feet as he groped his way up to the third floor in semidarkness. He was unable to find a light switch, so he felt his way along until a shaft of light from a cracked window above the landing of the third floor lit the way for him. He was able to make out a narrow corridor lined with wet clothing, stoves, vegetables, and all the odds and ends imaginable. Because of the rooms' cramped space, the corridor sometimes became a kind of battleground among the residents, who vied for an extra square meter or two.

He finally found and knocked on the door marked 3B in fading letters.

Shanshan opened the door with a surprised smile. She was standing there in a white terrycloth robe, barefoot and bare-legged, her hair still wet, with a soft ring of lamplight in the background.

"What a surprise, Chen! Come in," she said, reaching out her hand and closing the door after him. "But how did you find my place?"

"I remembered what you told me the day of our boat trip, 'Mine is 3B, but it's small as a piece of tofu.' This afternoon, I happened to learn the location of your dorm in a pub not far from here."

"You're really a detective, Chen."

She must have just washed her hair, which hung loose and shiny over her shoulders.

"Well, more like an unemployed detective," he said smiling. "I had lunch with the director of the center, but then I had nothing else to do the rest of the day. Standing by the window, I was thinking of a poem by Liu Yong, when I couldn't help thinking of you. The lake view is so fantastic, but what's the point when I had it spreading out before me all alone?"

"What poem are you referring to, Chen?"

"In one of his most celebrated poems, Liu Yong put it well: *'All the beautiful scenes are unfolding,/but to no avail./Oh, to whom can I speak/of this ineffable enchanting landscape?'* So I decided to come out."

It wasn't exactly true. After the lunch, at the foot of the hill in the back of the center, he was thinking of some different lines—lines of his own. But they were evoked by thoughts of her. And he had in fact thought of Liu Yong's poem a couple of times in connection with her.

"You're being poetic again, Chen. You could have called me first. Not that you're not welcome to my place, but I could have prepared. It's such a mess."

He smiled without making a response. It surprised him, too, that such a "poetic" role or identity came to him so effortlessly while in her company. Psychologically, it was perhaps due to his awareness of not being his true self for the moment. But then, he wondered what his true self really was. That of a Party member cop?

"It doesn't look like a mess to me," he said.

The room actually looked pretty close to what he had imagined it would be. It wasn't a mess because she was unprepared, rather because of the size of the room, which was five or six square meters in all. The main furniture was an old rusty bunk bed, which occupied about half of the room. The top had become a sort of storage, like a trunk stand in a hotel room, except that instead of a trunk, all sorts of stuff was heaped up there, along with a string of Chinese sausages that were hanging from a peg in the water-stained ceiling.

Parallel to the top of the bunk bed stretched a clothesline, which was empty, except for a pair of pantyhose.

In front of the lower bed was a rough wooden table that apparently also served as a desk. Sitting on it were books, an open notebook, an unwashed bowl, a small pot on an electronic burner like the one in the sampan the other day, and a bundle of noodles. Chen saw shoes peeping out from under the bed, including the shoes she had worn for the sampan excursion. It was nothing short of a miracle that she managed to store everything in such a small cubicle.

It reminded him of his college years, when he had lived in a dorm room like this, only with three other students. At least he didn't have to cook there, too.

He couldn't helping taking stock of this room in detail, as it was in such sharp contrast to the Lius' home.

"The problem with a dorm room is that you don't really treat it as your own room, because you believe you're going to move out one of these days," she said, motioning him to sit on the only chair there, from which she'd had to remove a pile of newspapers. "And another problem is, believe it or not, that you might never move out."

It was an ironic comment, possibly a witty justification of the room's messiness, but to him, the tiny room lent an air of intimacy to the moment.

She'd been cooking in the room, and the water in the pot began to boil.

"You've not eaten, have you, Chen?"

It was a conventional greeting Chinese people made when running into each other on the street. It wasn't exactly a question to which a response was expected. In the present context, however, the question meant something. So did the answer.

"No, not really."

In the pub he'd only had the cup of beer. The other two had eaten the food on the table.

She pulled a cardboard box out from under the bed, grabbed another bunch of noodles, and threw them into the pot of boiling water.

"You know how to watch noodles?" she asked, pointing to a dented kettle on the floor. "There's the cold water."

It became his responsibility to keep pouring cold water into the pot whenever the water started boiling. It wasn't difficult. He just needed to repeat that two or three times, and the noodles would be done.

She pulled out several jars of sauces, which she kept under the table, spooned a little out of each jar, and mixed them together in a bowl. She was absorbed in her work, which appeared to be an improvised concoction. He'd done similar experiments at home, tossing together whatever ingredients were available. In the somberly lit room, he couldn't make out the labels on the jars, and he couldn't help shifting his attention to her white thighs, revealed through the robe, which ended just above her knees.

After adding cold water and then repeating the process one more time, he began to ladle out the noodles into two bowls. She then poured the sauce on top of them. In addition, she opened a small plastic package of Wuxi gluten and put pieces of gluten onto the noodles.

So that was their dinner. She sat on the bed, and he on the only chair in the room, the noodles on the table between them.

To his surprise, the noodles were quite delicious. The meal was more agreeable than the banquet at the center. For one thing, he liked noodles. He was a gourmet when he ate out, but not an enthusiastic chef when he had to cook for himself.

It was probably the same for her. He then dismissed the thought almost instantly. She was much younger. An attractive girl like her probably had a lot of men her own age eager to invite her out to candlelight dinners. He felt a twinge of jealousy.

Or was he suddenly feeling so much older?

"Thank you. These are the best noodles I've had in a long time."

"Come on. How can someone who dines with the executives of the center really enjoy a bowl of plain noodles with me?"

"It's the truth, Shanshan. Noodles shared with you are no longer merely plain noodles."

"Someone who enjoys the special connections that you do," she went on, without responding to his comment, "doesn't have to say such things."

"What do you mean?"

"Uncle Wang told me that, on the morning I got into trouble at the company, you made some phone calls for me. Shortly after you called, a police officer rushed over, showed you all the respect he would if you were his boss."

"Oh, that. Yes, as I told you earlier, I did make some phone calls. I was concerned about you. As for the police officer," he said, trying to think what the old man might have seen from across the road, "we happened to meet when were both getting a haircut in the same barbershop. He knew of my work—I've translated some mysteries, you know—so I talked to him about it."

"According to the police officer who released me, I have a *guiren* in my life that I didn't know about. He said to me, 'But for your *guiren*, you might have remained in custody for god knows how long.' I don't know that many people here. Certainly not anyone that powerful, Chen."

In traditional Chinese culture, *guiren* meant someone powerful or influential who helps out in an unexpected way. It was understandable that Huang couldn't help using such a term, which suggested Chen but didn't give him away.

"Well, clearly they had no right to detain you. When they realized their mistake, they had to come up with some excuse, which is probably why they credited a *guiren*."

He couldn't tell whether she believed him or not, but her comment gave him an excuse to turn the conversation to the topic he had in mind. He had been unwilling to bring it up that evening.

"Let's talk business," she said, stealing the initiative from him. She sat up and drew her legs up under her on the bed, her hands clasped around her knees. "I don't think you came here for a bowl of noodles."

"Well," he said, looking at her, and then past her to the wall behind her, "the partition wall looks as thin as a piece of paper."

"No one will hear," she said, lifting up a wisp of black hair that had strayed over her eye, "provided we don't talk too loud. But why? If it was anything that important, you could have called me and asked me to meet you elsewhere."

"Here's a phone for you," he said in a quiet voice, pushing across the table a newly bought cell phone. It was shining scarlet, which somehow reminded him of her in her trench coat that day in the sampan. "In the future, when you call me, use this phone only."

"Why?"

"You aren't only getting prank calls on your cell. It's been bugged too."

"You're really scaring me, Chen. How the devil could you know about all that?"

"Through my connections. Don't worry about what connections, Shanshan. I just happen to have them. When I made inquires into those nasty calls you'd been getting, I was told about your phone being tapped." He went on after a short pause. "For instance, they mentioned you had been speaking to someone named Jiang."

She stared at him in shock, not uttering a word. She hadn't said anything to him about Jiang. Of course, she didn't have reason to— not to a tourist she'd just met by chance.

"How could you have—" she started without finishing the sentence, her face instantly bleached of color.

"About the threatening phone calls you've been getting, they were all made from a public phone booth. So there's no way to trace the identity of the caller. If anything, though, it proved that they weren't merely prank calls. Kids wouldn't have made such an effort or spent money on a practical joke."

"But how could someone have stooped so low?"

"It's someone who is capable of anything. That's one of reasons I decided to come over the moment I learned about it—without calling you first. But it's also true, needless to say, that I missed you. As an old proverb goes, One day elapsed without seeing you feels like a separation for three autumns to me."

"You're still being poetic with me."

116

"Setting sentimentality aside, tell me as much as you can about what has been happening of late—with you, around you, or at your company. I don't know if I'm in a position to help, but to be able to do anything at all, I need as much information as I can get from you."

"Why are you going out of your way to help me?"

"You know why," he said, grasping her hand across the table. "I want to."

"But I don't know what you want to know."

"Let me ask you this first. Now that Liu is dead, is there anything new at your company?"

"There's been nothing new under the sun. The wastewater keeps flowing into the lake, day and night. Fu, the new general manager, won't change anything."

"I heard that Mi was promoted to office manager."

"You've been hearing about things promptly. I only heard about it yesterday."

"She was only Liu's little secretary, wasn't she?"

"Fu's only been here for four or five years. He needs her help for the transition, I think. After all, there are a lot of things that Mi alone knows."

"So Fu's quite young? He must have been promoted very quickly."

"Fu majored in economics. When he was still a college student, he published an article on the economic reform in the *People's Daily*. This made him an instant celebrity, and he was named as a representative to the national Youth League conference. Upon graduation, he was assigned to work as an assistant to Liu. Because of his Youth League background, it didn't take too long for him to be promoted."

"So he's one of the 'rocket cadres,'" Chen said, nodding. "A lot of young cadres are chosen from the Youth Leagues, they are the so-called young vanguard for the Party. Fu must have worked closely with Liu then."

"Liu wasn't an easy one to work with or to share power with. I don't know much about the politics among the executives at the company, but Fu seems to have remained an outsider. That was just my impression, of course. Luckily, he knew how to play second fiddle."

"But he plays first chair now."

"Yes. It was clever of him to promote Liu's little secretary as gesture to the men and women in Liu's camp."

"I think you're right," Chen said. "Now, on a different topic, tell me what you know about Jiang."

"Well, he got into trouble for the same reason I did—his environmental protection efforts," she said, still without withdrawing her hand, "except that he pushed even harder. But as for what he's been doing of late, I have no idea."

He noticed her emphasis on time with the phrase "of late." That she didn't know was probably true. Had there been anything of late between the them, Internal Security would have pounced on her and wouldn't have let her go.

"Jiang's an 'environmental activist.' Anybody labeled as such can easily get into trouble, and not just him. Look at this dorm room. When I was first assigned to work here, Liu promised me an apartment. But as soon as I spoke out, the promised apartment vanished into thin air. It's my fourth year here, and I'm still in the same dorm room."

"Have you had any contact with Jiang?" he asked, making the question sound casual.

"We're in the same field, so we would discuss problems that we had in common," she said, without concealing a touch of hesitancy. "But I haven't been in touch with him for quite a while. I did call him the day before yesterday because of something that I heard. He didn't pick up and he didn't call back."

"You have no idea what's happened to him?"

"No. What?"

"He was taken into custody."

"Oh—like me?"

"Yes, like you. And now they're checking into the people close to him."

"They really are capable of anything," she said, shaking her head.

118

Her hair was still slightly wet and tangled. "I should have studied something different at school."

"No, that's not true. It's a critical subject area for today's China." He wondered if she was trying to steer the conversation away from Jiang for some reason. "But back to Jiang. Did he have an argument with Liu?"

"I can't imagine that. They might have met once or twice, but I don't know of anything recent."

"According to Internal Security, he tried to blackmail Liu recently."

"No, that's not possible," she said.

She didn't elaborate. Nor was Chen in a good position to push her, having not yet revealed himself to be a cop.

"Don't call him again. At least, not before telling me first if you think you must," he said instead. "I'll keep you posted on the latest developments."

"Things are really serious, aren't they?"

"Yes, I think so."

"But do you know how serious the environmental crisis is for our country?" She went on heatedly, without waiting for a response: "The government talks a lot about the improvements in human rights. I don't know much about that. But I do know that at the very least people should be able to breathe pure air, drink clean water, eat good food, and see the stars at night. These are the most basic human rights, aren't they? But not in China. Let me give you an example. When the Beijing government called for a ten percent reduction in sulfur dioxide in China's air, I was still in college. Now, five years later, sulfur dioxide pollution has *increased* twenty-five percent. As for water, well, you've seen the lake. And it's not just Tai Lake, of course. Decades of unchecked, unbridled pollution have left much of the water in big lakes and rivers unfit to touch, let alone drink. They have pollution levels of Grade 5 or worse, meaning that the water is unfit even for human contact."

"Hold on a minute, Shanshan. Are all these figures based on research?"

"Yes. They are no state secret, I can assure you. If you do your research, you can find all of this in the officially published material."

"It's shocking." He searched his pockets for a scrap of paper, but without success. "Can I have a piece of paper to write down some of those figures?"

"Why, Chen?"

Chen was thinking of the report he had to turn in to Comrade Secretary Zhao. At the moment, the chief inspector didn't have any solid evidence to support his argument. However, he wasn't going to tell her the real reason, even though he would never do anything to get her into trouble.

"I've been trying to write a poem about the pollution in China, but I'm not an expert like you. Still, I don't want to publish something unsupported by facts."

"Are you serious?" she said. "That might get you into trouble. Besides, I doubt if such a poem would be publishable."

He was serious and had, in fact, already written several stanzas.

"I have the connections to get it published, I think. Connections aren't something to be proud of, but they do help get things done." After a short pause, he went on. "After our conversation in the sampan, I did some serious thinking about the issue. Environmental protection must be an uphill battle. It is as difficult as it is complicated. But what is at the root of the ever-worsening pollution problem? Human greed. Pollution isn't a problem that pertains to our country alone—as the proverb says, crows are black all over the world—but the shape the problem takes here is certainly characteristic of China."

"Characteristic of China," she said, looking him in the eye, "as the newspapers say about China's socialism."

"Because China lacks any history of a sound legal system and because of the general ideological disillusionment, particularly resulting from the disastrous Cultural Revolution, people take whatever they can grasp in their hands, by hook or by crook, in this brazen ultra-acquisitive age. Some economists even declare greed a necessary evil for our economic development. Marx himself said something to that effect too, though he was very critical about it."

"Wow, you even dragged Marx into it, Chen. But I know the passage you mean. According to Marx, for a three hundred percent profit, a capitalist would do anything, commit any crime, even at risk of being hanged."

"Exactly. I don't think doing everything possible for profit will lead to anything good—not for the environment or anything else. But the issue is complicated. The Party authorities must be aware of the environmental problem, but, to some extent, the legitimacy of the Party's regime depends on maintaining economic growth, so any regulatory effort that gets in the way of growth will be suppressed."

"You've hit the nail on the head, Chen!" she said, her eyes bright.

"I've been thinking a lot about all this, Shanshan," he said earnestly, "because of your company, and because of the poem I'm working on. I've just started, but it could be a longer, more ambitious poem than any I've ever done before."

"Let me get my folder for you."

She got down on all fours, reached under the bed, and pulled out a cardboard box, her bare legs sticking out and her elegantly arched soles faintly dabbed with dust. She emerged out from under the bed with a blue folder in her hand and a smudge on her face.

"Anything you might want to know," she said. She seated herself at the table and opened the folder.

Chen moved his chair nearer to the table so he could read the small print on the pages in the folder.

He was reminded again of his college years, when he spent hours bent over a similar table in a similar small dorm room: idealistic, passionate, and doing what he believed to be the right thing.

Outside the room's small window, the color of the sky was changing, dimming into a deep blue with sparse glittering stars starting to show.

He didn't know how long they had talked. He was only aware of her hair touching his cheek, once or twice, like a refrain in a half-forgotten poem, and of her slender finger pointing at the material, as she explained it all in detail.

She then sat up, drawing one foot under her in a casual pose. But then she immediately thought of something else and leaned over the table again. As she bent over the folder, her robe parted slightly. He thought he caught a flash of her breasts. If she was aware of his glance, she said nothing.

A spell of silence fell over the room when she finished going over all the material in the folder.

"I really appreciate your coming over tonight," she finally said, her eyes lambent in the flickering fluorescent light.

He glanced at his watch. It was past nine. She didn't say anything about it's being late, so he could choose to stay, perhaps, for a bit longer.

It wasn't comfortable to sit in the same unchanging position for long, particularly in the cramped space between the desk and the bed. He was reminded of a so-called lovers' room in a restaurant on the Bund in Shanghai. The tiny size lent itself to intimacy. He had been there with another woman—though not his lover—who was murdered shortly afterward. He shivered at the sudden, inexplicable premonition. He shifted on the chair, which warbled with a screeching sound.

She sat further back, her back touching the bare wall, her arms no longer clasping her knees, and her legs parted. She patted the bed, an invitation for him to sit alongside.

As his glance fell to the bed, he noticed a sauce stain from the noodles she had made earlier in the evening on the fleshy spot below her big toe. In the soft light, her toe looked rounded and snowy like a creamy scallop in a chef's special. The absurd association only made her look appealingly vulnerable. As a Jin dynasty poet said, she's so beautiful that she could be devoured. He thought he could read a message rippling in her eyes, reflecting back what he fantasized.

Instead he rose to leave.

They looked into each other's eyes.

"It's late, Shanshan. I think I have to leave. The center locks the entrance around twelve."

It would be out of the question at this stage, Chief Inspector Chen knew, for him to do anything unacceptable for a cop, particularly for an incognito cop on vacation.

If he was going to help, he had to stick to his role as a policeman. There could be no conflict of interest, even if he kept his identity a secret from her.

ELEVEN

FRIDAY MORNING, SERGEANT HUANG parked his car in the shade near the center's entrance, rolled down the window, and waited. According to the plan Chen had discussed with him, the first interviewee of the day would be Mi, Liu's secretary at the chemical company.

It wasn't exactly a surprising move to Huang, who'd already talked to Mi before Chen involved himself in the case. Huang lit a cigarette, trying to guess which approach the chief inspector would use.

At the appointed time, Chen showed up at the gate, where an elderly security guard hastened to salute him obsequiously. Huang stepped out of his Shanghai Dazhong, which, as Chen specified, didn't look anything like a police car.

"Thank you, Huang," Chen said, sliding in to the front passenger seat. "Before we go to see Mi, I want to take a look at Liu's home office."

Huang jumped at the suggestion. His team had hardly finished working at the crime scene, with several reports still waiting to be processed by the lab, when Internal Security intervened and pushed them straight to a conclusion that left little for them to do. Being the youngest member of the team, Huang knew better than to protest when the other team members, older and far more experienced, chose to keep their mouths shut.

But it wouldn't be difficult for him to show Chen Liu's apartment, which wasn't being watched at the moment. They had talked about the photos of the crime scene, but Chen's going over the scene in person could make a difference. In Sherlock Holmes stories, the detective never failed to find something important yet previously unnoticed by others who examined the crime scene.

"No problem," Huang said. "We've gone over it closely, but you should definitely take a look."

Less than ten minutes later, they arrived at the apartment complex, which was located near the back of the chemical company plant. Sure enough, there wasn't any sign of police stationed near the complex, and no residents were out walking in the area.

"It's a relatively new complex and it's not fully occupied yet," Huang remarked. He showed his badge to the security guard standing as stiff as a bamboo pole under the white arch of the entrance.

"There has been a lot of new residential construction in the last few years, but with the soaring housing prices, few can afford one of the new apartments."

"But Liu had his for free, and that was in addition to his large house," Chen noted.

The apartment building in question was six stories tall with a pink-painted exterior that looked new and impressive in the daylight. They went up to the third floor without seeing anyone else.

Liu's was a three-bedroom apartment. Huang opened the door with a master key. They stepped into a hallway with hardwood floors that led into a living room and an open dining room, which in turn was connected to a kitchenette. On the other end of the living room were the three bedrooms, one of which was a guest room, and another the office where Liu had been murdered.

Chen looked at each of the rooms before he came back to the office. The office was practically furnished. On the L-shaped oak desk facing the door sat a computer with a large monitor, a printer, and a combination telephone and fax machine. A couple of chairs stood against one wall near the corner and beside a custom-made bookshelf, which had books and magazines on it. A flat-screen TV hung on the opposite wall.

"The people who live in these new apartment buildings don't talk to one another much. That was particularly true in Liu's case. He was only here once or twice a week, and usually in the evening. On that particular night, no one in the building saw him or heard anything from his apartment. But when their doors are shut, people can hardly hear anything from the outside. According to a neighbor on the fourth floor, a young woman was walking down the stairs around nine, but the staircase was dimly lit, so he didn't get a clear look. She could have been visiting anyone in the building."

"Yes, she could have come from the fifth or sixth floor," Chen said while picking up a framed picture from the bookshelf. It was a photo of Liu and a young man standing in front of that same bookshelf in the office. Liu was a robust man of medium height with wide-set, penetrating eyes, deep-lined brows, and a powerful jaw, and the young man was a lanky one with a pensive look on his fine-featured face.

"The young man is his son, Wenliang," Huang said. "He interned here at the company last summer."

Placing the picture back on the bookshelf, Chen started examining the books themselves. It was a curious mixture, including a number of fashion magazines.

"He read fashion magazines?"

"Well, Mi came here from time to time," Huang said.

Chen nodded in acknowledgment, then said, "Tell me again what you see as unusual about the crime scene."

"There is no sign of forced entry, and no sign of struggle, either. The murderer was likely somebody Liu knew well, and it was probably a surprise attack. The security guard didn't register any visitors for Liu that night. So it was possibly someone who lived in the complex, or even in the same building."

"But as you said, he didn't mix with his neighbors," Chen said. "Of course, that doesn't mean it's impossible for the murderer to be one of them. But what would be the motive?"

"That suggests another possible scenario. Someone familiar with the complex could have come in without stopping at the entrance. The security guard might make things difficult for a diffident visitor, but wouldn't try to stop a Big Buck who was striding in with an air of confidence."

"Or driving in a luxurious car," Chen said, as if he had done the same himself before. "Do you have the pictures of the crime scene with you?"

"Yes," Huang said, producing a folder of pictures. "You've already seen all of them."

Chen placed a few on the desk, examined them, and then looked around the room a couple of times.

He immersed himself in the comparative study for ten minutes or so. He walked out into the living room, but didn't stay there long before heading back into the office. Huang followed, without interrupting, notebook in hand.

"Has anything been moved here?"

"No, of course not. Nobody—not even Mrs. Liu—has been in here, not since she was brought to check over the things in the apartment. That is, of course, except for those items bagged and taken to the lab for testing."

"Do you have that list with you?"

"Yes, here it is."

Chen checked it carefully, then placed it on the desk and rubbed his chin with a finger.

"Now, let me ask you a question. Where do you think the host would usually receive a guest?"

"The living room, naturally. But we thought about that too. Liu might have simply stepped into the office to get a document or something."

"In that case, he would have entered the room first, and the murderer would have followed behind him—"

Chen didn't go on, apparently having a difficult time visualizing the murderer striking Liu from behind.

"What do you think of the position of the other chairs in the office?" Chen resumed, sitting down on the swivel chair at the desk. "They haven't been moved, right?"

"No. But what do you mean?"

"It doesn't make sense. If Liu were sitting here, like I am, then the murderer would have been sitting opposite him. So why are the other chairs in the corner of the room?"

"That's a good point," Huang said, writing it down in his notebook.

"If he'd been talking to someone who was standing in front of him and who then swooped down on him ferociously—"

"Then," Huang said, nodding, "how come there is no sign of a struggle?"

"Exactly."

"But what about the possibility that Liu was showing his visitor a file on the computer—something like a document about the antipollution efforts—when the visitor struck him from behind? That's a scenario that I discussed with my colleagues."

"In the pictures, the computer isn't on." Chen picked up one of the photographs. "So, in your scenario, Liu had to have been struck at the very moment his hand was just touching the computer button."

Huang could see the chief inspector wasn't convinced. As a matter of fact, neither was Huang.

"That's a good point. I'll write it down," Huang said, opening his notebook again.

"In the pictures, there wasn't a glass or a cup on the desk in the office. Or in the living room. Or in the list of the items bagged for testing. For a man who was working late at night, a cup of coffee or tea on the desk would seem logical."

"That's true."

"And another thing. The estimated time of death is between 9:30 and 10:30. That's very late for a visitor such as the one theorized by Internal Security to arrive. Maybe Liu and the visitor had already been talking and arguing for an hour or more. But then where? Surely not in the office. That brings us back to your hypothesis—that they moved from the living room to the office. But then why wasn't there a cup of tea in the living room for the guest?"

"Or at least a cup of water," Huang said, scratching his head.

"Now look on the shelf. An impressive array of Puer tea cans, a very expensive tea from Yunnan—"

But Chen left his sentence unfinished, as he started to examine a row of gilded statuettes that were lined resplendently along the top shelf. He picked one statuette up. It was a tall, muscular worker holding aloft a shining globe and standing on a solid marble base. It bore an inscription: "In recognition of the outstanding increase in production and profit achieved by the Wuxi Number One Chemical Company for the year of 1995. Issued by the Wuxi People's Congress." The statuettes were all identical in design, size, and caption, except for the year.

"The chemical company under Liu's leadership won that prestigious award nine years in a row," Chen said

"Wow, they are gold-plated too, " Huang said, picking one up. It was quite heavy. "Such a statuette could be quite expensive."

"Let's take some more pictures," Chen said. "I'll study them some more back at the center."

Chen took out a camera he had brought with him. He took photos for no less than fifteen minutes before he placed the framed picture of Liu and his son flat on the desk and photographed it as well. He then glanced at his watch.

"By the way, I've contacted Liu's attorney through some people I know in Shanghai," Chen said. "While the Lius hadn't made any specific moves regarding their marriage, Mrs. Liu made a joke over dinner about getting half of the IPO shares from Liu if he ever tried to divorce her."

A wronged wife out for revenge: that might throw a new light on a lot of things in the case. It gave Mrs. Liu a more plausible motive than Jiang's. There was the possibility that Liu was going to divorce her before the IPO, with the little secretary pushing in the background. In that case, Mrs. Liu could have lost everything. She had the access to his home office, along with knowledge of his whereabouts that night. Furthermore, it would explain the points raised by Chen about the crime scene—Liu's body being found in the office rather than in the living room, there being no sign of struggle, and the position of the chairs in the office. All of that would then make more sense.

"That was a brilliant stroke, Chen. Contacting the attorney, I mean. What she said about getting half of the shares from the IPO probably wasn't a joke," Huang said. "Liu was good at cover-ups, and so was she. The couple must have been trying to sound out possible divorce arrangements with the attorney. Liu was going to do it, and she knew it."

There was a glitch with that scenario, however. Mrs. Liu had an alibi. Then again, the people who supported her alibi were close friends, and unlike witnesses in those mystery novels Chen translated, some Chinese didn't worry too much about perjury. For one thing, there was no Bible for them to swear upon. For her friends, doing Mrs. Liu a favor might have outweighed other considerations. Besides, even if she were in Shanghai that night, she could have dispatched someone in Wuxi to achieve her ends.

"Time for the next item on our agenda, Huang," Chen said, breaking out of his reverie. "Let's go to the company office."

"Fine," Huang said, closing his notebook.

Huang had been there several times, so he suggested they walk from the apartment complex to the back door of the chemical company plant. "It's only about five minutes away. We can leave the car here."

Huang didn't want to leave his name at the front gate of the chemical company while he was in the company of Chief Inspector Chen.

His colleagues would be upset if they learned about this excursion, but he didn't have to explain that to Chen.

"As when we spoke to Mrs. Liu, you're the one in charge of the investigation," Chen said as they made their way to the company's back door.

At the door of the chemical company they saw an elderly security guard, who nodded at Huang's badge and let them in without further ado.

"The back door is locked after eight P.M.," Huang explained to Chen, "but people can still open it from the inside. On one occasion, when Liu had to come back to the company for some important documents, he had to call the guard at the front gate to come around and open the back door for him."

"I see," Chen said. "So it's really a shortcut."

The general manager's office was in a two-story building in the middle of the chemical company complex. They had arranged to meet Mi in the outer office, and she was already there waiting for them.

"What can we do for you today, Officer Huang? Oh, this is—" she said, rising from her desk.

A tall, willowy girl in her early twenties, Mi had almond-shaped eyes, a sensual mouth, and a fashionably thin body like a runway model. She was wearing a short, white, neckless halter top, which revealed her belly button; jeans; and high-heeled sandals, which showed her toes painted bright red.

There wasn't much about her, however, that really appealed to Huang.

"You know why I'm here, Mi. This is my colleague Chen. We want to talk to you about Liu's murder."

She pressed a key on a brand-new computer, which Huang didn't remember seeing last time. She motioned them to sit down in two black chairs opposite.

"We've already talked about it, Officer Huang," she said.

"I'm new to the team," Chen cut in, "so anything you say will be of great help to me."

"Anything specific," Huang echoed. He noticed another difference about her desk. A silver-framed photo of Liu speaking at a national conference had disappeared, and a golden plaque stating *Office Manager* was in its place.

"Let's start with what you can tell us about Liu," Chen said.

"He was an extraordinary boss. When he first took over, the company was teetering on the brink of bankruptcy. In a large state-run enterprise like ours, with more than three thousand employees, his was not an easy job. But he managed to turn it around."

"We learned about his work from all the media coverage. But what do you think of him as a man?"

"He was a good man—generous, intelligent, and always ready to help."

"Now, let me ask you a different question. As someone who worked closely with him, what do you know about his family life?"

"He didn't talk much about his family life."

"Do you think he had a satisfactory one?"

"I don't know," she said, then added, "But a busy man like him should have had better care taken of him."

"We talked to his wife," Chen said, looking her in the eye. "She told us something."

He paused deliberately, letting a silence eat away at her reserve like a crumbling wall in the room. Huang thought he knew what Chen was up to.

"Whatever she may have told you," she said, without meeting his eyes, "I don't think she was a good wife to him. Everybody here could see he wasn't happy at home."

"Can you give us any detailed examples?"

"It's just something I heard. They were schoolmates in Shanghai—she from a good family in Shanghai, and he from a poor village in Jiangxi. In spite of her family's opposition, she married down and followed him to Wuxi. She got it into her head that she should be compensated for her sacrifice, so to speak, by him waiting on her hand and foot, and obeying her in everything, big or small. She was a typical Shanghai woman."

"But then in Wuxi he became successful."

"Exactly. For a busy, overworked man like him—a virtuous wife would have taken good care of him at home, especially after she quit her job and became a housewife, leaving the family dependent on Liu's income alone. But no. She frequently went back to Shanghai during the week and over the weekends too. He was often left all alone in the house. "

"She has family in Shanghai. It's natural that she would go back from time to time."

"Who could tell what she was really up to in Shanghai? She used to be a high school flower, I heard, with a number of secret admirers hanging around."

"Really!"

"And I can tell you why he sometimes stayed overnight at his home office. With all the responsibilities on his hands, he frequently worked late. But more often than not, he simply didn't want to go back home. The home office was the only place he could really relax. But she wouldn't leave him alone even there. One time when he was away on a business trip, she came over and turned the whole apartment upside down."

Huang listened without interrupting. It was intriguing that Chen kept his focus on Mrs. Liu, even when interviewing Mi. It was possible that Mrs. Liu had killed him, as Huang had suggested at the crime scene, but after his initial excitement with it, it more and more seemed to him to be a theory that wasn't supported by any evidence.

Mi's accusations against Mrs. Liu were understandable, even though she had denied any knowledge of Liu's family life. She knew that the cops had heard stories about her, so she was trying to downplay the relationship between her and Liu. Presenting Mrs. Liu as an irresponsible wife was designed to justify her own role in Liu's life—if not morally, at least psychologically. But that self-justification was irrelevant to the murder investigation, with the exception that it presented a totally different version from that of Mrs. Liu.

Still, they learned some new things from the interview: for one, the frequency of Mrs. Liu's trips to Shanghai. It wasn't a long-distance trip, but it was nonetheless odd to so often leave her husband all alone at home.

And that led to the revelation about her having been a high school flower with many secret admirers. What could that possibly mean? If she had another man in Shanghai—which wasn't unimaginable for a couple like the Lius, whose marriage was already on the rocks—it introduced a motive that had been so far overlooked. Mrs. Liu's lover, whoever it might be, could have murdered for love or for money.

"Do you think Liu was planning to do something about his family problems?" Chen went on.

"What you mean?"

"Did he plan to divorce his wife?"

"No, not that I was aware of. As I've said, he didn't discuss his family problems with us other than complaining a little, now and then, when he couldn't help himself."

Chen took out a cigarette, tapped it on the pack, and looked at Mi before asking, "Do you mind?"

"No. Go ahead. Liu smoked too."

Chen changed the subject abruptly. "As you may have heard, Jiang is a possible suspect. Tell us what you know about him."

"Oh, Jiang," she said. "He called our office quite a few times. He was calling to speak with Liu, of course. What they talked about, though, I've no idea. I told Internal Security about all that."

"Can you give us any more details?" Huang cut in. "Particularly, anything in connection with the night Liu was murdered."

"Jiang called two or three days before the night Liu died, I think, but other than insisting on speaking to Liu, he didn't say anything to me. That's about all I know. And—" She cleared her voice before going on. "And as I told the police, Liu mentioned that morning he was going to see someone on some unpleasant business."

"Did he say when or where?"

"No, not that I remember."

"And who?"

"No, no names were mentioned either." She added, "Oh, but two or three months ago, I saw Jiang arguing with Liu in his office."

"His office here at the plant?"

"Yes, the inside office."

"What were they arguing about?"

"They stopped talking the moment I stepped in, but I caught a word or two. It was, I think, about pollution."

"Do you remember the date?"

"It was March, early March," she said. "It was the day before the Women's Day. Yes, now I recall . . ."

At that moment, a tall man burst into the outer office, greeting Huang in a loud voice.

"Hello, Comrade Officer Huang. What wind brings you over here again today?"

"Hello, General Manager Fu."

"It's only Acting General Manager for the moment. Please just call me Fu. And this is . . ."

"Chen, my colleague," Huang said.

"Welcome. Come into my office."

"Thank you, General Manager Fu," Chen said. He then turned back to Mi. "We might come back to you if we have more questions. If you think of anything, please call us—or rather, call Sergeant Huang."

Huang and Chen then turned and followed Fu into the inner office. Fu motioned for them to sit on two leather chairs opposite his oak desk. The wall behind the desk exhibited a striking array of framed awards, with Liu's name on most of them, but under the glass on the desk, Huang saw several pictures of Fu.

"Is that Bund Park?" Chen asked unexpectedly, indicating a picture of Fu standing in front of the park, his hand pointing proudly to the river.

"Yes, I came from Shanghai."

"So, do you go back there frequently?"

"I went back last Saturday, and I'm going there again this weekend. Nowadays, it's so convenient to go back and visit. It's only one hour by the new high-speed train. That is a picture I took two weeks ago."

"You know what we're here for, General Manager Fu," Chen said, moving on to the heart of the matter.

"Yes. We need to get justice for Liu. He worked really hard and did a great job turning around the company. We owe our success to him, and we will never change the course that Liu charted out for us. We will, of course, cooperate with your investigation in every way possible."

Fu spoke about Liu in a respectful and quite grateful way, as a young successor should, though his words were fulsome and couched in official language.

"We were just talking to Mi about Jiang," Chen said, coming straight to the point. "Can you tell us something about him?"

"Not much, I'm afraid. Jiang talked to Liu, not to me."

"So you knew about his contacts with Liu."

"Well, I saw him talking with Liu in the office one day, but as a matter of fact, I didn't even know at the time that his name was Jiang. Mi filled me in afterward."

"Did Liu tell you anything about Jiang's threat to expose the company's industrial pollution problem?"

"Now, let me first say something about this so-called pollution, Officer Chen. There is a city environmental protection office in Wuxi. They have checked and double-checked our production procedure. Our samples have always proven to be up to the state standard," Fu said with a serious look on his face. "Liu's job was an extremely difficult one. In today's market, it's not easy for a state-run factory to survive, let alone to succeed. But Liu was successful, and it was no real surprise that he became a target for cold-blooded criminals like Jiang and other irresponsible critics who know nothing about our industry."

"We understand all this, Comrade Acting General Manager Fu," Chen said. "And we've spoken to Mrs. Liu too."

"Really! That's good. Considering Liu's contribution to the company, we're going to offer his family an adequate sum. In addition, there will be a position for Mrs. Liu—that is, if she wants to work here."

"That's so thoughtful of you. She's originally from Shanghai. I wonder whether she might prefer to move back there."

"That I don't know," Fu said, suddenly shifting the topic as he looked at his watch. "Have you had lunch, Officers? I worked late last night, and then skipped breakfast this morning."

It was an obvious attempt to end the interview.

"We had a late breakfast," Chen said, also glancing at his watch. It was near one thirty. "Yes, I think it's time for us to leave."

As they left the office, Chen didn't speak. Both he and Huang were lost in thought as they moved to the front gate.

"I'm sorry," Huang said. "I forgot that the car is parked near the apartment complex. Let's go back."

Chen came to an abrupt stop and then looked up. There were several visitors signing a register book at the front entrance. Instead of turning and heading to the back door, Chen walked over to the security guard standing there.

"So, is it required that people sign in and out here?" Chen asked the security guard, pointing at the register book.

"We're from the Wuxi Police Bureau," Huang said, producing his badge in a hurry.

"Anything you want to know, sir," the security guard said, "and yes, that's the rule. All visitors have to sign in."

"Oh, and there's a video camera here too," Chen said, pointing at it.

"Yes, our late boss ordered a lot of equipment, including the video cameras. They're state of the art, appropriate for a large state-run enterprise, but we still stand here on guard twenty-four hours a day."

"I see. That's good. I'd like a copy of the visitor registration book for the last seven days, along with the tapes from the camera."

"That can be easily done, sir," the security guard said, nodding his head like a rattle drum.

But it took more than a few minutes to duplicate the tape and the pages. Huang was watching, bewildered, when his cell phone rang. He looked at the number, excused himself, and walked over to a shaded corner, out of their hearing.

It proved once again to last longer than he had expected.

When he returned to the front entrance, Chen was already holding a large envelope in his hand.

"Let's have a bite at the canteen here," Huang said. "I still have the company canteen coupons Fu gave us the first time we were here. So I can afford to be your host today."

"That's a good idea," Chen said.

They made their way to the canteen. It was past the lunch hour, but there were still a handful of employees eating and talking. They chose a table toward the side, close to the window, where there were no people around.

"What do you think?" Huang said over a steaming-hot bowl of beef noodles strewn with chopped green onion.

"To begin with, Mi may be an unreliable narrator."

"What do you mean?"

"It's a term I picked up in my literature studies in college, which means a narrator who doesn't provide a reliable account from an unbiased perspective," Chen said, adding a lot of black pepper to his noodles. "Mi put on a passionate defense of Liu, but it was more a defense of her own actions, at least subconsciously, on the grounds that a happy, contented husband wouldn't have an extramarital affair. Like an echo of the old saying, 'If the fence is tight, no dog will stray in.' But it's undeniable that Liu hadn't been a good husband, and that he kept the home office for his rendezvous with Mi. In her attempts to defend her position as a little secretary, Mi may not be able to give us truthful statements."

"I see your point, Chief. There are some inconsistencies in the statements regarding Liu. I put them together on a piece of paper while she was talking, in an effort to connect them, but some of them simply couldn't be connected." Huang then said, "I still like the theory that Mrs. Liu was responsible."

"That's just one of the possible theories," Chen said, seeming to back away from his earlier assertiveness. "It's unsupported so far."

"True. By the way, the phone call I took earlier was about a new development. Well, not exactly new, since it's based on an old scenario being pushed by Internal Security. As of now, they have reached their conclusion, obtained approval from above, and officially taken Jiang into custody."

"Have there been any new evidence or breakthroughs?" Chen asked, apparently surprised at how quickly Internal Security was moving the case along.

"No, not any I'm aware of. From what I just learned from the head of our local team, the case has been attracting a lot of attention internationally; the longer it drags on, the more damage it could do to the government's image. So people from above gave the green light to Internal Security's plan. I don't like it. If this is how it's going to work, then what the hell are we cops for?"

"I don't like it either," Chen said, putting down the chopsticks even though he hadn't finished his noodles. "Can you me get a copy of Jiang's statement regarding his argument with Liu?"

"Yes. He insisted that he hadn't talked to or met with Liu for months. I'll get you a copy."

"Also, can you get a copy of the phone records for the company? Particularly the general manager's office, if that's available."

Huang wasn't sure he was following Chen's thinking. He had assumed the scenario in which Mrs. Liu murdered her husband was beneath Chen's approach, his examination of the crime scene, and the questions he asked at the company.

Perhaps Chen had another objective in mind, Huang mused. Maybe he wanted to rule out the possibility of Jiang's being the murderer.

But was it too late? The "approval from above" that Internal Security had received sounded ominous. A chief inspector on vacation, no matter how well connected, could hardly match that. Perhaps that was what made Chen a different kind of cop—persistence. Chen plodded on, conscientiously, if circumspectly, in his own way.

"But Internal Security is ready to conclude the case in the interests of the Party. It'll be over in just a matter of days, I'm afraid," Huang said, broodingly. "Not that I'm not willing to confront them if we could obtain any real evidence or witnesses, and with you at my side—"

He broke off his sentence, however, at the sight of Shanshan walking into the canteen and striding over toward them.

"Oh, you're here, Chen!" Shanshan said, fixing her stare on him, "and along with Officer—"

Her face showed surprise, which was quickly turning to something like anger.

There was surprise on Chen's face too, though perhaps for a different reason.

"This is Shanshan, my friend. And this is Officer Huang." Chen rose and made a hurried introduction, which wasn't necessary for either of them. "He is a fan, having read every one of my mystery translations."

The second part of the introduction was meant for her benefit, Huang realized. He wondered whether she would buy that explanation, but he picked up on the cue not to reveal that Chen was a cop.

"Mr. Chen is truly a master. I've read all the books he's translated. He's also a poet, you know, and that makes a huge difference in his translations. The language is superb."

"You seem to know your fans among the police very well, Master Chen," she said, with undisguised sarcasm. "Or is this another 'chance' meeting?"

"I think I have to leave now, Mr. Chen," Huang said, rising. "You may call me any time."

"No, stay, Officer, and please continue discussing your important police work," she said. "I'm leaving."

They watched her retreat from the canteen in a hurry.

"I have some explanations to make, I think," Chen said, rising and smiling a bitter smile.

"Catch up with her," Huang said. "We'll talk later."

All of a sudden, the legendary chief inspector looked defeated and crestfallen, not that legendary after all.

TWELVE

CHEN DIDN'T CATCH SIGHT of Shanshan when he hit the street after hurrying out of the chemical company. She must have turned at the intersection, but in which direction, he had no idea. She had walked away fast, in a state of high dudgeon.

Her reaction wasn't beyond comprehension. She'd asked him about his connection to the police officer who had released her, a question he'd parried, keeping his real identity a secret.

But he had his reasons for doing so, at least during the course of the investigation.

He turned onto a small road, which he thought might lead to the center. He was pondering what he had just learned from so many different sources. He had to sort out the information.

Then he saw her walking in front of him.

"Shanshan," he said, breaking into a run. "Let me explain."

"You're horrible," she said without slowing her steps. "Officer Huang listened to you so reverentially, nodding all the time like a puppet. Do you still want to tell me that you met him by chance in a barbershop?"

"I owe you an apology," he said, deciding to reveal his connections, if not his identity. "I have connections with the police here. That's not something I really want to show off, or talk to you about, but in today's China, you can't do anything without connections. You know that."

"You don't have to waste your breath explaining anything," she said, walking on with her head down. "I'm surprised that a master of connections like you actually has time for me."

"You don't have to say that, Shanshan. As for Sergeant Huang, he happens to be a fan of the mysteries I've translated. That part is absolutely true, and that's the reason he calls me a master. As a matter of fact, I didn't know Huang before this vacation. After meeting you, however, I thought I had to establish and develop the connection here."

"You're full of connections, both old and new, as you've already told me," she said, with a distrustful edge still in her voice. "What do you want from me?" She seemed to be gradually recovering from her initial shock.

"We need to talk, Shanshan. Let me tell you something I've just learned from Huang. According to him, things are getting uglier for Jiang."

"How?"

"He'll be convicted of murder in Liu's case." He resumed after a pause, "I don't know Jiang from Adam. Whatever happens to him, it's not my business. But it involves you. That was why I had to tell you that it was a chance meeting between me and Huang. Because it wouldn't do anyone any good to reveal such a connection. Especially at this juncture."

They must have walked for some distance without paying attention to the direction. At an intersection ahead, another turn brought them to the beginning of the small, quaint road that lead back to the center.

She slowed down before finally coming to a halt, hesitant as to whether to walk any further with him. This was the only road in the city of Wuxi that was familiar to him. He remembered some of the tourist attraction signs he had seen.

"There's a pavilion, I think, halfway up the hill. It should be a quiet place to talk."

She followed him without saying anything. They started up the steps, which were half-covered in moss and weeds.

To their left, the flat surface of the rock cliff had lines engraved in red- or black-painted characters left by people years earlier. Among them was a couplet by Qian Qianyi, a Qing-dynasty minister who had first served in the Ming dynasty. The couplet was partially blocked out by "Long March," one of Mao's poems, which had been carved by Red Guards during the Cultural Revolution. Beneath Mao's poem, a young couple had recently chiseled out a romantic pledge, with their names carved under a red heart. Perhaps they believed their names would last forever this way.

The trail, winding between clumps of larches and ferns, became rugged, slippery, even treacherous in places, with the stone steps in bad repair. Fortunately, as they labored up the trail in the heat, a breeze occasionally found its way through the groves of small spruce.

An old, ramshackle pavilion came into view. It had a yellow-glazed tile roof supported by vermilion posts, and the posts were set into curved wooden benches with exquisite lattice railings above. Chen was momentarily confused by a sense of déjà vu. Which was odd. It was nothing like the dilapidated pavilion overlooking the lake and its turtle-head rock in Yuantouzhu.

Shanshan sat down, leaning sideways against the post, fanning herself with a newspaper that she pulled out of her pocket. He sat down beside her, his arm stretched out onto the railing.

In the trees behind them, small birds chirped. Among the trees, there was an ancient stump surrounded by an abundance of yellowish weeds and a flattened white fungus across the top.

"I'm afraid Jiang will be charged and convicted," Chen started, "in a couple of days."

"How could that possibly be?" she demanded. "They don't have a shred of evidence."

"They think they have. And that's what matters. They aren't ordinary cops, you know. They are Internal Security."

"But why?"

"It's the politics behind the case, Shanshan," he said carefully. "Jiang is a troublemaker, not only in Wuxi, but to the people high above in Beijing too."

"Because of the environmental issues he brings up," she said. "I guess you do know everything."

"Once he is sentenced, it will be impossible for anyone to turn the situation around—whatever their connections. I know hardly anything about Jiang, so I'm in no position to speak for him. That's why I really need to talk to you."

"I understand, Chen. Sorry that I was too upset to listen."

"You don't have to apologize for anything."

They didn't speak for several minutes.

He shook a cigarette out of his pack. For once, he didn't ask for her permission, just lit it. The distant sky was dappled with white clouds like lost sails, purposelessly moving, torn at the edges.

"I'm trying to help, Shanshan," he repeated. "Please tell me what you know about Jiang."

She sat unresponsive, statuelike. The hills behind them were spread out like a traditional landscape scroll.

"Only by clearing Jiang," he went on in earnest, "can I hope to help you and get you out of trouble."

"I don't know how you can help," she said softly, but she started to tell him what she knew.

"Jiang had started as an entrepreneur in Wuxi in the late eighties. Having made a small fortune for himself in the early waves of China's economic reform, he began to take note of the deteriorating environment in the area. A native of Wuxi, he had grown up by the lake, so he took it as his responsibility to draw attention to the issue. Initially, his efforts were not without support, and he had limited success. The media mentioned him as a fighter for the environment, and he even appeared on provincial TV and radio programs. With his firsthand knowledge about the problems with local industry, and by talking and writing about them, he was able to get several local factories to mend their ways—at least to some extent.

"Jiang then began taking the issue more seriously. He sold his business and devoted himself full time to environmental protection. He managed to make a modest living from the fees for talks and articles, but his efforts started to upset an increasing number of Big Bucks, especially those he mentioned unfavorably. So they launched a fierce counterattack, claiming that he was seeking publicity at the expense of law-abiding companies, and that his writings were amateur and half-baked, not based at all on scientific research.

"Then they took it even further by appealing to city authorities. After all, the success of Wuxi was dependent on its booming industry, and the city couldn't afford for it to be discredited. The officials didn't hesitate to put pressure on him.

"Jiang persisted, however, targeting factories that continued to dump pollutants into the lake. After doing extensive research, he sent detailed reports to many newspapers and magazines. To his dismay, though, his submissions were invariably returned. He was told that they had received specific instructions from above banning his work and that those companies were untouchable because they produced the majority of the local industrial revenue. Still, he kept on sending letters and reports to government authorities—higher and higher authorities—a persistence which eventually got him labeled a 'political troublemaker.'

"According to his research, most of the companies in Wuxi were problematic. They were far from meeting the environmental standards, and the situation was aggravated by the acquiescence of the government.

"He started to reach out to foreign media, contacting Western correspondents, who sometimes paid him for his work and published it abroad. Ironically, it then found its way back into China, even into some 'inside journals' compiled for high-ranking leaders in Beijing. This made the local officials consider him even more troublesome, and he was consequently blacklisted. But those factories went on operating as before, at the expense of environment.

"So he modified his tactics. He started doing specific field studies, collecting pictures and data, undeniable evidence, before confronting the companies in question and demanding that they mend their ways. If they then didn't do anything about it, he would post vivid pictures and concrete information on the Web. Those Web posts became quite influential, even more than his earlier articles in the newspapers and magazines, drawing thousands and thousands of responses. As the information spread to an ever-increasing number of people, it became a serious headache to the authorities.

"Then, out of the blue, the accusation came up that Jiang was making a mountain of money by blackmailing those companies. A local business tycoon even went so far as to produce a letter from Jiang which said: 'If you don't respond, you'll have to pay for it.' There was no question that it was a warning, but it was too vague for it to be read as blackmail.

"So for the last two years, he has been in trouble," she concluded, "and there has been one attempt after another to bring him down. But I don't think he would blackmail someone for his own benefit."

Chen listened on attentively, without interrupting or commenting. Her narrative about Jiang had gone on fairly long. The afternoon light that silhouetted her against the quaint pavilion was gradually fading. In the distance, a light haze began softening the hills.

"But as you said, he had sold his business and had to make a living," Chen said. "Nowadays, he doesn't make any money from his speeches or articles."

"I guess he made enough before he became an activist."

"What kind of a man do you think he is?"

"He's no murderer, I'll say that." Then, as if in afterthought, she said, "Of course, he has his flaws. For instance, he's too fond of the limelight. And he's self-important too. When a company offered to pay him a consulting fee, he never said no. He might have planned to use the money for his environmental work, but it wasn't a good idea."

"How did his activities affect you?"

"I got to know him about a year ago. Because of our common interests, we would meet up and talk from time to time. On one occasion, I talked to him about the problem at my company, citing a bunch of research data which he later put into a special report."

"Do you know if he approached Liu with it?"

"He did. Liu was furious with me over my 'betrayal,' though there was nothing secret or confidential about the data. Anyone could accumulate the same information through their own research. But I, too, was upset with Jiang. He should have considered the consequences before confronting Liu with it. Jiang claimed that he never mentioned my name, but that didn't change the fact that he got the data from me. I was so pissed off, I stopped seeing him."

He noticed her choice of words—*stopped seeing him*. They carried a subtle hint as to the nature of their relationship.

"That was several months ago?" Chen asked.

"Yes. What he's been doing since, I have no idea."

"About two months ago, in March, I believe, he contacted Liu again. They met at the chemical company office and had a heated argument."

"What? That's not possible! Jiang promised me that he would target other companies instead. He said that it wouldn't be a problem since there are so many of them around."

"Well, maybe he did it because of the timing. With the coming IPO of the Wuxi Number One Chemical Company, Liu would have been more likely to compromise at that critical juncture. At least, that is how Internal Security has it figured."

"But I still don't think Jiang would have come to the office."

"Mi says she heard him arguing with Liu in his office."

"When was that?"

"At the beginning of March—the day before Women's Day. She was positive about it."

Shanshan made no response, instead staring first at him, then seemingly at something beyond him, in the distance. The air on the hill became slightly chilly for the time of year.

There was something suddenly vulnerable about her, he noticed. She sat up against the post, her arms hanging at her sides, hands slightly open, as if in supplication. She hadn't yet said anything explicit about her relationship with Jiang. Chen decided not to push. What she would tell him, eventually, she would.

The personal factors aside, a clear picture was forming of the economic background behind the case against Jiang. For the local government, environmental protection efforts were made only to the extent that they wouldn't jeopardize the appearance of "a harmonious society." The local authorities depended on the ever-increasing production and profits contributed by the factories, which cut costs by dumping industrial waste into the lake. Exposing this to the Western media, as well as on the Web, made Jiang politically intolerable, and Internal Security must have been following him for quite a while. Which would explain how they came to intervene so quickly in the case.

"It's difficult," she said, as if reading his thoughts. "Isn't it?"

It was difficult because he couldn't rule out the possibility of Jiang's being a criminal, even though political persecution appeared to be a far more likely scenario.

"Who else did you talk to at the company?" she said, with an alert look in her eyes, suddenly changing the subject. "You didn't meet Officer Huang just for lunch in the canteen, did you?"

"You're right. We went and inteviewed Mi and Fu. But I'm not the one who's a cop here, so Huang did most of the talking. We didn't learn anything new or useful from them. Huang and I also spoke to Mrs. Liu at her home."

"You've been doing some investigating, like a cop."

"There's something strange about Mrs. Liu, but I'm not sure what it is," he said, ignoring the question in her remark. "She travels back to Shanghai frequently—almost weekly—to play mahjong. How could she afford it?"

"Money is nothing to her. Liu earned a lot—he got as a bonus ten percent of the company's annual profit. And that's only his legitimate income, not including what he got in gray-area money."

"She must have known about his little secretary, so how could she have left him on his own so much in Wuxi?"

"She did know about his little secretaries. But I've heard that they had a deal. He gave her a lot of money, and she provided the secure, stable home environment that was a necessity for his position."

"Hold on, Shanshan. Little secretaries? Plural? Liu had someone else in addition to Mi?"

"There was at least one before Mi—that I know of."

"What happened to her?"

"Dumped liked a worn-out mop."

"Can you find out more about her?"

"I could try. Somebody told me she had been a karaoke girl. Mi used to work in a foot massage parlor," she said. "As a Party cadre in charge of a large state-run company, it was very shrewd of him to maintain a quiet, stable home life by providing generously for his wife. At the same time, he had Mi serving him hand and foot like a concubine at his home office."

"Yes, I see."

"But tell me, Chen, what did you hear from Mi and Fu?"

"Mi described a most unhappy family life for Liu, which I think was an effort to justify her role as a little secretary. Fu said little. He's also from Shanghai and mentioned going there—to Shanghai—this evening."

"Fu goes back quite often. Now, as the boss, he can travel there whenever he likes." She paused, then said suddenly, "Oh, I don't know what will happen to the company or to China."

It reminded Chen of something written by Fan Zhongyan, a Song-dynasty poet-statesman who described people *"joyful with the joy of the country and sorrowful with the sorrow of the country. Alas, in whom can I find such a companion?"*

Shanshan, herself besieged by troubles, was sorrowful with the sorrow of the country. She was so different from many of her contemporaries, standing out from the crowd in this acquisitive age by fighting for things beyond her own materialistic considerations. He couldn't help but be reminded of himself from his long-forgotten years at college, when he, too, had cherished idealistic, passionate dreams.

Their eyes met, and they beheld each other. The air was abruptly filled with the sound of birds chirping, and a fitful breeze blew through the trees like a lost song.

A couple of lines he had written earlier came to mind—*when you no longer belonged / to a place, nor a time, nor yourself.* It was a poem about her, he realized.

At that moment, however, he didn't know what to say, so he repeated the words he, as a cop, had said so many times.

"Thank you for telling me all this, Shanshan. If you think of anything else, anything unusual, let me know."

THIRTEEN

IT WAS ONE OF the few mornings that Detective Yu, of the Shanghai Police Bureau, didn't have to get up early. Nor did he want to. It was Saturday morning, and the clock on the wall read eight thirty, but he was still in bed with Peiqin. Qinqin, their only son, had left around six for an intensive review session in Pudong to prepare for the coming college entrance exam.

There was only a plasterboard partition wall between their room and Qinqin's, so they couldn't enjoy any real privacy. But this morning, it was different.

Peiqin was sitting up, reclining against a couple of pillows and watching TV with the volume turned up fairly loud. She didn't want to go out to the food market early, either. With Qinqin away for the day, she had no motivation to prepare a special meal.

Yu understood. He lay beside her, contented. The moment would be perfect if he could smoke a cigarette in bed, but he knew better. He thought about talking to Peiqin about the recent work at the bureau but then thought better of it. It was a quiet moment, which he cherished. There were several none-too-special "special cases," for which he wasn't in a hurry to do anything. Chief Inspector Chen would come back in a week.

"Any special cases of late?" she said, turning off the TV. It was as if she was synchronized with his thoughts.

"No, not really," he said. "There's one involving an official in the city government, but he's already a dead tiger, so to speak. It's just a matter of process—first a list of his wrongdoings will be released to the public, and then an editorial will appear in *Liberation Daily* hailing the Party's determination to fight corruption. Another case involves some dissidents planning to release a petition calling for improved human rights. The authorities in Beijing put them on a blacklist long ago, so the results are a foregone conclusion. I don't think there is anything our squad can do. Even Chen couldn't do anything to stop it."

"So why the sudden vacation for your chief inspector?"

He had sort of anticipated the question. The inscrutableness of the inspector had become one of her favorite topics. "I don't know of anything happening here that Chen had to get out of the way of. Not recently."

"Did he give you any explanation for his sudden vacation?"

"No, not at all."

"But you never know what your boss is really up to. Remember his trip to Beijing not too long ago?" she said, then added, "Not that I have anything against him, you know."

"Some people are saying that he will soon be removed from his position because he has ruffled too many high feathers and that the vacation is just a face-saving maneuver. But I don't think so. His vacation was arranged by Comrade Secretary Zhao. If anything, that should indicate that Chen remains in favor in Beijing. So it might be nothing more than a vacation. It's not unimaginable for him."

"He needs a break, what with his nervous breakdown not too long ago, and his ex-girlfriend having married somebody else. A vacation will do him good. But still, I wonder what he's doing in Wuxi. I can't picture him relaxing, drinking tea, and sightseeing like a tourist. Your boss seems to bring trouble with him wherever he goes."

"Well, I've heard from Sergeant Huang, a local cop in Wuxi. According to him, Chen might be having a vacation fling with a young pretty woman—much younger than Chen."

"Really!" Peiqin said, sitting up straighter. "He has a way with women."

"But this time he might not be in luck. According to Huang, there's a snag. She's connected to a man in trouble. Big trouble—"

Before Yu could continue, the phone rang.

"Oh, Chief Inspector Chen," Yu said after picking up the phone. "We were just talking about you."

"Yu, I need a favor."

"Yes, Chief?"

"I need you to do a background check on someone. She lives in Wuxi, but was originally from Shanghai and comes back regularly."

"A young girl?"

"She's middle-aged, one Mrs. Liu. Her husband, head of a large chemical company, was murdered a few days ago."

"I see. So you're in Wuxi to investigate the murder?"

"No. I'm on vacation in Wuxi. It's not my case. It's up to the Wuxi police, but I do need your help," Chen said. "Last Tuesday, Mrs. Liu was in Shanghai, playing mahjong with three others. I'll text you her Shanghai address, along with the name and number of one of the three with her that evening."

"So you want me to check her alibi."

"Yes, but not officially, if you can avoid it. The Wuxi police have already made some enquiries, but she's not a suspect. Not exactly." Chen then added quickly, as if in afterthought, "Also, see if you can find any background information about a man named Fu. He also works in Wuxi, but was originally from Shanghai. And he too was back in Shanghai this weekend."

"Why? Is there some connection between the two?"

154

"There might be—something that I'm still failing to grasp. The Wuxi police haven't made any enquiries about him. He's not a suspect, and I'm just curious, you know. It's probably nothing more than a hunch."

It was strange. Despite what he was saying, Chen sounded more than casually curious to Yu.

"Oh, Fu lives in the Old City area, quite close to the intersection of Renmin and Henan Road. I'll also text you his Shanghai address," Chen went on. "Unless I'm remembering wrong, it shouldn't be too far from Peiqin's old home."

"I'll get on it, Chief. Is there anything specific you're looking for?"

"Anything you can find out. I know it's a Saturday, so I owe you one, Yu. Give my regards to Peiqin."

"What's up?" Peiqin said the moment Yu put down the phone.

Yu repeated Chen's requests, which had come out of nowhere, especially if Chen was truly in Wuxi on vacation. He wished that Chen had explained further, but as always, the chief inspector must have his reasons.

"I see," Peiqin said. "Sure, we'll do our best to help."

Yu got up, smiling at the pronoun in her quick and crisp response. As in the past, she was eager to join in.

In years past, Peiqin had been reluctant to get involved in his duties as a policeman. But since he started working for the chief inspector, she had completely changed. In fact, she had helped—in her way—with the investigation in several difficult cases.

After getting Chen's text message, Yu dialed the phone number of the woman who had been with Mrs. Liu the evening of the murder. Bai was her surname. She was not at home, so Yu left a message asking her to call back at her earliest convenience.

"We might try to talk to her neighbors," Peiquin said.

"Good idea."

The lazy Saturday that Yu had envisioned was suddenly no more. But it wasn't the sort of thing that Yu would complain about.

They set out to Mrs. Liu's old neighborhood in Zhabei. It was a part of Shanghai not familiar to either of them. Zhabei had been something of a slum—full of old, shabby, ramshackle houses and dirty, ugly factories. The construction of plain-looking concrete "workers' homes" there in the sixties and seventies had hardly helped. There weren't any well-known stores or attractions there, and with the terrible traffic congestion in the city, they had previously no reason to spend a couple of hours going there.

But Zhabei had changed a lot in recent years. As Yu and Peiqin stepped out of the subway, recently extended to this part of the city, they saw a number of new high-rises.

The overall impression was, however, singularly mixed. Just two or three blocks from an ultramodern skyscraper, they saw shabby side streets with dilapidated buildings, tiny lanes with sordid entrances, and scenes that they imagined were typical of the old neighborhood.

They approached a small family grocery store near the entrance of the lane in which Mrs. Liu had lived. To their surprise, Xiong, the owner of the store, a garrulous woman in her early fifties, claimed to know Mrs. Liu well, having been her childhood neighbor and friend. According to Xiong, Mrs. Liu came back quite regularly, though her parents had passed away. Her old home was unoccupied most of the time, with only occasional visitors staying there. Among her old neighbors, Mrs. Liu had plenty of face, having once invited a large group of them to a fancy restaurant. She also owned a high-end apartment in Xujiahui, one of the top areas in Shanghai, but she didn't seem to go to that apartment often, and none of her old neighbors here had ever visited. Still, the very location of it spoke volumes about her wealth.

"You should see the way she plays mahjong—a hundred yuan a game, not including tips. It's as if she was printing money at home," Xiong said, in proud excitement.

"She comes all the way back here to play mahjong? Does she lose a lot too?"

"She won't bankrupt herself on a mahjong table. You don't have to worry about that. For a woman, having a good husband is far more important than having a good job," Xiong concluded. "She always has an eye for men. In the early years, Liu was still a nobody from the countryside, yet she followed him all the way to Wuxi. No one else had that kind of far-sighted vision. No wonder he provides her whatever she wants."

But all of this information was neither here nor there, and despite her claims of profound friendship with Mrs. Liu, Xiong hadn't even heard about the death of Mrs. Liu's husband.

After taking their leave of Xiong, Yu and Peiqin then approached some of the other neighbors. They didn't learn much, and some of the neighbors were suspicious of them and refused to answer their questions. Yu and Peiqin managed to get into the stunted two-story building and up to the room Mrs. Liu kept there. The door was locked, of course, but from the outside it looked no different from her neighbors'.

Mrs. Liu appeared to be a success story, all the more so when compared to her neighbors, Yu thought. He went fishing for a cigarette in his pocket, but he decided not to take one out around Peiqin. Why Mrs. Liu kept coming back to the impoverished old neighborhood remained a mystery. Her family hadn't been that well off, though in the context of the neighborhood, they might have done okay. The only possible explanation Yu could think of was that she wanted to show off, but what would be the point of showing off repeatedly, continuously, for years?

"If she was happily married," Peiqin said, as if reading his mind, "why would she come back so often?"

"I don't know," Yu said, shaking his head. He had no idea what Chen wanted him to find out. But then Chen himself might not have a clear idea.

It was then that his cell phone rang. It was Chen again.

"I have to ask you another favor, Yu."

"Go ahead, Chief," he said, then added, "I'm in Mrs. Liu's old neighborhood right now."

"Thanks, Yu. The Wuxi Number One Chemical Company here is about to go public. The head of the company, Liu, was the one who was murdered. I have only a little information about its IPO plan. It could help if I knew more about how such a plan works. Now, as I recall, Peiqin said that her restaurant belongs to Plum Blossom Pavilion Group, which is also going public soon. I'm wondering whether Peiqin could, as an accountant, find out something about the IPO for the Wuxi company. Perhaps she knows a thing or two about it."

"I'll tell her. In fact, she's right beside me. Do you want to talk to her?"

"No, that's about all I could tell her. Please let her know that I appreciate her help. I owe you both."

Chen said his good-bye, and Yu returned the phone to his pocket. He looked over at Peiqin.

"Something for me to do again?" Peiqin inquired with a smile.

Yu explained Chen's request.

"Ours is just one of the numerous small restaurants owned by the Group," Peiqin said, shaking her head. "These things are determined by the bosses of the Group and have nothing to do with me."

"But do you know something about the way an IPO works?" He knew she had been dabbling a little in the stock market.

"Different companies have different ways. It's something new and unprecedented in China, at least since 1949," she said. "I've heard a little about the so-called large noncirculating shares and the small noncirculating shares. The bosses who initiate an IPO each get a number of shares, an amount in accordance with his position, at a symbolic price which is practically for free. Once a state-run company goes public, the Party member CEO can become a millionaire or even a billionaire. No one can tell the difference between socialism and capitalism anymore."

"That's totally against the Party tradition. Cadres are supposed to serve people wholeheartedly, selflessly."

"That's why people want to be Party cadres nowadays," she said with an ironic smile. "But as for an IPO, that's about all I know. How could I know anything about a company that's far away in Wuxi? Your boss must be desperate. As the proverb says, When one's seriously sick, he will go to any doctor."

"You mean you think that Chen's in trouble?"

158

"He's desperate for something. Perhaps it's because of the affair with the young woman. Anyway, the stock market is closed on Saturday, so it would be useless for us to go there. Besides, I don't know anyone who works there."

"And I can't approach anyone there. Chen made a point of saying he didn't want me investigating officially. Even if I did try to ask a few questions, they wouldn't have to cooperate with me. I have no authority whatsoever in these matters."

"No, it would be of no use," Peiqin said. "Unless we could find someone who has inside connection and information."

"So, what are we going to do now?"

"Let's go to visit the other one's neighborhood. Fu's."

That area happened to be Peiqin's childhood neighborhood, where she had lived until the start of the Cultural Revolution. Her family, being a "black" one, had never mixed much with their neighbors and then during the Cultural Revolution had been driven out of the neighborhood. The memory of being a "black puppy," with its head hung low and its tail tucked in, still stung. Peiqin hardly ever went back there.

"After so many years," she said pensively, "I may not find anyone who still knows me, let alone someone who will tell us anything about Fu. The address you have is in a side lane, if I'm not remembering wrong, and in those years I didn't go there often."

However, after having made several calls on the way, Yu had better luck. One of his colleagues was acquainted with the neighborhood cop there, Wei Guoqiang, who promised to help.

Wei was waiting for them at the neighborhood committee office. Though no longer as powerful as it had been in the years of "class struggle" under Mao, it was still something of a grass-roots organization responsible for neighborhood security. Wei had no problem obtaining information for a general background check on a local resident.

According to Wei, Fu had been born to and raised by a poor family here in this mainly lower- and middle-class neighborhood. Three generations of Fu's family had been squeezed into a single room of fifteen square meters in a *shikumen* house: his grandfather, his parents, and

Fu and his younger brother. Even though Fu worked in Wuxi now, he still came back quite regularly. When there, he shared a retrofitted attic with his brother.

"Hold on," Yu cut in. "Fu serves as the head of a large state-run company in Wuxi. He should have been able to buy an apartment for himself, if not for the family."

"Is he already the head?" Wei asked, then went on without waiting for an answer. "But there's a reason he hasn't bought an apartment here, that I can tell you. This neighborhood is included in the city reconstruction plan. The old houses may soon be pulled down and replaced by new construction. When that happens, the Fu family will be given at least two apartments as compensation, and Fu could have one of them when he gets married. If instead he bought one now and moved out, it would be a different story. Housing compensation is based on the number of people in the family."

"I see. But he works in Wuxi. Does he have to come back to Shanghai regularly as part of the housing plan?"

"Well, it is said that he has a girlfriend in Shanghai, someone who used to live in this same neighborhood. She would come to see him here whenever he was back, but I've not seen her for a while. Perhaps a lovers' fight or something like that. Between two young people, you can never tell."

This was something Chen hadn't mentioned—a girlfriend in Shanghai, Yu noted to himself. It could be totally irrelevant, however.

"Is there anything strange or suspicious about him, Wei?"

"What do you mean? Is there anything strange or suspicious? No, I don't think so. He passed the entrance exam and was accepted to Fudan University. As his parents are both barely educated, it wasn't easy. He studied hard. He became a representative at a national Youth League conference and then joined the Party. And he must have worked really hard at his job, too, if he's already the head of a large state-run factory."

"How long have you worked here?" Peiqin cut in.

"Three—almost four years."

"I used to live here," she said with a wistful look on her face, "but it was almost thirty years ago."

"Really!"

"I'd like to take a walk around, Yu. It's such a fine day today."

"Good idea," Yu said.

"Come back if you have any other questions," Wei said, smiling.

They took leave and walked out of the neighborhood committee office.

As Peiqin had supposed, a lot of old neighbors had moved away. After half a block, she hadn't recognized anyone. It was almost lunchtime, and there was a group of people standing around. Some were cooking on a coal stove, some were using a common sink, and some were enjoying early lunch. Only one or two looked up in curiosity at the two strangers passing by.

Finally, she noticed a makeshift scallion and ginger booth on a street corner facing a side lane. The old woman sitting at the booth used to live in the building next door to her family. Back then, Peiqin called her Auntie Hui. Now, white-haired, toothless, sitting on a small stool with a pronounced stoop, she must have been in her seventies. The booth looked the same as always, though, with the green onion still succulent, and the ginger still golden, spread out on the same narrow wooden board. The one difference after all these years was that the small bunch of green onion that had cost only one cent at that time now cost fifty cents. Peiqin stepped up to the booth and introduced herself.

"I was a slip of a girl then, Auntie Hui. Once you gave me a bunch of green onion for one cent and a large piece of ginger for free. After that, my mother called me a capable girl for days."

"You still remember that after all this time," Auntie Hui said, her face wreathed in smiles like a dried-up winter melon. "And this is . . . ?"

"Oh, this is my husband, Yu."

Auntie Hui was pleased by the unexpected reunion, and the two spoke of little other than memories of the bygone days. The continued existence of the tiny booth spoke for how little the old woman's life had improved since then. Peiqin finally brought the conversation around to the question she had in mind.

"The Fu family lives just opposite here, right?"

"Yes, three generations of them now."

"I've just heard that Fu Hao, the eldest grandson, is now the managing director of a large state company in Wuxi."

"Yes, I heard about that too," the old woman said, eyeing Peiqin somewhat warily.

"Our old neighborhood has produced some successful people," Peiqin said with a smile.

The door of the *shikumen* house opposite opened with a grinding sound, as if echoing from twenty years ago, and a tall, angular man wearing a light gray wool suit and a pair of gold-rimmed glasses walked out.

Auntie Hui looked up at Peiqin and whispered, "It's none other than Fu Hao. Do you know him?"

"No, I moved away many years ago, you know."

"We have to get going, Peiqin," Yu said. "We've spent too long here as it is."

Peiqin picked up Yu's cue as he spoke.

"Yes, let's go. It's Saturday. We have to do some shopping," she said, like an understanding wife. "We'll come again, Auntie Hui."

They sauntered away, hand in hand like a loving couple, which they were. It was as in a popular song, *"It's the most romantic thing to live, love, and grow old with you, side by side."*

They followed Fu at a discreet distance, even though Yu didn't have a plan in mind. It wasn't something Chen had asked him to do, but he had nothing else planned for that afternoon. Yu redialed Bai, who wasn't home yet. So it might not be a bad idea, he thought, to continue following Fu for a while.

They cut across Yanan Road, and then on to Fuzhou Road. Fu walked steadily, heading north, without looking at the bus stop or for a taxi, seemingly unaware of being shadowed. Fu then turned left on

Nanjing Road, which, at the intersection with Henan Road, became a pedestrian street thronged with shoppers and tourists.

No one could move quickly along Nanjing Road. The street was lined along both sides with stores, some of which were very crowded; it would be easy to lose sight of someone. With the two of them following Fu, however, Yu thought they could still manage.

"We haven't been to Nanjing Road in months," Peiqin said.

"We're here today, so we might do some shopping," he said, "if we lose sight of Fu. We shouldn't worry about it. Chen didn't say he was a suspect, and sending us out to look into him was probably nothing more than a whimsical hunch of our eccentric chief inspector."

But Fu slowed down near the corner of Zhejiang Road and started looking around, as if anxiously awaiting someone. Sure enough, he spotted a slender girl standing near Sheng's Restaurant and walked over to her. She was smiling and waving her hand at him. However, instead of walking into the restaurant, they went into an old building next to it.

Yu and Peiqin hurried across the street. To their surprise, the old building was a hotel. They peered inside, but there was no sign of Fu or his companion at the front desk or along the dimly lit corridor. They must have already checked in.

In front of the hotel, there was a large sign that declared in bold characters: "*Serve the people, hourly rate available, both day time and nighttime, full of leisure, convenience.*" The first part sounded like an echo of a saying from Mao, but the part about their business hours was puzzling.

Yu couldn't help walking up to take a closer look, leaving Peiqin behind.

"It's really convenient," a young hotel attendant with a sweet dimple in her cheek came out and said to him. "And very clean too. We change the sheets after every customer. If you don't have a companion, we can recommend one to you. "

The full meaning of the hourly rate advertised in the sign finally dawned on him. The hotel was charging for a couple of hours in bed and then a quick shower. That's all that their operation was about. "Oh, no, thank you," said Yu, retracing his steps in a hurry.

For a hotel like that, Yu doubted that Fu and his companion had registered under their real names. It would be pointless to ask at the front desk, and he didn't want to raise unnecessary alarm. In the city, such places were sometimes closely connected to the police, and he thought there was a good chance that this hourly hotel was one of them.

But why would Fu have gone there if that was his girlfriend that he picked up? Was she possibly one of the girls "working" for the hotel? Would Fu come back to Shanghai just for that?

"You know what kind of a hotel it is?" Peiqin said, as Yu walked up.

"I think so," Yu said, a bit sheepish. "Let's sit down somewhere and wait for a while."

He decided to wait and watch for them to come out. Fu's behavior was strange—even suspicious.

Across the street, there was a small square. It sported a huge LCD screen mounted high and in the background. Next to it stood the celebrated Seventh Heaven, a notorious dance hall back in the pre-1949 era. After 1949, it was turned into the Shanghai Number One Pharmacy Store, but nowadays, it had reverted back to its original function as a nightclub attached to a hotel, though it was no longer that notorious. Nor as classy as its original name suggested. The seven-story building was now dwarfed by all the new surrounding high-rises.

At the edge of the square, there was a somewhat fashionable teahouse, so they went over and took a table outside. No one would pay much attention to a middle-aged couple sitting at a teahouse.

Yu ordered a cup of Lion Hill tea and Peiqin, a bowl of white almond tofu.

"I wouldn't have the pleasure of sitting with you here if it weren't for your boss's request," she said in mock peevishness.

"After Chen comes back, I will also request vacation time—a whole week. And I'll sit here with you just like today, every day, all day, if that's what you really want, Peiqin."

"No, I'm not complaining. You don't have to envy your boss's vacation. True, his may be an all-expenses-paid vacation with all the privileges of a high-ranking cadre, but does he have someone sitting beside him there, looking over that beautiful lake?"

"One can never tell what Chen is up to," Yu said. "What he has asked us to look into today, I suppose, may have something to do with that girl, the one who is connected to the man in trouble. It might possibly even be a murder case."

"That's true," she said with a low sigh.

"Do you like the area?" Yu asked, changing the subject.

"Yes, but for me, it might be more because of nostalgia. When I was still a small girl, back in the neighborhood we just visited, I sometimes passed by the Seventh Heaven, which then loomed up so high, seemed so unreachable, to me."

Sipping at the Lion Hill tea, Yu glanced back at the pedestrian street, which seemed to not have changed as dramatically as much of the rest of the city. Several of the old-brand stores remained standing there, though even those had been refurbished.

In the square, a group of people began dancing to music that blared from a cassette player on the ground. A middle-aged, bald man, apparently the leader, dressed in an old sweat-drenched T-shirt with the character *Dance* printed on the front and in white silk pants with flared legs, danced intently, earnestly. For him, his green belt streaming in the breeze, the movement of the moment seemed to carry the meaning of the world. Across the square, another group was practicing tai chi, striking one pose after another, like floating clouds or flowing water. Continuing to look around the square, Yu then noticed something else going on across the street.

Two young girls, probably only seventeen or eighteen, were approaching a stoutly built Westerner, pointing at the hotel sign. China had been changing so rapidly and radically, it was like the proverb his father, Old Hunter, liked to quote: *changing as if from the azure ocean into a mulberry field.*

"I can hardly remember what the store was that used to be where the hotel is now," Peiqin said, following his gaze.

"It was just a stationery store, as I remember," Yu said.

Apart from the scene unfolding in front of the hotel, sitting there, drinking, relaxing, and looking around was pleasant.

"The only place that looks unchanged is Sheng's Restaurant. At least the name is the same. And the outside as well."

"Nanjing Road is no longer the busiest, most important street in the city, but then the city itself has always seemed young and vital, always with young people moving in and out," Peiqin said, sipping at her drink, "and around here new stores, hotels, and restaurants are springing up."

It was Yu's turn to follow her glance to another new hotel, this one near Fujian Road. It was a high-end one built in the European style. He must have walked by it a number of times, but he never thought about going in. As Yu watched, a Big Buck emerged from the revolving door of the hotel, turned and blew a kiss to someone inside, a large diamond ring shining like a dream on his finger.

"Oh, the stock market," Peiqin exclaimed, as if suddenly inspired, "We don't know any businesspeople, but Chen does. Remember, he knows a Big Buck called Mr. Gu whose company, New World Group, is in the market."

"That's right. I met him once during an investigation. He helped us, claiming to be an admirer of Chen's. He'll help out again, I think, if I let him know that the information is for Chen."

Yu was taking out his cell phone when Peiqin touched his elbow.

"Hold on. He's coming—they are coming out."

Fu was walking out with the girl. Instead of parting outside the hotel, they started strolling around, her arm locked in his. They walked across the street to the Yongan Department Store, another old building from the pre-1949 days, newly redecorated from the inside out.

An elderly African man in a white suit had stepped out onto a white balcony on the third floor of Yongan and was playing the trumpet like in an old movie. His performance soon drew a crowd of people, including Fu and his girl.

His cell phone still in his hand, Yu seized the opportunity to quietly take pictures of the two without their knowledge. Even if they had noticed, it was common for people to take photos in the area around Nangjing Road.

It wasn't what Chen had asked him to do, but it couldn't hurt. Besides, it wasn't a bad idea to have a few photos of the street. Nanjing Road was changing at such a rapid pace that in a couple of years, he and Peiqin wouldn't be able to recognize it.

As Yu watched, the couple under the balcony were parting. They hugged passionately several times.

"We should be parting too," Peiqin said, looking up at him, "if you want me to follow the woman."

"No, I don't see the point," Yu said.

However odd the hotel episode might have appeared, he couldn't think how it could be relevant to Chen's investigation. Later, he might check in with Wei, the neighborhood cop. That should be more than enough.

"You sure?"

"Yes, I'm sure. It's Saturday. Let's do some shopping now, Peiqin. And then I'll call that woman, Bai, one more time."

FOURTEEN

ON SATURDAY MORNING, SHANSHAN awoke with both her eyelids twitching. It was another ominous sign, she thought, as she tried to remember the horrible dream that was fast fading.

She reached for the watch under the pillow. It wasn't yet eight. Lying back on the bed, she tried to go over in her mind what had happened in the last few days.

She glanced over at the china saucer used as an ashtray during Chen's unexpected visit the other day, her finger tapping the edge of the bed, unconciously, the same way that Chen tapped his cigarette. As if through mysterious correspondence, the scarlet cell phone that Chen had bought her started to vibrate.

She picked it up and, when she'd answered, heard his voice.

"Morning, Shanshan. I woke up this morning thinking of you."

"Thank you for waking me up with the great news," she said, then added in a hurry, rubbing her eyes, "Oh, I'm just kidding."

"I'm standing at the window, holding my first cup of coffee for the day. The view is fantastic. I wish you were here with me at this moment. '*Don't lean on the railing, alone—/with the boundless view of waters and mountains.*'"

"How romantic of you! I'll think about your invitation," she said, suddenly aware of footsteps moving along the corridor and then coming to a stop outside her door. It might be one of her neighbors in the dorm, where young people, many of them single like her, would sometimes borrow sugar or salt from each other. "One of my neighbors might be at my door."

Dressed in the shorts and a white tank top she wore to bed, Shanshan stood up, still holding the phone, and moved to the door.

"Think about it, Shanshan," Chen said. "Come over this afternoon or evening, whenever you like. Also, if you happen to think of anything unusual that you noticed about your company—anything you hadn't thought to mention before—call me."

They said their good-byes, and Shanshan hung up. Chen's last line about calling him reminded her of something she'd heard in a popular police drama, she mused, before her thoughts were interrupted by a knock on the door.

Opening it, she was surprised to see two strangers standing there. One was tall and stout, and another, short and thin. Both were dressed plainly yet were ferocious-looking, as if emerging out of Shanshan's half-forgotten nightmare.

The tall man flashed something like a police officer's badge at her, then handed her a business card that identified him as Ji Lun of Internal Security.

"Han Bing, my partner, is also from Internal Security," Ji said, pointing to his companion. Neither made a move to enter her dorm room. Ji continued, "Our car is parked outside. Follow us."

She had no idea what Internal Security could possibly do to her, but the two men standing outside her door meant that she was in trouble, far more serious trouble than she could have imagined.

"Can you wait there for one minute? Let me put something else on."

She closed the door and when it opened again, she was dressed in a short-sleeved white blouse, jeans, and sandals.

They led her outside to a new black Lexus. She went without protest. Resisting would only make things worse, she supposed, as some of her neighbors were hanging around outside, watching while holding their breakfast in their hands.

They drove in silence, the only sound an occasional screech of the tires on the stretch of gravel road before the car turned onto the main road. The inside of the car was wreathed in cigarette smoke, both men smoking heavily.

It took them fifteen minutes to arrive at a towering hotel, somewhere close, though she had never been there before. It was a sprawling multistory building, squatting like a surrealistic monster over the lake.

The two officers nodded at the people manning the front desk, and they took her directly to a grand suite on the top floor. Ji Lun motioned her to a gray chair in the living room, while he and his comrade seated themselves opposite her on a velvet sectional sofa.

"You'd better come clean immediately, Shanshan," Han Bing started.

"I don't know what you're talking about, Officer."

"Don't kid yourself into thinking that you can get away with it. There's no way, Shanshan," Ji said. "Stop dreaming your spring-and-autumn dream. Jiang has already confessed. Spill everything now, or it will be too late for you."

"I parted with Jiang about half a year ago. Whatever he's done since, I have no knowledge of."

"But you provided him with the industrial pollution data on the lake, which he still uses against the interests of the government. That's something you can't deny."

"That's not a state secret. All the data was gathered from official publications. As for the pollution in the lake, all anyone needs to do is look at it for themselves."

"Not a state secret? The document you provided him was marked 'inside information.' We've already double-checked that. It is very much a state secret. There's no mistaking it. "

It was like a recurring nightmare, except that it now was Internal

Security, not Liu, who was accusing her of "giving away state secrets." It was a deadly serious charge and even more so coming from Internal Security.

"How am I supposed to have obtained secret documents? The 'inside information' stamp is just something routinely printed on the front cover of the newsletter. It only means that it's the newsletter for company employees."

"Well, that's your interpretation," said Han.

"That's a serious crime in itself," Ji went on wildly. "Has Jiang discussed with you selling state secrets abroad?"

"How much has he made selling secrets?" Han pushed further.

"Jiang told me nothing. We only went out a couple of times and then we parted, as I've already told you."

"I'll tell you something! He's going to be convicted and sentenced for the murderer of Liu. And you, too, will be punished as his accomplice."

"What are you talking about, Officers?"

"Jiang blackmailed Liu using the state secrets you gave him, and then killed Liu when he refused to give in," Ji said deliberately, each word pronounced in a serious, official way. "If you're not an accomplice, then who the hell is?"

By such logic, she was unquestionably involved, guilty no matter what explanation she offered. There was no use arguing about it.

"And you called him after Liu's murder," Han chipped in. "Do you still claim that you had already broken up with him?"

Her heart sank. What Chen had told her was all true: she had been under surveillance and her phone bugged for a long time, including her phone call to Jiang just a few days ago—the call he had not picked up.

"Didn't you tell Jiang about Liu's schedule that night—that he was going to be at his home office?" Ji snarled. "You not only called him, you were also seen meeting with him near the company just the day before Liu's murder."

"No, I didn't," she said emphatically. That was definitely not true.

"You two met secretly in a small eatery close to the company. We know everything about you, Shanshan. The monkey cannot escape the palm of Buddha. You can be assured of that."

It dawned on her that it was Chen they were talking about, the time she met him at Uncle Wang's place. There was actually a slight resemblance between Jiang and Chen.

Whoever had been following her made a mistake. She decided, however, not to contradict them. Chen couldn't be dragged into this mess, or she would never forgive herself.

"But we are still willing to give you one more chance. Work with us, Shanshan," Han said, tapping his cigarette into a makeshift ashtray in the non-smoking room. "Tell us what Jiang has done."

"But he's confessed. You just told me he did," she said, biting her lips. "Why do you need me?"

"Don't think you have a wise head, young woman, or you'll wash your face with rueful tears all the day long. All the year long," Ji snapped again. "And I'll see to it personally."

"Now, you might think that you've got someone in the background who could help you out of this mess," Han said in a more persuasive tone. "You're wrong. In a murder case like this one, no one can possibly help you. If anything, you'll make things worse by trying, and get him into trouble too, no matter how capable he might be. We are your only chance."

With one playing the red face, and the other, the white face, the two Internal Security officers had set up a subtle division of labor in their efforts to intimidate her. Their talk about this "someone in the background," however, worried her more than anything else, even if they seemed not to be sure who he really was. Chen had been justified in taking all the precautions he had. If it weren't for the newly purchased cell phone, his identity might have been revealed. But did Chen know that Internal Security was already aware of his existence and possibly of his interference?

As for Jiang, she didn't think they had anything solid on him. At least not yet. That was why they wanted her to cooperate.

"Everything depends upon your attitude," Ji concluded. "Use your brains, young woman."

"Attitude" meant whether or not she cooperated with Internal Security, and it was entirely up to their interpretation.

"This is my cell number," Han said, writing the number down on his business card and handing it to her. He stood up to open the door for her. "But we won't wait long. Jiang will be convicted, with or without your cooperation. Working with us is in your own interest."

She hardly knew how she walked out of the hotel on her own.

She must have wandered, her legs moving mechanically, her mind a total blank, for a long while until she noticed that she was walking along a narrow, nameless trail that skirted the lake. The willow shoots looked long, tender, yet sorrowful. The hotel behind her wasn't visible. She slowed down to a stop and stared out at the lake. Her reflection in the water rippled out in a soft sigh of breeze.

There was no point in struggling anymore, she decided.

A lone wild white goose flashed into flight. Where would be the end of its journey? There was nothing but factory chimneys, far and near, along the shore.

She then did something that surprised her. She sat down on a slab of rock overhanging the lake, kicked off her sandals, and put her feet into the water.

The cool touch of the water brought back memories of her childhood in Anhui. There was a gurgling brook behind their farmhouse. As a little girl in that rural village, she used to sit there alone, dabbling her feet in the clear, crystal stream, dreaming of a different future for herself when she grew up . . . Time flowed like the water between her toes. And then, after elementary school, after middle school, after college, a different life spread out ahead of her, far away from home, when she had first come to work at the chemical company in Wuxi. But soon, everything had changed.

She had done the same thing just a couple of days ago, she then recalled, dabbling her feet in the water in the sampan with Chen.

She was beginning to cool down, her mind no longer so confused. If anyone could help her at this stage, it had to be Chen.

He was a mysterious man, but well connected in his way. Even Internal Security, who might not know his name, reluctantly acknowledged his resourcefulness.

Thinking of him, she pulled her feet out the water and put on her sandals. She had a feeling that she could hardly understand, one that surged through her all of a sudden, like a swift spring tide. He had come into her life at a time when she was unprepared. Having just parted with a man who had caused her nothing but trouble, she was in no hurry to start another relationship. And the trouble in which she found herself made her even less inclined. Still, she was not unaware of something in Chen that attracted her, from their first encounter at the eatery. As for Chen, he had since made his feelings transparent to her, going out of his way to help, even putting himself at risk.

Among the scenarios he had laid out for her, one was particularly convincing. She had been thrown into the same boat with Jiang. His sinking would inevitably bring her down too. If he was convicted, she would surely be prosecuted and punished as an accomplice.

But she didn't believe Jiang was the murderer. In fact, she couldn't even believe that Jiang would have come to the offices to talk to Liu. Not in the beginning of March, not after the promise Jiang had made her. What she believed, however, didn't matter. She had no proof.

She stood up, and an idea sprung up like a rabbit out of the tall, wild weeds. She stumbled, then collected herself, turned around, and made her way straight to the company offices. All the way, she kept thinking hard.

The security guard at the front gate was surprised to see her, but he didn't ask any questions.

"It's the weekend, Shanshan. You're working too hard."

"I need to check something. It won't take long," she said readily.

An engineer could choose to work in their lab over the weekend if, for one reason or another, they needed to. It was something she had done in the past—last weekend, in fact.

In her office, she started by checking the company calendar. The one on her desk had certain dates marked in red pencil, and occasionally, a few sloppy words understandable only to herself. Then she logged on to the company Web site and looked through the events listed for the month of March.

She was right. Heaving a sigh of relief, she stared at a Web page with the dates and events for March clearly marked.

At the beginning of March, she had planned to report to Liu about a new, cost-effective method of wastewater treatment, but Liu wasn't in the office. He was at a meeting in Nanjing. The date marked on her calendar was March 7. It was crossed out with a note: "Liu out, till 8th." Liu didn't come back until late that night. The information on the company Web site confirmed that. Mi, who worked in the reception area, claimed to have overheard their argument in the inner office, but there was no possibility that Liu met with Jiang at the offices on March 7, the day before Women's Day. She picked up the office phone and began making calls, to see what she could learn from other colleagues.

When Shanshan left the building, the dusk was already spreading out against the sky. It was a long walk from the company back to the dorm, but she was barely aware of the distance, absorbed as she was in her own thoughts.

When she reached her room, she was exhausted. She locked the door after her, let down the curtain, and flung herself across the bed. Never had she felt so helpless. She tossed the faded blanket aside and tried to drive the confusing thoughts from her mind. For several minutes, she stared up in bewilderment, waiting for the end of the day to reveal inscrutable images against the ceiling.

As the evening progressed, she gradually became aware of the noisy cooking along the corridor, particularly of a strong smell of salted fish coming from a neighbor's sizzling wok.

She thought back to Chen's visit the other day. Would there be another light knock at her door this evening? She didn't think so. But she hoped there would be.

She got up, changed into her robe, and sat down on the chair Chen

175

had used that evening, putting her feet on the bed. There was a red patch above her left ankle and another on the back of her right foot. Idly scratching, she wondered whether they were from her exposure to the lake water today, or earlier, when she was in the sampan beside him. The water was unfit for human touch, as she had told him.

The fragmented memories continued to resurface, undulating in the stillness of the evening in the small room. That evening, he was having a hard time taking his eyes off her, she recalled, fingering the belt of her robe.

What kind of a man he really was, however, she still had no clue. He surely wasn't the bookish school teacher he claimed to be. On the contrary, he was more likely an emerging cadre with extraordinary connections, a "successful man" in today's society. That was a far more plausible explanation for the mysteries about him. Whatever his true identity was, though, why had he concealed it from her?

But then, did she tell him everything about herself?

Whether he could do something to help or not, she wanted to see him that evening. He was, as the cliché put it, a solid shoulder to lean her head on.

She then turned her thoughts to Jiang, who didn't fit the same cliché. She had been trying not to think about him, but she hadn't always been successful. Not for one single moment could she bring herself to believe that he was a murderer. Especially after the research she had just done at the company.

More than ever, she was convinced that this conclusion was being pushed by Internal Security based solely on political considerations. Jiang must have been aware of this all along. In fact, he had told her about the perilous situation in which he had landed himself. Could that have been the reason he was so willing to break up with her? It wasn't his fault, not exactly, that she had got into trouble, too. He had just been too eager to do the right thing for the environment, not for himself.

She decided not to think about her relationship with Jiang anymore tonight. Her head had started aching from the circular thoughts. Besides, she had another idea for this evening.

FIFTEEN

LATE SATURDAY AFTERNOON, CHEN decided to take a break. He got up and opened the windows. As the leaves rustled in a low pitch and the lake stretched out against the horizon, Chen saw a lone silver fish jumping up, in the distance, over the darkening water.

He shook out a cigarette from a new pack.

Chen had spent most of the day inside the villa, shutting himself off from the world as he pondered the information he had gathered so far, speculating over its meaning without any interruption except for breakfast and the herbal medicine delivered early that morning. But his efforts yielded little. Turning, he stared at the ashtray on the windowsill, the shell-shaped tray full of cigarette butts, which stared back at him, like a pile of dead fish eyes.

He couldn't rule out the possibility that Jiang was the murderer. Internal Security had political considerations, but they also had circumstantial evidence, witnesses, and a plausible motive with the story of blackmail gone wrong. In contrast, Chen had only unsupported theories.

Of course, he could tell himself that it wasn't his fault. He didn't have any authority here, and his hands were bound; consequently, his information pointed to possibilities, but only to unsubstantial possibilities.

Whistling absentmindedly, he poured himself a glass of red wine. The bottle was compliments of the center, and the label said Bordeaux. All these nice extras were provided in recognition of his special status.

As he gazed into the red wine rippling in the glass, he realized that he missed her.

She cared about him without knowing his status. Not that he had intended to keep his identity a secret. His situation was not like the one in an English novel he had read years ago, where a rich and powerful nobleman had disguised himself as a poor vagrant to try to find true love, someone who would love him for the man he was, not for things like wealth or status.

Shanshan hadn't told him that much about herself, either. Considering the circumstances in which they'd met, she had her reasons.

A young, attractive, bright woman like her must have had men pursuing her, presumably many of them, including Jiang. That was not suprising. But when they first met at Uncle Wang's eatery, he was sure there wasn't anyone in her life. Like there wasn't anyone in his.

He stopped himself from thinking further along those lines. At this moment, there were so many more important things for him to do. It wouldn't be a good idea for Chief Inspector Chen to lose himself in a burgeoning affair. If Internal Security happened to find out about their relationship while they were in the middle of the investigation, he might not be able to wash himself clean, as the proverb says, even if he jumped into the Yellow River.

It was late in the afternoon, and he was beginning to feel slightly hungry. He had skipped lunch; after the interruption of breakfast delivery, he had instructed the front desk that he wanted no disturbances whatsoever.

It would be only a matter of minutes for him to walk over to the canteen and have them prepare something, but he didn't like the idea of being treated as a "special guest." Instead, he boiled a pot of water and put in a package of shrimp dumplings he had bought at the center's convenience store as an instant snack.

He ate the meal without really tasting it. When he thought about it, though, there was still an agreeable aftertaste lingering on his tongue. Afterward, he dumped the bowl and pot into the sink without bothering to wash them. Out the kitchen window, he noticed a fitful wind dispelling the languid clouds in the distance.

Chen changed into an old T-shirt and short pants, then picked up the phone. But he hesitated. He'd already left her a message, which she hadn't yet returned. Putting down the phone, he wondered what she'd been doing all day. It was tempting to make another surprise visit to her room, but he decided not to go out. There wasn't anything new to tell her, and besides, the dorm might be under surveillance.

Instead, he opened up the laptop on the table. He had an unexpected impulse to continue on with the fragments he had written earlier in the week. Thinking of her, he opened the file. The earlier lines remained unpolished, but they could develop into a long poem, perhaps even something as ambitious as "The Waste Land."

Again, images sprang forth. Random ones, clustering around the lake, and with her in the middle of every line. The moment she was sitting with him in the sampan, the lake water murmuring after her, as she was telling him about all the environmental problems . . .

The morning comes to the lake
in waves of toxic waste, waves
of poisonous air, surging to smother
the smile in the waking boughs.
She walks in a red jacket
like a bright sail through the dust
under the network of pipes, long
in disrepair, spreading cobweblike,
dripping with contaminated water.
A mud-covered toad jumps up

at the dew-bespangled report in her hand
opens its sleepy eyes, seeing
all around still murky, slumps back into sleep.

There was something contagious about her youthful idealism. For a long while, he'd thought he was no longer capable of being genuinely lyrical. But it might not be too late for him to start all over again. He thought of her, and kept pounding at the keys.

The broken metal-blue fingernails
of the leaves clutching
the barren bank of the lake,
the dead fish afloat, shining
with the mercury bellies trembling,
their glassy eyes still flashing
with the last horror and fascination,
still gazing up at the apparition
of a witch dancing in a black bikini,
her raven hair long, streaming
on her snowy white shoulders, jumping
into the dark smoke from the chimneys,
against the dark waste currents
across the lake, a dark wood of
nightmare looms up.
A dog is barking the cell
in the distance.

Who's the one walking beside you?

The moonlight streaming like water,
and worries drifting like a boat . . .
who's whistling "The Blue Danube"?
So close, yet so far away.
All the joy and sorrow of a dream.

A snatch of the violin sweeping over,
a water rat creeps along the bank.
The city wakes up sneezing in the morning,
and falls asleep coughing at night.

Who's the one walking beside you?

The lines kept pouring out, as if rolling up on wave after wave. He worked on with intense concentration, pouring himself another glass of the red wine, until the spell was broken by the ringing phone. It was Detective Yu in Shanghai.

Apparently, Yu wasn't calling from home, but from somewhere in the street. Chen could hear traffic in the background, and occasionally, Peiqin's excited voice.

Yu began relating to him what he and Peiqin had learned.

It turned out to be a fairly long narrative. Yu made a point of including Peiqin's analysis, sometimes even quoting her directly. Chen listened without interruption, sipping at his wine, until Yu finished relaying the part about Mrs. Liu.

"So what's your take on her frequent trips back to Shanghai?" Chen asked.

"It's difficult to say, Chief. According to Peiqin, it may be complicated. It might be more than just an escape from the unpleasantness in Wuxi. Only in Shanghai could she afford to keep up her image as a successful woman. She's surely a character, desperate to keep up appearances—to preserve face—in the eyes of others." Yu then added, "Oh, Fu, it seems, is another character."

"How so?"

Yu summed up what he and Peiqin had seen while sitting at the café on Nanjing Road.

"I took a number of pictures of him and the girl," Yu said. "Peiqin calls me a private eye. Which is, you know, a fashionable profession in the city now. Old Hunter is thinking about making it his new career."

"That would be a good idea. Nowadays, there are quite a number

181

of rich wives looking to find out about their husbands' infidelities. Your father is experienced and energetic—an old hunter indeed. So why shouldn't he?"

"Oh, before I forget, one more thing. Peiqin and I contacted Gu, the chairman of the New World Group. As far as he knows, there's nothing out of the ordinary about the IPO plan for the Wuxi Number One Chemical Company. The top Party boss always gets most of the shares when a company goes public. It's something that is taken for granted, but Gu promised that he would ask around."

"Thanks for everything you've done, Yu, and of course, thank Peiqin for me too."

After Chen hung up, he tried to fit this latest information into the puzzle, but without success. Instead, he found himself worn out by the fruitless speculations. To his surprise, he felt a little sleepy. Perhaps he really had needed this vacation.

After another futile call to Shanghai, he made for himself a cup of Cloud and Mist tea, hoping that it might revive him a bit. It didn't work. So he brewed himself a fresh pot of coffee as well. It wasn't a day for him to go to bed early. Internal Security was already reaching their conclusions. He had to be up and doing, he told himself, pouring out a cup.

Then a thought struck him. The night he was murdered, Liu, too, had tried to work. Of course, he might have dozed off while he was there all alone in the apartment. There was nothing really inconceivable about that scenario. But he probably wouldn't have taken sleeping pills, certainly not that early. Allowing a half an hour for them to take effect, Liu would have to have swallowed the pills around nine, or even earlier. That was inexplicably early for a man who planned to work late into the night on an important document.

Another argument against Liu's having taken pills was the missing cup in the apartment. Occasionally, Chen swallowed pills without water, but that was due to specific circumstances, like being on an overcrowded train. It was hard to imagine that Liu, in his own apartment, would have chosen to swallow the pills dry rather than getting a glass of water.

In a case of unpremeditated murder, the perpetrator was likely to have killed with whatever weapon they had found there and then left the apartment with it. A missing cup would have been too light for such a fatal blow. According to the autopsy report, the blow was definitely inflicted with a heavy object. So what else—heavy, blunt—was now missing and could have been used?

Again, he tried to fit Jiang into the details. The unpremeditated murder scenario could work, but could he have entered without being stopped by security? As for the missing murder weapon, Chen had no clue about that at all.

Chen started to feel slightly queasy, his head swimming. Perhaps it was the result of too much coffee and an empty stomach. He tried to take another short break. Leaning against the window, he looked out it again. This time of year, the light lasted long into the approaching dusk. He was fascinated by the scarlet clouds beyond the distant ragged lines of the hills, which seemed to be spurting out a huge flame, gilding an immense area of the lake. The lake had never looked so fantastic, as if sporting its natural grace in an unappreciated effort to keep itself from being contaminated.

Turning his attention back to the laptop, Chen found himself unable to settle into the unfinished poem. The fragmented lines could be saved on the laptop, but he had no idea when he would experience another impulse to complete the whole piece.

It might not matter that much. He thought of what Shanshan had said about the irrelevance of poetry in today's China. He pressed the save key and went off to take a shower.

After the shower, he wrapped himself in a gray robe provided by the center, lit a cigarette, and settled on to the couch before turning on the TV.

There was nothing worth watching, except perhaps a "much-awaited" football game. But Chen wasn't a sports fan. A faint breath of cool air, barely noticeable, came wafting in from the lake. He fetched a bath towel. Chen sometimes drifted off to sleep more easily with the TV on. He didn't want to go to bed for the night, but a nap might refresh his mind.

SIXTEEN

THERE CAME A LIGHT knock at the door.

He must have dozed off. It was an evening when most of the people in the center would be watching football on television. Rubbing his eyes, he wondered who the visitor could possibly be.

He opened the door and standing there was Shanshan. She was wearing a short-sleeved white blouse, jeans, and sandals, with a light-green satchel slung across her shoulder. She looked casual, as if she'd just come back from a leisurely walk by the lake. A few loose hairs curled down at her cheeks, giving her a vivacious look despite the suggestion of dark rings under her eyes.

"I sneaked in by taking the shortcut through the fence door you showed me the other day," she said. "No one stopped me or asked any questions."

The security people must be watching the football game, he realized.

"Welcome, Shanshan. But you've caught me by surprise. Come on in. I'm sorry that the room is in such a mess."

"I wanted to see you when you weren't expecting a visitor. Now we're even." She stepped in. Still smiling, she added in a low voice, "You mentioned the possibility of the phone being bugged. So I thought I'd better come over without calling you first."

"Yes, we can't be too careful, but—"

"What have you been doing this evening?"

"Oh, nothing in particular, I've been watching TV. But there's nothing good on."

Shanshan turned her head left and right, taking in the villa.

"What a place—and you have it all to yourself!"

"It's not too bad, I daresay. Please, take a seat."

"It's a place for a high-ranking cadre indeed," she said. She pulled a scarlet swivel chair over opposite the sofa, but she didn't sit down immediately.

"You're being sarcastic, Shanshan. Yes, staying here is a special treat. As I've said before, it wasn't originally intended for me."

She let her eyes roam around the room, and they came to rest on the empty instant dumpling bowl on the desk and the plastic wrapper crumpled into a ball next to it.

"You should have someone taking care of this place."

"They provide room service here, but I don't like it, especially not when I have to concentrate."

She picked up the bowl and wrapper and threw them into the trash can under the desk, her hand inadvertently brushing the keyboard. The monitor lit up in response, displaying Chen's unfinished lines.

"Oh, you're writing poetry."

"Just some fragments," he said, then added on impulse, "They were inspired by you."

"Come on," she said, leaning down. "Can I take a look?"

"Of course, but the poem is unfinished and unpolished."

She settled down to read, picking up a red pencil as though she were going to make some comments. He pushed a notepad over to her.

She didn't write anything down. Nibbling at the top of the pencil, she read intently. He stood behind her, taking in the fragrance from her hair.

It took her a while to read through to the last line. She looked up. "It's fantastic, Chen."

"No, it's only a part of it, and a rough draft. It's completely disorganized."

"You'll finish the poem and publish it," she said earnestly. "Environmental protection remains an extraneous issue to a lot of Chinese. It's too technical for some and too impractical in this materialistic age for others. But they'll read your poem and think about it."

"I hope so," he said. "Oh, I left a message on your phone this afternoon."

"Sorry, I didn't get it until about an hour ago. What a lousy day!"

"Tell me about it." He took a can of Coca Cola from the refrigerator and handed it to her.

"What a day!" she repeated, staring at the can in her hand. She continued, "But once in a while you want to forget about all your worries and do things you haven't been able to do."

"Yes, me too," he said, wondering what she meant by "once in a while."

She started telling him what had happened to her today. It didn't really surprise Chen to learn that Internal Security had made such a move. Shanshan was no longer being vague about what had happened between her and Jiang. Chen should have figured out long ago how close the two were, but people see only what they want to see. Still, he was a cop. He should have known better.

Was it possible that she came here for Jiang's sake? Chen stopped himself from thinking along those lines.

Shanshan continued on and declared that she was concerned about Chen, giving him a detailed description of how Internal Security talked about "someone in the background" who was helping her.

So it was equally possible that she came here for his sake.

"You have to look out for yourself, Chen," she concluded.

"Don't worry about me," Chen said. "I don't think they can touch me that easily."

"But I'm worried sick about you. All the way here, I kept looking behind me. I had to make sure I wasn't being followed." Visibly shaken after the encounter with Internal Security, she went on, "In your phone call, you asked me to think about unusual things going on at the company. And I've thought really hard. There is something I've been going over in my mind, but I'm not sure."

"Tell me about it."

"Liu's dead. People shouldn't speak ill of the dead."

"I understand," he said, "but the life of another man—possibly an innocent one—is at stake."

"Also, as a woman, I hate to speak against another woman behind her back."

"Who are you talking about?"

"Mi, the little secretary. It's an open secret that Liu used the home office as a convenient place to have sex with her. But Mi never worked late in the company office—I've confirmed this with her colleagues. That night of all the nights, however, she said that she stayed late."

"That's a good point, Shanshan. But Mi has an alibi. Fu saw her working late that evening. They were really busy working on the IPO."

"That seemed possible. I've double-checked on that, too. The office staff were busy working out a restructuring plan, something that would go into place prior to the IPO. I don't know what the plan will involve exactly, but some employees might be let go. At least, I have been warned about it, as you might imagine."

"This may be very important," he said. "Can you tell me something about Mi, either in connection with the IPO or the restructuring plan?"

"She won't get fired. Whatever the final restructuring plan, she'll stay and get her shares when the IPO goes through. That much I'm sure of. Even someone like me, if I haven't been fired by that time, may get a couple of hundred shares. This is nothing, of course—it's two or three hundred shares for an ordinary employee versus two or three million shares for Liu. The number of shares will be determined by the position held. As for Mi, what Liu might have given her privately is another story." After a short pause, she continued. "But back to that evening in question. According to what I've learned from the others in the office, Mi has never been involved with real business decisions. She's nothing but a little secretary, and you know what that means."

"But now as the office manager, she may take on more responsibilities."

"That's true. Interestingly, Fu gave her that job only a couple of days after Liu's death."

"Did Fu offer any explanation for the appointment?"

"He said that it was a promotion that Liu had decided on long before and that Fu was just carrying it out. Of course, he might need her help. There might be things in the company known only to Liu and her."

"Yes, he needs her help." Chen went on, "By the way, I've just heard Fu has a girlfriend in Shanghai."

"How could you—" She didn't finish the sentence, saying instead, "I didn't know that. He never told anybody about it. What's the point of keeping it a secret?"

Fu's companion could have been one of "those" girls that get picked up in front of a sleazy hotel, Chen thought, but Yu's description didn't make her sound like one.

"Are you sure he kept it a secret, Shanshan?"

"Fu himself told me that he didn't have a girlfriend, as he was sort of making a pass at me. It wasn't too long ago, though it was before I got into trouble."

"Well, I'm not surprised that he made a pass at you or that he told you what he did. As *The Book of Songs* says, '*A man cannot but go / after a beautiful girl.*'"

"Come on, Chen, you don't have to say such things to me. To be fair to Fu, he didn't push it too far," she said with a slight frown.

188

"Sorry I've digressed. There's something about Mi I need to discuss with you."

"It's my fault, Shanshan. Please go on."

"Let's say she happened to have worked late that evening, which I doubt. Still, she lied about something else."

"What's that?"

"You told me that she witnessed Jiang arguing with Liu in the office on March 7, the day before the Women's Day. That's what she remembered, right?"

"That's right."

"But that's not true," she said. "I checked both the company calendar and the company Web site. According to them, Liu was in Nanjing that day, and he didn't come back until late that night."

"Hold on—Fu backed up that statement, I think." He stood to go get the folder provided by Sergeant Huang and started checking through it. "Let's see. Here, Fu didn't say anything about the particular date, just that it was early March. He said that he saw Jiang in the office without knowing who he was, and Mi told him it was Jiang later that day."

He was aware that Shanshan was paying close attention to the folder marked "confidential." The sight of the label on the folder could add to her suspicion of his identity. It wasn't the time, however, for him to worry too much about it. Instead of sitting down, he remained standing with the folder in his hand. After all, the folder might contain something that she shouldn't read.

"I don't know why Mi made that statement about Jiang. But with your connections, you might be able to find out."

"Yes, I'll ask Officer Huang for help," he said, still standing. "We'll double-check Liu's itinerary on March 7. If need be, I can also call the Nanjing police bureau. No stone will be left unturned."

Shanshan then stood up, a serious look on her face silhouetted by the soft light through the window.

"I've also come to ask a favor of you, Chen."

"Anything I can do for you, Shanshan."

"I've gathered some information about the industrial pollution here." She produced a bulging folder from her satchel. "Firsthand, authentic data. None of it has appeared in even the so-called inside newsletters."

"Yes?"

"Internal Security might come to search my room at any time. I want you to keep the folder for me. If you have an opportunity, publish the information. Not for me, but for the people who've been suffering as a result of the pollution."

"Nothing will happen to you, Shanshan."

"It might not be easy, even for someone like you, but I'm still asking you to do it."

"I will do whatever is possible to get it published. I give you my word."

"You're the only one I trust," she said, looking into his eyes.

"I promise," he repeated and gripped the folder in her hand.

And he then grabbed her hand too.

She leaned toward him unexpectedly, her hand in his, her head touching his shoulder. He became aware of her breath, warm on his face.

They were standing close to each other, by the window. Behind her, the lake water appeared calm and beautiful under the fair moonlight. In the deep blue evening sky, the night clouds grew insubstantial.

She tilted her face up to him, her eyes glistening. He tightened his grasp of her hand, which was soft, slightly sweaty. She raised her other hand, her long fingers moving to smooth his face, lightly, as a breeze from the lake.

Several lines came back to him, as if riding on the water: *Come to the window, sweet is the night-air! . . . /Ah, love, let us be true/ To one another . . .*

Another poet, long ago, far away in another land, looking out the window at night, standing in the company of one so near and dear to

190

him, thinking of the reason why they should love each other: . . . *for the world, which seems / To lie before us like a land of dreams, / So various, so beautiful, so new, / Hath really neither joy, nor love, nor light, / Nor certitude, nor peace, nor help for pain . . .*

It was a melancholy love poem, presenting love as the only momentary escape—from a faithless world, hopeless with "human misery, and the eternal note of sadness." But at this moment, this world of theirs by the lake was even worse—an utterly polluted one. There was no certitude even in the air, in the water, or in the food. They were here . . . *on a darkling plain / Swept with confused alarms of struggle and flight, / Where ignorant armies clash by night.*

Still, they could be true to one another.

He had had some vague anticipation since her arrival, but they had been so busy talking about the murder, conspiracy, and politics around them. Now, in the sudden silence, the significance of the night fell upon them.

A moment ago, she had looked preoccupied, but now she was intensely present. The moonlight seemed to focus on her face in a stilled glare. He put the folder on the windowsill and touched her lips, and she murmured his name against his hand.

"Well," he said.

"Haven't we talked enough about other people and things?" She tugged his hand, turning.

Turning to their right, he saw the door of the bedroom standing open, inviting, the lambent light shedding like water.

SEVENTEEN

HE AWOKE AT MIDNIGHT.

She was sleeping beside him, her head nestling against his shoulder, her legs entangled with his. Through the curtain, slightly pulled aside, a shaft of moonlight peeped in. Her naked body presented a porcelain glow, a small pool of sweat beginning to dry in the hollow between her breasts barely covered by a rumpled blanket.

Through the window, he glimpsed a faint light flickering in the distance, then vanishing across the nocturnal water. The stars appeared high, bright, as if whispering down to him through the lost dream. A ship sailed by in silence. The tick of the electric clock was measuring the invisible seconds.

So it had happened. He still found it hard to believe. It seemed as though he had been another man earlier, and now he was reviewing in amazement what had happened to somebody else. He looked at her again, her black hair spilled over the white pillow, her pale face peaceful yet passion-worn, after the consummating moment of the cloud coming, and the rain falling.

In the second century BC, Song Yu, a celebrated poet of the Chu state, composed a rhapsody about the liaison of King Chu Xiang and the Wu Mountain goddess. At parting, the goddess promised she would come again to him in clouds and rain. A breathtaking metaphor, which had become a sort of euphemism for sexual love in classical Chinese literature.

The memory of the night surged back in the dark, intensely, illuminating Chen in fragmented details. The intensity of their passion had been accentuated by a touch of desperation that affected them both. There was no telling what would happen—to her, to him, to the world. There was nothing for them to grasp except the moment of being, losing, and finding themselves again in each other.

With her above, she turned into a dazzling white cloud, languid, rolling, soft yet solid, sweeping, almost insubstantial, clinging, pressing, and shuddering when she came, into a sudden rain, incredibly warm yet cool, splashing, her long hair cascading over his face like a torrent, washing up sensations he had never known before. Then she undulated under him like the lake, ever-flowing, rising and falling in the dark, arching up, her hot wetness engulfing him, rippling, pulling him down to the depth of the night, and bearing him up to the surface again, her legs tightening around him in waves of prolonged convulsion.

Afterward, they lay quietly in each other's arms, languorous, in correspondence to the lake water lapping against the shore, lapping in the quietness of the night.

"We're having the lake to ourselves."

She whispered a throaty agreement before falling asleep in his arms. "Yes, we're the lake."

A night bird hooted, close, yet sounding eerily distant. Chen hoped it wasn't an owl, which were supposedly unlucky at this hour. An inexplicable sense of foreboding brought him back to the present.

Again, he turned to her curled up beside him, the serene radiance of her clear features vivid in a flood of moonlight. He was awash in gratitude.

All this was perhaps too much for him to think about now. But he had to, he told himself. At least, to think of a plan to protect her, and then, if possible, a plan for their future.

Eight or nine times out of ten, however, things in this world don't work out in accordance to one's plan, as an ancient sage once said.

In his college years, Chen had planned to be anything but a cop, but he failed.

Then he tried to be a good cop. Was he failing at that too?

That he wasn't ready to admit. Not yet. Nothing could be judged out of context. That was something he'd learned—by being a cop.

For him, being a good cop came down, invariably, to the conscientious conclusion of a case. The present case now came with an obligation to make sure that nothing would happen to her.

Would he be able to do that? What was involved in this case, in the final analysis, was politics, which kept turning like colored balls in a magician's hand, unfortunately not in his hand. So all he could do was to play a cop's hand. It wouldn't be easy. The approach taken by Internal Security might be political, but they at least had witnesses and evidence. Politics aside, he had practically no trumps in his hand. Not to mention, for the first time in his career, a possible conflict of interest.

Now, there was something in what she had told him earlier tonight, something concerning one statement crucial to the investigation . . .

She stirred, turning, her shapely leg sprawling out. He couldn't help reaching out and tracing his fingers along her bare back, which rippled smooth under his touch, like the waves that *begin, and cease, and then again begin, / with tremulous cadence slow.*

Once again, he found himself too distracted to concentrate on the case. So he got up, found the laptop in the living room, and brought it back to bed. Propped up by a couple of pillows stacked against the headboard, he placed the laptop on his drawn-up knees, overlooking her moon-blanched face.

He didn't start all at once. He was sitting still, thinking, unaware of the time flowing away like waves in the dark. It started to rain. He

194

listened to the rain pattering against the windows, imagining the lake furling around like a girdle.

To his surprise, she flung one arm over, her fingers brushing against the keys as her hand fell, then grasping his leg, as if anxious to reassure herself that he was beside her in her sleep. Her accidental touch brought up the lines he had composed earlier.

So he began working with a multitude of images surging up into his mind, thinking of the lone battle she had been fighting for the lake.

Soon, the spring is departing again.
How much more of wind and rain
can it really endure? Only the cobweb
still cares, trying to catch
a touch of the fading memory.
Why is the door always covered
in the dust of doubts?
The lake cries, staring
at the silent splendid sun.

Who is the one walking beside you?

The moon wakes up from a nightmare
immersed in ammonia, pale,
pensive in speculation,
in the acid reflection of the lake,
the stars blinking tearfully
trembling in the cold.

By the lake, an apple tree is blossoming
transparent in the light, expecting—
only a gesture, nothing
but a gesture, the test always done
by selecting the pure sample
up to the standard.

The lines were disorganized, but it was imperative for him to put them all down without a break. He went on typing, juxtaposing one scene with another, jumping among the stanzas, worrying little about the structure or the syntax. Realities, too, were disorganized.

He felt as if the lines were flowing in from the lake, flowing through her. He simply happened to be there, pounding at the laptop. The stillness around was breathing with a subtle fragrance from her naked body. Amidst the images rushing up to the monitor, he paused to look at her again. He could hardly remember how she had seemed to him when he first saw her in the small eatery just about a week ago.

And he tried to visualize the hard battle she'd been fighting here, working at her environmental protection job, day after day, alone by the lake.

But what had he contributed? As a successful Party member and police officer enjoying all the privileges, and now even standing in for a high-ranking cadre at the center, he had paid little attention to environmental issues. He was simply too busy being Chief Inspector Chen, a rising Party cadre in the system. Pushing a strand of sweat-matted hair from her forehead, he wished he had met her earlier and learned more about her work.

He then put an intimate touch into the poem, imagining a conversation she'd had with him about the lake.

Last night, a white water bird
flew into my dream again,
like a letter, telling me
that pollution was under control—
I awoke to see the night cloud breaking
through the ether, thinking
with difficulty, shivering.
It seems as if the key was heard
turning only once
before the door opens, only

to the anemic stars lost
in the lake of the waste . . .

Finally, he moved back to the beginning of the poem, typed out a tentative title, "Don't Cry, Tai Lake." It wasn't finished, he knew, but he also knew he was going to have a busy day as a cop tomorrow. He set the laptop on the nightstand, held her hand, and finally drifted off to sleep.

EIGHTEEN

NOT UNTIL SUNDAY MORNING did Detective Yu receive a callback from the message he'd left for Bai.

"I know you're a good friend of Mrs. Liu, so I'd like to talk to you," he said, repeating the message he'd left for her.

"I would like to talk to you too, Mr. Yu, but I'm going to church right now. And I have to leave for Nanjing this afternoon," Bai said. "If it's something really urgent, though, we could meet after the service this morning. I will be at Moore Memorial Church, near the Peace Movie Theater. I may go directly to the train station from there."

So that Sunday morning Yu and Peiqin arrived at the church, which had been named to memorialize an American donor in the late eighteenth century.

It was a gothic building of umber brick on the corner of Xizhuang Road, with a huge cross installed on the top of the bell tower. It might have been something of a landmark in earlier years, but like other old buildings such as the Seventh Heaven, it appeared lost among the new modern and ultramodern high-rises looming around. Still, the church looked as if it had received an extensive face-lift in recent years.

The service had just started when they got there, but there were a considerable number of people still standing around, greeting each other, and talking outside.

"I've been to the movie theater several times," Peiqin said, "but I've never once stepped into the church."

"Neither have I."

"Well, better to believe in something than to have nothing to believe in, I would say."

"What do you believe in then, Peiqin?"

"I don't have any grand theories, but I believe it's wrong for people to kill other people. That's why I wanted to come out with you today."

"Thank you."

They moved inside. The church looked impressive with its rectangular pillars in the hall and the colorful stone balusters in the balcony, and it was packed. According to the brochures they picked at the entrance, it could accommodate about a thousand people, including some in the hall and some in the balcony.

Yu and Peiqin failed, however, to find seats for themselves, so they had to stand in the back. To their surprise, they saw a large number of young people. Beside them, a fashionable girl in a low-cut yellow summer dress prayed devotedly, clutching a Bible in her hands, her head hung low, her hair dyed golden. She was perhaps in her early twenties.

They waited patiently, hand in hand, till the end of the service.

As soon as people began to pour out of the building, Yu pressed a number on his cell phone.

"Who is it?" Bai said.

"Oh, it's Yu. We talked earlier this morning. I'm waiting for you near the entrance."

A middle-aged woman came over to them with questions in her eyes. She was in her late forties or early fifties, slightly plump, with a pair of gold-rimmed glasses on her round face.

Small groups of people still lingered outside, conversing loudly. They might have come to go to the movie theater, or they might have just left church. At least some were holding tickets in their hands. The traffic rumbled on continuously along Xizhuang Road.

"This is no place for us to talk," Peiqin said. "Let's go to People's Park across the street."

They went through the underground tunnel to the park, which looked much smaller than Peiqin remembered. The park was built after the racetrack built by the British in the nineteenth century was torn down. Originally, the park was extraordinarily large, considering its location in the center of the city. In recent years, however, a lot of new construction had started to chip away at the park.

They found a stone table with stools around it near the back, where they could look out onto the People's Square.

"I'm confused," Bai started the moment she sat down with them. "Does Mrs. Liu know you two?"

"No, but a friend of ours is trying to help her in Wuxi," Yu said.

"But what can I do to help you?" Bai said. "And to help her? Liu's dead. No one can do anything about it."

"Well, some people are trying to push the investigation ahead with her as a suspect."

"What? That's too much! She's already lost her husband."

"The Wuxi cops must have contacted you to talk about her alibi," Yu said. "To them, there must seem to be something inexplicable and suspicious about her. The night her husband was killed in Wuxi, she wasn't at home but with you here in Shanghai. Could that have been a coincidence? And they're puzzled by her frequent trips back to Shanghai, trips taken during weekdays and over weekends simply for a game of mahjong. They are also aware that their marriage had long been on the rocks."

"I'm lost, Mr. Yu," she said alertly. "If that's the case, I don't know how you or your friend can help."

Yu took out his badge. This revelation couldn't be avoided, he decided. He also produced a business card of Chen's.

"Wow. Chief Inspector Chen Cao of the Shanghai Police Bureau! I think I've read about him in the newspapers."

"Yes, he's my partner, and he's the one who's now in Wuxi. He's not there on official business, but he's trying to help Mrs. Liu in any case. That's why he wanted me to contact you."

"Now I see, Detective Yu."

"So tell us what you know about her," Yu said. "Right now, I'm approaching you informally, and talking to you as a friend of hers. Let me assure you that you are helping us and helping her too. It will be in everybody's best interest. Once other officials take over, it will be a different story."

"Thank you for your frankness." Bai started slowly. "I've been her friend since middle school. So of course I would like to help, though I may not be able to answer all of your questions. But as for her frequent trips back to Shanghai, particularly on the weekends, I can tell you why. She comes for the church service here."

"But aren't there churches in Wuxi?"

"People at a church are like brothers and sisters, having known one another well for years. Wuxi isn't that far away now, just a little more than an hour by train. I live in Minhang, and it takes me about the same amount of time to get here. But more importantly, being the wife of an important Party cadre, she didn't think it would be a good idea to let the local people in Wuxi know about her church attendance."

"No, it wouldn't have been good for her husband's official career if it became known that his wife went to church every week," Peiqin said. "But what about the mahjong game?"

"People like playing mahjong with old partners. It's not just a game, you know. Around the mahjong table, people chatter a lot too. But for her, it was mostly because she didn't want to stay in that big house in Wuxi, all by herself, imaging what her husband was doing with another woman."

"So she knew about his affair?"

"Yes, she knew about it. She suffered so much because she was too proud to admit it, or to face it."

"For a Big Buck like her husband, something like a little secretary can be common nowadays," Peiqin said.

"But I've known her from the very beginning. A beauty has a thin fate, like a piece of paper. In the early years, so many young men were after her in school. But of all the candidates, she chose Liu. When he began to succeed in Wuxi, we were all so happy that she had made a good choice. Things in this world are like flowers, however, that blossom only for a short while. He soon began to have little secretaries, karaoke girls, massage girls, and whatnot. After he got the so-called home office, he came home less and less. With their son having left for college in Beijing, she was all alone. What could she do except imagine her husband in bed with another woman, wallowing in the cloud and rain of sex? To give the devil his due, however, he tried to be good to her in his way. He swore never to divorce her, declaring that she's the only one that really cared for him, that all the others cared only for his money, and were capable of doing anything behind his back. So he provided for her generously and bought her a high-end apartment in Shanghai. Of late, things between them had improved somewhat. Their son is graduating from college and coming back to Wuxi, which might be another reason that they hadn't divorced. She didn't tell this to anybody except me. She cares too much about face, which would have been totally lost if people in Shanghai learned that Liu had chosen another woman over her."

"She could have divorced him if she were that miserable."

"No, not a woman like her, who puts face before anything else. That would have been an admission of disastrous failure in marriage. Her life had to remain a success story, something enviable to other women, who would do anything to be in her shoes. Of course, they don't know what's behind the glossy and glorious appearance."

"Even if they knew," Peiqin said, "I bet some of them would still be willing."

"You're so right about that. What a shame that men are all like that! Once they become successful, they start looking for girls their daughters' age. It's as if they were rejuvenated overnight." Bai went on after a short pause, "She really tried. I have to say that for her. Last Sunday, after the church service here, she went back to Wuxi with a Wufangzai urn of wine-immersed pork tongue, Liu's favorite. As I mentioned, of late, things seemed to be improving between them. She'd planned a dinner at home with him. But he called her and said that he would be staying at the home office that night. She was so upset that she came to my place late in the afternoon. She knew we were having a mahjong game that night."

"One more question," Yu said. "You mentioned that there were many young men after her years ago. Some of them must still be in Shanghai. Are any of them still in contact?"

"Come on. You know the difference between men and women. Men in their forties and fifties are in their prime, especially those with a rising career. But women our age are like yesterday's flower trodden in mud. She is too proud to be pitied by those who had once cared for her. No, she never contacts them."

"A different question," Yu said, not giving up. "Are any young men seen with her at the mahjong table?"

"Well, there are sometimes some hanging around the table. For a rich woman like her, that's not really surprising. But they're all no good, just sucking up to a 'Big Auntie' for a little tip. She knows better."

"So her coming back to Shanghai is more a retreat into a shelter," Peiqin said, "where she could still cling to her imagined image or appearance of old."

"Yes, you're a woman and you understand." After glancing at her watch, Bai added, "Playing mahjong may help her forget, but more importantly, she is beginning to find peace in the church here. It's a long story. But I'm afraid I have to leave for the train now."

"Thank you, Bai. What you told us really helps."

They then rose and watched Bai hurry out of the park.

"What do you think, Peiqin?" he said.

"Mrs. Liu is desperate to keep up her appearance in others' eyes. A lot of the things she does, like the frequent trips home and mahjong games, may not make sense to others, but they are full of meaning to her."

"When did you become a psychologist, Peiqin?"

"I'm not. You heard Bai. Mrs. Liu kept casting herself in the role of a successful woman so she could continue to bathe in the admiration and envy of others. But it's different with Bai, since they've been friends for so long. As for her churchgoing, she might find some real solace there that is unavailable to her elsewhere."

"That's quite an analysis, Peiqin," he said. He couldn't help adding an ironic edge to his tone. "I might just report it to Chief Inspector Chen verbatim."

"You know what? I'm glad that you're not that successful," Peiqin said, changing the topic. "Or I'll have to worry like Mrs. Liu."

"Come on, Peiqin. But what we have learned probably won't help our Chief Inspector Chen a lot."

"Let's go to my old neighborhood again."

"Why?"

"I have a feeling," Peiqin said, "that it wasn't a karaoke girl that Fu picked up in front of that cheap hotel."

NINETEEN

WHEN CHEN WOKE UP, it was almost nine A.M.

The curtain still drawn, the room appeared enveloped in a gray opaqueness, as if its contents were waiting to be mailed into the morning.

He remained lying in bed, disoriented by the lingering sensations of the night, before he turned and reached out for her.

But she was gone.

He sat up with a jerk, looking at the rumpled sheet.

"Shanshan!"

The echo of her name resounded like a dream in the empty stillness. But their evening wasn't a dream. The white pillow against the headboard remained rumpled with the shape of her head, still slightly warm, as he touched it again.

He put on his robe and hurriedly searched through the house, but she was nowhere to be found. Stepping outside, he shivered with a premonition, seeing the stone steps strewn with fallen petals after the night's clamor of wind and rain. The sound of birds chirping was heard here and there.

He moved back inside to see on the desk a note, upon which was placed her black plastic hair band. She'd taken it off last night while standing beside him at the window. The note said:

> Don't try to look me up. It wouldn't be good for you to be
> seen in my company. You've been so kind to me. Thanks for
> everything. But you have your destination, and I, mine.
> Shanshan

What? He was totally confounded. The last sentence seemed somewhat familiar, yet he failed to recall where he'd come across it.

Beside the note lay the bulging folder she'd entrusted to him last night. It was heavy when he weighed it in his hand.

So what was Chief Inspector Chen going to do?

He started pacing about, as if anxious to catch the echo of her footsteps from last night.

He could hardly make sense of her appearance last night. Or her disappearance in the morning. Was she so depressed that she simply wanted to let herself go in the company of a man she cared for, for one night?

The willow shoots are looming through the mist. / I find my hair disheveled, / the cicada-shaped hairpin fallen to the ground. / What worries should I have / about the days to come / as long as you enjoyed me, tonight, to the full?

But the folder in his hand didn't speak to that scenario. She wasn't going to give up the environmental cause. It meant more than that— perhaps it was her way of saying thanks for his help in the uphill battle to come.

It wasn't a moment, however, to indulge in such speculations. Chen had to decide on an immediate course of action. To leave the whole matter behind was one possibility, as was suggested in her short note. No obligations. No commitments. They hadn't talked about future plans. He would, of course, keep his word by taking the folder with him—there was no need for him to hurry and make a specific move.

In the long run, doing a good, effective job as Chief Inspector Chen would be in the best interest of the country and the people.

Alternatively, he could try to help her through the crisis. He should be able to keep her out of the clutches of Internal Security, who had targeted her because of her relationship to Jiang. Her "cooperation" wouldn't be that crucial; with or without it, Jiang would be convicted. As a last resort, Chen could go so far as to appeal to Comrade Secretary Zhao, though such an option did not appeal to Chen.

But he could also choose to get further involved, as he had said to her, by clearing Jiang of the charge. That was an effort that Chief Inspector Chen should make if Jiang proved to be innocent. Chen wondered, however, whether he would be able to throw his weight about here in Wuxi. It wasn't just a homicide case, and it wasn't his territory.

Besides, if he endeavored to help Jiang, Chen might actually be helping out a potential rival. He paused, then brushed aside that consideration. If he were to give up because of that, then he would never be able to consider himself worthy of her or of being a cop.

But he had no authority here. It wasn't feasible to confront Internal Security, by whom he had long been considered a troublemaker, having blocked them on several occasions. There was no way to argue with them about what was considered a "state secret," as that was something defined by them and in the interests of the Party.

It wasn't possible to pressure the local cops, either. It was out of the question for him to rush onto the scene. What he had told Huang about Comrade Secretary Zhao and his "special mission" wouldn't really stand up.

"Room service, sir—"

The young attendant came in bearing the breakfast tray along with the thermos bottle of herbal medicine. Smiling a sly smile, she might have noticed something different about the room.

"Thank you," said Chen, reaching for the thermos.

He finished the herbal medicine in two or three gulps as he watched her withdraw. He then dialed the cell phone he had given Shanshan, but it was turned off.

It might not be a good idea for him to visit her dorm, since it was most likely being watched by Internal Security. Instead, he decided to go to Uncle Wang's eatery. There he could wait, or at least learn something about her. Before he stepped out, he picked up a soft leather briefcase—a gift from the center—and put in a bunch of the photos as well as other information related to Liu's murder. What he was going to do that day, he had no idea, but he might as well restudy some of the material while he waited for a call from her.

That morning, the same old route felt almost unbearably monotonous. He walked on without looking around, lost in thought. A maroon convertible suddenly sped past him with a strident rumble. The driver, a young man in his early twenties, waved his hand dashingly at him. An extremely slender girl in a light-blue dress sat reclining in the back, dangling her bare feet off the side. To his surprise, the car came to a screeching halt and backed up a couple of yards. The driver looked over his shoulder.

"My dad stays at the center too, you know," he declared with a proud grin. "Would you like a lift?"

An HCC—high cadre's child, or Communist prince. Chen knew their ways. A high-ranking Party cadre probably brought along his family for a vacation at the center.

"No, thank you."

"We live in the villa next to yours. It's not too bad, but there's no real fun inside the complex. It's old and filled with old-fashioned people. We have to party outside to entertain ourselves."

"You're right. Perhaps another time," Chen said.

He watched as the car drove away in a cloud of dust.

Surely it was a waste for one man alone to occupy a whole villa, but then according to the policy, only a high cadre—a cadre of a certain rank—was entitled to such treatment. Of course, Chief Inspector Chen himself wasn't a high cadre, and he was only there because of his connection to one. He wondered how far he could go with all his connections, and whether he really wanted to go that far.

Whistling, he tried Shanshan's number one more time. Still no answer.

The phone still in his hand, a call came in. He recognized the number shown on the screen. It was Sergeant Huang.

"Oh Chief, I've just learned something," Huang said, with a strange edge in his voice. "I told you that Shanshan's phone was being bugged because of her connection to Jiang, you remember?"

"Yes?"

"Her connection to Jiang wasn't just because of their work. According to Internal Security, she'd had an affair with him. That's how her name appeared on a list—not our list, but Internal Security's. They took pictures of her sneaking out of his apartment late at night several months ago."

Even though Chen knew Shanshan and Jiang had dated, he was momentarily at a loss for words. Whatever their relationship, he hastened to remind himself, they had parted.

If anything, it only proved that Internal Security must have been following Jiang for a long time. And perhaps Shanshan as well. He thought of the suspicious peddler he'd seen a couple of times in the last few days. But then again, he might simply be jumpy.

"She made a phone call to him just a couple of days ago," Huang went on, having not gotten any response from Chen.

"What did they say to each other when she called?"

"He didn't pick up."

"Thanks, Huang," he said. "If there's anything new, let me know."

Still, the timing of the call couldn't have been worse. How would Huang have reacted had he learned about Shanshan staying overnight at the center with the Chief Inspector?

All of a sudden, a siren shrieked, piercing the grayness of the overcast morning sky. Chen looked up to see that he had arrived at the shabby eatery, with Uncle Wang bending over a large stove outside.

"You're early today, Chen," Uncle Wang said, busy setting up the fire with old newspapers and dry twigs before he threw in a ladle of coal balls. He must have just started. "We don't serve breakfast. There's nothing for you at the moment. But I can have a bowl of salty bean soup microwaved if you'd like."

"Don't worry about it, Uncle Wang. I've had my breakfast. Has Shanshan been here?"

"Not this early and not today. It's Sunday. I didn't see her yesterday either. Do you know if there's anything going on with her?"

"No, but I saw her last night."

"Oh, I'm so concerned about her," Uncle Wang said. "And about you, too. The day before yesterday, a couple of strangers came here. They asked me a number of incriminating questions about her, and about the man seen with her in the last few days."

"Really!"

"Of course, I didn't tell them anything."

So they were already checking on him. Perhaps it was naïve of him to think he could provide protection for her. If Internal Security found out about their relationship, it might only be to her disadvantage. Nor was he untouchable, in spite of the assurances he'd given Shanshan. In China, everything was politics. His enemies could hit him hard by saying that his involvement with her was another example of his "bourgeois lifestyle."

A lanky middle-aged man on a tricycle rode up with the morning's food supply piled in the trunk. Uncle Wang picked up a carp, smelled it, threw it back, and then began bargaining with the supplier.

As Chen watched, his cell phone rang again. It was Detective Yu. He must have been calling from the street again, given all the noise in the background.

Yu summed up his encounter with Bai after the church service.

"According to Bai, Mrs. Liu may be attending church in Wuxi today," Yu said.

"So she seems to find some peace in the church."

"Yes, at least Bai thinks so." Yu summarized what he had termed Peiqin's analysis before he shifted to another topic with renewed excitement in his voice. "But you know what, Chief? I've just talked to

Wei, the neighborhood cop, again. He recognized the girl with Fu in front of the sleazy hotel from the pictures we took. She's none other than Fu's longtime girlfriend. There's something weird about that. Why would they be so stealthy?"

"It might not be that odd. It could be as simple as Fu having to sneak off for a quickie with his girlfriend at such a hotel, because of his housing situation in Shanghai." It was not uncommon for two or even three generations of a Shanghai family to squeeze together in a single room.

"True. Still, people always find ways to do what they want to do. Peiqin and I lived in the same apartment with my parents for years, as you know. But Peiqin insists that she would never spend money for something like that."

"Peiqin is so perceptive. I'll check it out here," Chen said. "Anyway, you'd better keep the pictures of the lovers. Someday, you might be able to sell them for a lot of money."

Closing the phone, Chen thought that it must have been an anticlimax for Yu, who had spent his weekend learning nothing really useful, at least not from a cop's perspective.

As for Mrs. Liu, Chen didn't know what else he could do. If anything, this new information made her more of a character but less of a suspect. It wasn't the first time, however, that the chief inspector had an elaborate theory end up as nothing more than just that: an unsubstantiated theory.

Then he thought about the "something weird," as Detective Yu had phrased it, about Fu's behavior yesterday. There could be a number of explanations for it. For one, Fu might be a sly dog who kept his affair "in a stealthy way," so that he could approach other girls at the same time. When Chen was first assigned to the Shanghai Police Bureau, he also tried to keep secret his relationship with his HCC girlfriend in Beijing, though for a different reason.

Chen decided not to think too much about it. He could see no interpretation that applied to the investigation.

"You're no schoolteacher, are you?" Uncle Wang said, breaking into his thoughts.

"Sorry, I've just had a phone call from Shanghai."

The old man, perhaps having overheard some of the phone call, studied him closely.

"Shanshan can be stubborn, but she's a nice girl," Uncle Wang went on wistfully as he seated himself on a bench opposite Chen. He picked up a cup from another table. "Let me tell you something about myself."

"Go ahead," Chen said, wondering what the old man wanted to tell him. He poured himself a cup of tea.

A few doors away, a middle-aged woman with a bamboo basket of wet, green shepherd's purse blossom looked at the two in curiosity, and then smiled pleasantly.

"I used to be a school teacher in the Anhui Province. During summer vacation several years ago, I came to Wuxi and fell in love with the city. To be honest, it was mostly because of the lake fish and shrimp. The three whites, you know. So after I retired, I moved here and started this eatery. I didn't do it for business reasons exactly. I have to cook for myself, and I like cooking anyway. A single retiree with grown children in Xinjiang with their own lives, I simply wanted to enjoy the remaining years of my life with a cup of Southern rice wine and a platter of steamed lake fish. But it was a decision no one seemed to understand."

"But I do, Uncle Wang. In ancient times, a poet-official missed a particular fish that was available only in his hometown, so he resigned his position to return home. I think his name was Jiying. No, your decision was no mistake."

"So you know the story. That's great. '*With the west wind rising, / Jiying's still not back.*' The world is meaningful only in what has meaning to you. Anyway, I didn't think it was a mistake, at least not at the time. Then the lake became less clear, and the fish and shrimp less fresh, and, at the same time, the city an increasingly commercial tourist destination. Alas, it's too late for me to go back."

Chen didn't comment, wondering what the old man was driving at.

"That's why I'm so sympathetic to Shanshan's efforts to protect the environment," Uncle Wang resumed, nodding. "I'm just an old man;

nothing really matters for me now. But it's an issue that affects so many people—all people, you might say. She really believes in what she does, no matter what others might say. It takes an extraordinary man to appreciate someone like her in today's climate."

Chen was more than impressed, and not just because of Uncle Wang's story. One way or another, people pick up a given discourse, that which makes the world meaningful or sensible to them. Then they live in accordance to it, even though what they do may not make any sense to anyone else. Peiqin apparently just said something to the same effect, as reported by Yu in the recent phone call.

Indeed, things could be connected by an invisible net. Years earlier, Uncle Wang happened to recall a story about a fish-loving scholar while enjoying the lake fish here, so he decided to move and set up a small eatery in Wuxi. That might appear to be the last link in the chain of cause-and-effect for the old man, but no one lives in a vacuum. Years later, because of the environmental crisis at Tai Lake, he formed a bond with Shanshan, and eventually, the chief inspector from Shanghai, on a compulsory vacation, walked into Uncle Wang's eatery by chance, where he met Shanshan. So many links, mysteriously connected. If only one piece had been missing or misconnected, it could have turned into a different story. In Buddhism, as is sometimes said, one peck, one drink, is all predetermined, and is predetermining too.

"For whom the bell tolls, it tolls for thee—"

"What do you mean?"

"Oh, that was just a quote. I'm thinking of the environmental disaster in China."

But he was also thinking of the present murder case.

The people were connected and interconnected. Liu, Mrs. Liu, Mi, Jiang, Shanshan, Uncle Wang, Fu, and perhaps many others, all in a long chain of yin/yang causality. It could be difficult for him to determine whether or not those links existed in reality. For instance, he had tried to look into the remote possibility that there was something in common between Mrs. Liu and Fu due to their frequent trips to Shanghai, but there didn't prove to be a link there.

However, one piece was falsely connected in the official investigation—Mi's statement about Jiang having met and argued with Liu on March 7. That is, unless Shanshan was purposely trying to mislead the investigation. After all, she might be another "unreliable narrator." But he chose to believe in her. More importantly, he appreciated "someone like her in today's climate," as Uncle Wang put it. So Chief Inspector Chen would check into it.

Now, Mrs. Liu might not remember clearly a particular date from a couple of months ago. But her husband coming home at midnight, which might have woken her up, might be a different story.

But how was he going to approach her? The last time he was in the company of Sergeant Huang. Would that be necessary this time? The way things went, it was probably only a matter of time before his involvement became known to Internal Security. If he could manage it alone, it'd be better not to drag Huang into it.

Decided, he abruptly stood up and said, "Thank you, Uncle Wang. You've really been a help, but now I have to leave. Call me if Shanshan comes here."

He took leave of the old man and hailed a taxi.

TWENTY

CHEN RANG THE DOORBELL at Mrs. Liu's place.

A tall, thin, long-limbed young man opened the door. He was wearing a white Chinese-style shirt with black characters printed all over. He was in his early twenties, and looked like a college student.

"She's at church and I don't think she'll be back until later this afternoon. What do you want with her?"

"So, you're her son, Wenliang?"

"Yes, I'm Wenliang."

"So nice to meet you, Wenliang. My name is Chen," Chen said, producing two business cards—one that identified him as a chief inspector, and another provided by the Writers' Association. "I recognize you from a photo of you and your father. Since she's not at home, I may as well talk to you."

"Wow, you're a chief inspector from Shanghai," Wenliang said, beginning to examine the second card. "And a poet too!"

He led Chen into the living room, where the detectives had spoken to Mrs. Liu a few days earlier. The only change Chen noticed there was a new large color photo of the Liu family on the wall, with Wen-liang posed between his smiling parents.

"Tea or coffee?"

"Tea, thanks," Chen said. "I'm in Wuxi on vacation, and I am helping to investigate your father's death. In the course of the investigation, I heard about you and your internship at the company last year. Is there anything you can tell us that might help us in our work?"

"What do you want to know, Chief Inspector Chen?"

"To begin with, why an internship at the chemical company here? You're studying literature at Beijing University, right?"

"My father had a plan for me after graduation."

"What kind of plan?"

"He wanted me to work at the company. According to him, he had a position ready-made for me, and so my internship was part of that plan. I believe he wanted me, eventually, to be his successor. As a man of his generation, he was anxious to keep the business in the family, and he talked to me about it several times."

"How would that work? As far as I know, the cadre appointments at a large state-run company, particularly for a position like your father's, are decided by the higher party authorities." Chen added, "It will still be a state-owned enterprise even after the IPO."

"I asked the same question, but according to him, everything is possible with connections, and he had a lot of connections in the city government, and even above. Needless to say, I wasn't supposed to become his successor overnight."

"I see. No wonder he kept that picture of you two at his home office. It was the only picture I remember seeing there."

"Which picture are you talking about?"

"The one of the two of you standing in front of the bookshelf—before a row of the shining statuettes. It was taken during your internship, I believe." Chen opened the briefcase, pulled out a bunch of pictures, and picked one out.

"Oh, that one. Yes, that was from last summer. He was so proud of the company's achievements, winning a statuette year after year. He kept all of them on the shelf in his office."

The sight of the glittering statuettes in the background of the picture touched something at the back of Chen's mind. He had photographed the framed picture as it was the only one he had of Liu. In his experience, pictures sometimes helped to establish a sort of bond between the investigator and the victim. He had examined it several times back in the center.

"Didn't he win another one," Chen asked, "at the end of last year?"

"Of course he did, but why do you ask?"

Instead of responding, Chen took out some of the other pictures taken by the police, along with those he had shot. In the background of all of them, he counted the statuettes. Nine of them.

"He insisted on us posing in front of the statuettes," Wenliang said, gazing at the picture of the father and son. "He lined them all up on the shelf."

But one was missing, Chen thought. In the crime scene photos, there should have been ten statuettes, including the one that was awarded last year. But there were only nine of them.

"He had each of them gold-plated—using a special company fund set aside just for the purpose. He called me at the end of last year to tell me about it. 'Now we've won ten statuettes in succession under my leadership, but the eleventh or the twelfth should be won under you.' "

So the tenth one was missing from Liu's home office. What could that possibly mean? It wasn't the time for him to get too engrossed in speculation, especially when it might turn out to be irrelevant to the investigation.

"So are you still going to have a position at the company, Wenliang?"

"I don't think so. A new emperor must have the ministers of his own choosing."

"What's your plan then?"

"Believe it or not, my real passion is for Beijing opera. So I'm thinking about studying for an MA in the field."

"That's interesting," Chen said, immediately aware that it was the exact same response people offered him when they learned about his passion for poetry.

"It may not sound like a reasonable choice in today's society, but with what my father left us, I think I can manage."

"I understand. But as with poetry, there would be little money in a career in Beijing opera."

"My father toiled and moiled for money his whole life, but could he take any of it with him?"

"Yes, I understand. You can't live without money, but you can't live for it."

"Besides, no one else really wants me to work at the chemical company anymore."

"Fu, the new boss, was going to offer your mother a job, I heard."

"What sort of a job will he offer her? Something at the entry level. It's nothing but a gesture."

"But Fu didn't seem too bad to the people who worked under your father. For instance, Mi was promoted."

"Don't talk to me about her," Wenliang said with an undisguised look of disgust on his face. "It's just like in the Beijing opera 'Break Open the Coffin.' Oh what a horror!"

" 'Break Open the Coffin'?"

"Don't you know the story of Zhuangzi's sudden enlightenment about the vanity of the human world?"

"I know of Zhuangzi, of course. I remember some story about his enlightenment. He dreamed of being a butterfly, but when he woke up, he couldn't help wondering whether it was the butterfly that dreamed of being him. But he was a great philosopher, and we don't have to take that story too seriously."

"There's a popular Beijing opera version you might not know. Indeed, this version is totally different. According to it, Zhuangzi had a young loving wife, who was the one thing that, for all his profound philosophy, he still couldn't let go of in this world of red dust. One day, he suddenly took ill, and she swore at his bedside that there was only room enough for him in her heart. The moment he breathed his last, however, she started searching around for a new lover. That same day, she had the luck to find one, but he, too, got sick overnight. According to a quack doctor, the sick lover could be saved only by a medicine that consisted of someone's heart, so she broke open the coffin, which was not yet buried, to cut out Zhuangzi's heart. It turned out to be a test Zhuangzi set up with his supernatural powers. Shame-stricken, she committed suicide, and he was enlightened about the vanity of human passion."

Chen remembered having heard a folk tale version of the story, but it was far less gruesome than the one he had just learned from Wenliang.

"So you mean—"

"You know what it means. Mi is nothing but a little secretary kept by her Big Buck boss," Wenliang said with a sneer. "So she needs a new one to keep her in the same style."

"Well—"

"A younger one was already waiting backstage in the dark before the old one exited."

"Oh, like in *Hamlet*."

"Exactly. They staged a Beijing opera of *Hamlet* several months ago at the university. It's a universal story. Mi, too, carried on with someone else. When I was working in the office last summer, I saw something. It was none of my business, of course. But Father didn't really trust her, he knew better."

Wenliang, of course, could be just another unreliable narrator, understandably biased against her, Chen mused.

"You're sure about that, Wenliang?"

"I saw it with my own eyes. I wasn't wind-chasing or shadow-catching, I can assure you," he said broodingly. "It's not a crime for a little secretary to carry on with the second-in-command behind the back of the boss. What could I have done? I hated to bring it up to my father, who might not have taken my word on it, and it could have been a huge scandal. One's father being cuckolded isn't something to be proud of, so why would I make up such a story?"

"That's true . . ."

With the sunlight streaming through the window, the chief inspector thought of what he'd heard over the last few days. They were mostly fragments, to which he hadn't paid any real attention, such as the story of a younger man seen at night in the company of Mi, the fox spirit. Pieces such as the stories narrated by the two drinkers in the pub, or like the melodrama in the hotel on Nanjing Road, as reported by Detective Yu a short while ago.

Now those pieces were beginning to connect, in a way he had never imagined.

"Thank you so much, Wenliang. We'll surely do our best to get justice for your—"

He was almost finished with the sentence when Mrs. Liu opened the door and, with a sour expression on her face, stepped inside.

"Oh, you're here again, Mr. Chen."

"Yes. I've had a good talk with Wenliang, Mrs. Liu. Now, I have just one question for you. In early March, Liu came back from a business trip in Nanjing. He got back quite late that night, I've learned, so he might have woken you up when he came in. Do you remember anything about it?"

"Yes, I do. He was coming back from a business meeting in Nanjing, and it was raining heavily that night. He took a taxi home."

"Can you remember the date?"

"It was March, early March, I think. He apologized for waking me up, saying that because of something unexpected in Nanjing, he had to take the last train back to Wuxi," she said contemplatively. "Oh, I remember, it was the day before the Women's Day. He had bought me a gift for the holiday, which was the next day."

"Thank you so much, Mrs. Liu. You've really helped our investigation. And thank you too, Wenliang." Chen stood up abruptly. "But now I have to leave."

TWENTY-ONE

SERGEANT HUANG WAS CONFOUNDED by Chief Inspector Chen's request when the older detective called early Monday morning.

"Bring Mi over to my place at the center. Immediately. You don't have to give her any explanation, just let me do the talking. Once she's here, then you can jump in and play your part when it's appropriate."

They had talked to Mi once before in her office. Why did Chen need to talk to her again, and why at the center? Over the course of the investigation, Chen had mentioned her a couple of times, but not once had she come up as a suspect. It might be because of Mrs. Liu, Huang thought. But he didn't believe that Mi had much more to tell. She would be the last one to cover up something for the widow.

Nor did he think there was anything Chen could really do to alter the conclusion of the case. Internal Security had already gotten approval from Beijing to proceed. Still, Huang was eager to see if the legendary chief inspector would, like in those translated mysteries, be able to achieve the impossible at this late stage.

Huang hurried over to the chemical company, where Mi was just leaving the office for a business meeting downtown. She looked surprised when Huang asked her to accompany him, but she complied without protest.

The Cadre Recreation Center wasn't far away, and she might not be as apprehensive about going there as she might be about visiting the police bureau.

It took them less than ten minutes to get to the center. Security examined Huang's badge and waved them both in.

The white villa looked majestic standing on the hill, set off from the other buildings, with its stainless-steel fence glittering in the morning light and an armed guard standing in front. Huang had heard that Chen enjoyed extraordinary status as a cadre who was rising fast, but he was still more than impressed. The villa was one of the most magnificent buildings in the center, standing out against other buildings designed for the use of high-ranking cadres.

"Sergeant Huang?" the guard said. "Comrade Chief Inspector Chen is waiting for you inside."

"Comrade Chief Inspector Chen?" Mi murmured uncomfortably. "In the villa here?"

Huang took this as a cue that Chen wanted his true identity revealed instead of simply passing himself off as Huang's colleague.

"He's somebody," Huang said vaguely, not sure if it would have the effect Chen wanted to produce.

As they stepped into the spacious living room, Huang saw a gray-haired man sitting with Chen on the leather sectional sofa, with a bouquet of carnations arranged in a crystal vase on the marble coffee table in front of them.

"This is Comrade Qiao, the director of the center," Chen said without even standing up when they walked in.

Huang knew of Qiao as a sort of local celebrity and had seen his picture in the newspapers. Mi must have met Qiao before, under different circumstances, and she couldn't conceal her surprise at the sight of the two sitting together there.

"Mi, let me introduce you," Qiao said, standing up and grinning from ear to ear. "This is Chief Inspector Chen Cao. He is a special envoy from Beijing. Comrade Secretary Zhao, the retired head of the Central Party Discipline Committee, made several personal phone calls to arrange his vacation here. It's an honor for us to have him stay at our center."

The way Qiao was talking was puzzling. In terms of cadre rank, Qiao's was probably higher than Chen's. There was no need for him to make such a show of obsequiousness. Nevertheless, Chen seemed to take it for granted.

"It's an honor for me to work under him," Huang echoed, believing that the scene before him must have been arranged, even though he was unable to figure out for what purpose. Up until now Chen had made a point of keeping a low profile, and Huang had been his only contact with the investigation.

"You've already met with Sergeant Huang, Mi. I don't think you need any further introduction." Chen added in a patronizing tone, "A capable young man, he serves as my local assistant."

"Why—I mean why?" she said, flustered, her glance shifting from one to another, before she settled on Qiao with an imploring look.

Equally puzzled, Qiao shifted awkwardly on the sofa, glancing sideways at Chen without knowing what to say.

"You may leave us now, Director Qiao," Chen said curtly. "Please see to it that we are not disturbed."

"Of course, I'll make sure of that, Chief Inspector Chen. If there is anything else I can do for you, just let me know," Qiao said, bowing his way out. "The center is at your service."

Signaling Huang to pull a chair over for her, Chen didn't start speaking at once. He took a cigarette out of an embossed silver case, lit it, and waved the match repeatedly in the air before dropping it into the crystal ashtray. Huang stood beside him, keeping his back as straight as a bamboo pole.

An oppressive silence was building up in the room.

"Oh, you sit down too," Chen said, patting the sofa for Huang.

Huang seated himself on the sofa edge beside Chen, like a respectful subordinate, and didn't say a single word.

Finally, Mi couldn't stand it anymore and blurted out nervously, "What do you want from me?"

"Well, I'm not just a cop, I'm also a poet," Chen said deliberately, not responding to her question. He handed her two business cards. "You know what? The first time I saw you at your company, I was reminded of an ancient line: '*Even I cannot help taking pity on such a beauty.*'"

It sounded flirtatious, but it wasn't, Huang knew. Rather, it came across as a serious warning.

"I don't know what you are talking about, Chief—"

"Chief Inspector Chen," Huang said, stealing a glance at the business cards in her hand. While the first one stated Chen's position with the Shanghai police, the second one represented him as a member of the Chinese Writers' Association and of the Shanghai People's Congress.

"My vacation here is only a pretext," Chen said. "You should be able to guess why I want to talk to you today."

"If it's about Liu's murder, hasn't Jiang already been arrested?"

"You are well-informed, Mi."

"Then what do you want to talk to me about?"

"Well," he said deliberately, "because I don't want to see a young, beautiful woman like you get into trouble for something that's not exactly your fault."

"I'm totally lost, Chief Inspector Chen."

"In a murder investigation, things may appear to be complicated, but what's behind it all can be simple when seen from the perpetrator's perspective," Chen said, a cigarette smoke ring spiraling out of his fingers. "It's always done for something—money, power, or whatever the criminal hopes to gain. Now, what could Jiang have possibly gained by killing Liu? Nothing. On the other hand, someone else could gain tremendously."

"What are you talking about?"

She kept playing dumb, Huang noted, and he himself felt no less dumb, having no clue as to what Chen was driving at.

"About the death of Liu, you made several statements. And I want to remind you, Mi, that perjury is a serious crime," Chen said. He reached over and pressed the start button on a mini recorder sitting on the coffee table.

"What's all this? I've told the police officers—including Officer Huang—only the truth and everything I know."

"Let me say this one more time, Mi. You're responsible for what you did, but you don't have to be responsible for somebody else. You have to ask yourself whether it's worth your sacrifice."

It was an intriguing dialogue. Chen pushed on like he was playing a tai chi game, pointing rather than striking. Huang wondered how this could work. It wasn't likely that Mi would fold in the face of such an insubstantial bluff.

"People take a lot of things for granted," Chen went on. "Like the water in the lake. I still remember a song about how clear and beautiful the water is here."

"Liu tried his best to contain the pollution," Mi said. "I worked closely under him, I know."

"You worked closely under him, in both the company office and at his home office. So let me ask you a question. You said that you saw Jiang arguing with Liu in his company office. And you were quite specific about the date. It was in early March, the day before Women's Day."

"Yes, that's right."

"In Liu's office at the company, correct?"

"Correct. Fu saw him too."

"So the local police took your statement at face value, especially because it was corroborated by your present boss, Fu. After interviewing Jiang, who denied meeting with Liu at the company that day," Chen said, turning to Huang, "Officer Huang double-checked with Fu on his statement. It seems that Fu isn't so sure about the date."

"No, he was not at all sure," Huang said, even more mystified than before. He hadn't double-checked anything with Fu. Nor had he discussed such a plan with Chen.

"But I remember it clearly," Mi said, shifting nervously in the chair.

"According to our research, Liu was at a business meeting in Nanjing that day," Chen said, taking out a folder without opening it. "He didn't come back until very late that night—practically the next day. We checked the company calendar and Web site, as well as the hotel records, which showed he had a late checkout, around nine P.M. We also obtained a copy of the night train ticket for which he had been reimbursed. What's more, we talked to Mrs. Liu about it. She, too, remembers the date clearly because he came back late that night. It was raining heavily, and he apologized for waking her up. He bought a present for her for Women's Day, which was the next day."

For a moment, Huang was too astonished to play along. Fortunately, Mi was so flabbergasted that she didn't notice anything about Huang.

"Oh, maybe I didn't remember the date too accurately. It was about two months ago, you know," she said rather lamely. "But I did see Jiang arguing with Liu in his office."

"No, that's a lie. But it was somebody in the background who wanted you to make that false statement, and you had no choice but to comply. Nor were you fully aware of the complications involved. Anyway, you had to support the people above, didn't you? You might not have been able to think too clearly under the stress."

"Yes, I've been so terribly busy of late and under a lot of stress. I might not have been able to get the date right. Whatever Jiang might have done, it wasn't any of my business, so I didn't try to pay close attention to it. I'm sorry about the possible mistake, Chief Inspector Chen."

"But it's a murder case, Mi. An innocent man could have been convicted because of your perjury."

"No, that's not true. How could it be perjury? People's memories may not always be reliable, you know that. What do you want me to

226

do? Both you and Officer Huang are here, so I can give you another statement. The meeting between Jiang and Liu was definitely in March, of that much I'm sure."

"Let's put it aside for the moment, and talk about another statement you gave. On the night of the murder, you said you were at the company office, working late on the IPO plan. That was just about a week ago. Your memory couldn't have failed you concerning that part, too? "

There was no mistaking the ominous hint; she got it and turned ghastly pale. Mi stared first at Chen, and then at Huang, wringing her hands, panic-stricken and tongue-tied.

"You told us that you were so busy working at the office that evening," Chen went on, "that you didn't leave until after eleven. You were so overwhelmed with work that you didn't even have time to go to the company canteen. Correct?"

"Correct," she said. "We were so busy preparing for the IPO. It was a Sunday, but a number of people were at the office working, including Fu. Fu talked to me that evening and we discussed the company's business plans."

"Now, I want to remind you again, Mi. Perjury is a serious crime. You have to consider whether it's worth it or not," Chen added, crossing his legs, breathing into his cup, and then taking a leisurely sip of his tea. "Confucius says, *A man lays down his life for one who appreciates him, and a woman makes herself beautiful for the one who loves her.* But it really depends on who."

"I'm afraid that what you're saying is over my head, Chief Inspector Chen."

"Fine, let me ask you a question. Liu went to his home office, as a rule, through the back door of the building, right?"

"I think so. It's a shortcut."

"So when you go there it's also through the back door?"

"Yes, when I had to work with him there. There's no point in going through the front gate, it would take at least ten more minutes."

"You don't know about the advanced security camera recorder at the back door, I'm guessing."

"No, I didn't know. But why are you asking?"

"The back door closes at eight, and then the security guard leaves for the night. We all know that. However, the camera there records people going through the door all night long, and I don't think you knew about that."

"Yes," Huang said, echoing Chen's statement. He was beginning to see the light for the first time, though he didn't know anything about a hidden camera. For all he knew, there could be one and he was determined to play along. "The camera there records all night long, Mi."

"I don't know anything about it."

"Why? Because Liu didn't think that you needed to know those things as a little secretary. If so, it was totally understandable that he didn't even mention it to you. But we've obtained the tape for that night and studied it carefully—"

"Everyone going in and out the back door that night is on the tape," Huang contributed hastily.

It was obvious that Chen had Mi trapped. She opened her mouth helplessly, but no words struggled out.

"Has your memory been refreshed, Mi?"

"So many things have happened of late," she said at last, repeating what she'd said earlier, "I've been so worn out that my memory might not prove to be accurate."

"A young, energetic office manager is supposed to remember a lot of things," Chen pushed on relentlessly. "Anyway, the videotape is admissible as evidence in court, you know."

"Do you need us to play it for you now?" Huang chipped in again.

"You—" She sprang up, as if galvanized, before she swayed, slumped back into the chair.

Chen waited, pouring himself a cup of tea, and another for Huang, without looking at her.

It took only a minute or two, however, for Mi to try to pull herself back together again.

"I worked so hard that evening, Chief Inspector Chen. I might have stepped out, briefly, for some fresh air, and not even thought about it. I'm still not sure, but something like that could have eluded my memory."

"Now you have perjured yourself repeatedly in a murder investigation."

"No, I just forgot."

"You signed your earlier written statements, and we also have your new testimony recorded here and in the presence of Sergeant Huang and me. One small lapse in memory is possible, but not so many lapses in both of your statements. Definitely not. It's up to the police to decide whether this amounts to perjury or not. Right, Sergeant Huang?"

"If this isn't perjury, I don't know what it is," Huang said.

Instead of responding immediately, she kept staring at them like a melting snowwoman, her eyes like two black coal balls.

She'd been caught lying, trapped in the very act of it. Huang tried to think of all the possible scenarios. Out of all of them, if she kept insisting that it was just memory lapse, she might still get away with it. After all, leaving through the back door didn't have to mean going to Liu's home office. Huang guessed there was no security camera there. There were no witnesses or evidence against her. No motive, either.

What's more, Internal Security could simply brush aside the scenario of her and a co-conspirator being the real culprits, since they had already reached their own conclusion and were ready to convict Jiang.

The silence weighed on all of them like a huge rock.

So what was Chief Inspector Chen going to do?

"Fu wasn't in Wuxi over the weekend, was he?" Chen said unexpectedly, changing the topic.

This was another thrust that left Huang perplexed. Why was Chen bringing Fu in at this critical juncture?

"Yes, he was in Shanghai for a business meeting."

"He was in Shanghai, that much is true, but I'm not at all sure about the business meeting part. I happen to have some pictures taken there last Saturday, the day before yesterday."

Chen produced a large envelope containing a bunch of enlarged pictures. The first two or three pictures showed Fu and a young woman emerging from a hotel onto a street thronged with people. Then photos of the two walking, hand in hand, with the hotel visible in the background, and one of them showing the two kissing passionately, regardless of the passers-by. The pictures weren't of high quality, but Fu was recognizable and the girl was someone Huang had never seen before. The last photo Chen brought out was of a large sign standing in front of the hotel.

"Look at this sign. This so-called hotel rents rooms by the hour," Chen said with emphasis on "by the hour," handing the picture to her. "On Nanjing Road. Who would go to such a hotel with him?"

"A prostitute?" Huang said.

The picture began trembling in Mi's hand.

"No, she's not one of those girls soliciting customers on Nanjing Road. That much I can tell you, Mi. She's his fiancée. The cop in his old neighborhood in Shanghai has confirmed that. Fu has kept his relationship with her a secret here at the company. Why would he do that, Mi? You know better than anybody else, I would think. Anyway, that Saturday afternoon in Shanghai, Fu and his fiancée sneaked into that sleazy hotel, where they stayed for more than two hours. What were they doing there? You can easily imagine that. Here's a picture of them leaving the hotel. Look at the happy, radiant smile on her face. There's a young attendant—you can see here—who stands at the hotel door, shouting, 'Clean, convenient, we change the sheets after every customer. Hot showers twenty-four hours. Mandarin Duck Bath . . . Worth every penny. Fifteen minutes in the spring valance is worth tons of gold.'"

It was astounding that Chen chose to launch into this vivid narrative at this juncture, almost like a Suzhou opera singer who got carried away by the details of the story he was narrating.

"That's so dramatic," Huang improvised.

"For everything under the sun, Sergeant Huang, there must be a reason. A reason may be inexplicable to others, but so transparent to the man or the woman involved in it."

Again, Chen didn't push further. Instead he spread those pictures on the table like a mosaic.

"Take a good look at them. And think really hard about it, Mi. No one else knows about our conversation. Not yet, anyway. Officer Huang is my loyal assistant, so you don't have to worry about him"

"What do you want exactly, Chief Inspector Chen?"

"All of this must have come as an overwhelming surprise to you," Chen said, looking at his wristwatch. "Sergeant Huang and I are going to have lunch at the center canteen. So you may take your time thinking things through. It wouldn't be a good idea for you to leave, but if you want anything for lunch, I can bring it back for you."

"Our chief inspector is a very considerate man," Huang said.

"When I come back, I think we'll have a good talk. I may be able to do something for you. I hate to see a beauty like you punished for what you haven't done."

Chen picked up his business card and added a number on it. "It's my cell number. Call me any time you think of something."

Pushing the card over to her, Chen stood up quickly and Huang followed suit. The sudden exit for lunch was just the latest in surprises for the young cop.

Mi was already visibly shaken, and she might have collapsed if Chen had continued to build up the pressure.

"But why, Chief Inspector Chen?" she repeated, unable to control an involuntary twitch at the corner of her mouth.

"You are a clever woman, Mi," Chen said, looking over his shoulder before he stepped out the door with Huang. "Use your brains. And you can find out for yourself whether what I've told you is true."

TWENTY-TWO

CHEN WALKED OUT OF the villa with Huang.

Instead of to the center canteen as he had told Mi, however, he led Huang around to a small bamboo grove close to the foot of the wooded hill, where they had a partial view of the white villa through the green bamboo. They seated themselves on rocks, around which patches of new tender bamboo shoots appeared golden in the sunlight.

"The center is a nice place, isn't it?" Chen said, reading the question in Huang's eyes. "Don't worry, Huang. I don't think she'll attempt to sneak out. Nor will the guard let her."

"How did you come to suspect her, Chief Inspector Chen?"

"Remember our discussion at the crime scene? That was the first time I started to have questions about her."

"Yes, you made several good points about the crime scene, but you didn't mention her at all."

"I wasn't sure about those questions. Internal Security then came up with their scenario, so I tried to fit Jiang into it, but without success. I was confounded by the lack of any sign of struggle at the crime scene. It appeared as though Liu had been killed, peacefully, in his sleep. Of course, there's no ruling out the possibility that Liu was asleep, given the time of night. But according to the scenario put forward by Internal Security, Liu was supposed to have had a serious showdown with a blackmailer. How could Liu have fallen asleep? And if so, how could Jiang have gotten in?"

"But for the sake of argument, what about Jiang sneaking in after Liu happened to leave the door open—" Huang didn't finish the sentence, as it sounded like too many coincidences even to himself.

"Even in that scenario, the killing would have happened after the argument—after they confronted each other, not before."

"No, not before."

"Then another related detail came to my attention. Mi mentioned that Liu had trouble falling asleep, so he took sleeping pills. This was confirmed by the autopsy report. I checked with Mrs. Liu, who said he took them occasionally. Then I looked more closely into it, and I found something else that was incomprehensible. According to the autopsy and the estimated time of Liu's death, which was nine thirty to ten thirty in the evening, he had to have taken the pills before then. But I couldn't imagine that he would have taken sleeping pills prior to Jiang's arrival or while he was there."

"That's a brilliant deduction, Chief."

"Now let's leave these questions aside and go back and follow the scenario maintained by Internal Security a bit further. Liu didn't have any evidence to prove that Jiang had tried to blackmail him—there was nothing in the folder provided by Internal Security. So it would have been his word against Jiang's. On the other hand, Jiang had all the research to back up his claims, as well as his media connections. Was Liu going to take a risk by letting Jiang go public with his information? It was a critical moment for Liu and his IPO plan. Once word about the company's disastrous pollution problem had spread, the local authorities would have been under pressure to investigate the accusations. And that would have totally ruined their business prospects."

"That's true. Liu was too shrewd a businessman."

"But back to the initial questions concerning Mi—or, I should say, some passing thoughts about a possibility that occurred to me at the crime scene," Chen said, fingering the pointed tip of a bamboo shoot at his foot. "With Internal Security's theory practically crossed out, I began to think in a totally different direction. What if Liu was already asleep or unconscious when the murderer struck? That could explain lots of things, but at the same time it led to another question. Who could have gotten into the room when Liu was sleeping? Or a variation of that question, who could have made Liu fall asleep and then delivered the fatal blow? Or instead, who could have then left the scene, with the door unlocked, for another to come along later?

"Given the force of the blow and the amount of sedative in Liu's system as estimated in the autopsy report, I was more inclined to this second scenario. But whatever the actual circumstances, these all pointed to one person. Someone very close to him, even intimate with him, and familiar with his whereabouts that evening."

"Mi, the little secretary," Huang said. "The only one who could have had access to that place at night and wouldn't have aroused suspicion. She could have given Liu a handful of sleeping pills in a drink, I would imagine."

"And here's the blind spot. Everybody knew Mi was his little secretary. She was nothing without him, only a massage girl originally from a so-called hair salon. Why would she murder him? As a materialistic girl, she knew better. She would be the last one to be suspected of his murder.

"Another stumbling block to those other possible scenarios is her alibi. Mi has a solid alibi for her whereabouts that evening, one provided by Fu. Of course, in turn she provided an alibi for Fu, as well."

"Chief, apparently I'm the dumbest of the dumb sidekicks, like the ones in the mysteries you translate. All along, I thought you were targeting Mrs. Liu."

"I was, and for quite a while too. In fact, Mrs. Liu also satisfied the necessary criteria of the scenarios I was working with. For that reason alone, she had to be included as a suspect with the means and a possible motive, considering Liu's infidelity. Furthermore, her frequent trips to Shanghai—two trips over one weekend—were naturally a bit suspicious. The question for me then was: Why now? She must have known about Liu's affairs for quite some time. Why kill him now? So I contacted Liu's attorney, from whom I learned that Liu had had no plans to divorce his wife. Other sources said the same thing. On the contrary, with their son coming back to Wuxi, the family seemed to be far from falling apart. Still, there were things I found puzzling about her, like her frequent trips back to Shanghai. So I decided to look deeper into it, and it was in the course of it that something else occurred to me."

"What?"

"Mrs. Liu used to be the 'queen' back in school. Could someone be after her even today? You might say that she's no longer young, but I once had a case where a successful Big Buck was chasing after a 'loyal character dancer' twenty years later, despite the fact that she'd been crushed by life—a haggard, sallow, middle-aged peasant with her beauty utterly ravaged. It's not impossible that there was an old suitor after Mrs. Liu, however implausible it might seem after all these years. It would explain why she endured Liu's affairs and why she went back to Shanghai so frequently. Thanks to the great efforts made by Detective Yu and his wife Peiqin, I was able to see that I was on the wrong track."

"So Detective Yu has been working along with you?" Huang asked, cutting in.

"No. I asked him to check into Mrs. Liu's Shanghai background. That's about it. Indeed, people are complicated. They are capable of doing things that seem totally inexplicable to others, hence suspicious, but once you manage to see it from their perspective, it all makes perfect sense. That's another story, of course," Chen said, glancing up toward the closed window of the villa. "But excluding a possible change in Liu's family life meant there was another probability: Mi would remain a little secretary indefinitely."

"I've never thought about that, Chief. But a girl like Mi might not necessarily see herself as the potential second Mrs. Liu. As long as Liu provided well for her, she might be content. She's still young and capable of saving a considerable sum over the next few years. Then she could start a new life for herself somewhere else and with somebody else too."

"That might be true. But there are some others factors to take into consideration. To begin with, she might not be able to take her position for granted, what with Liu's son joining the company—"

"His son was starting at the company? I'd heard he'd had an internship there last summer."

"It was all in Liu's plan. Eventually, the company would go to his son, so you can imagine what that could have meant to Mi. And then there was another indirect factor—the IPO, which affected Mi through a long complicated chain of links, particularly through one hidden link with Fu. Incidentally, your efforts to identify those who might suffer as a result of the IPO are what inspired me."

"I'm utterly confounded," Huang said. "How did you bring Fu into the picture?"

"Well, you focused on business rivals who might gain from Liu's death. I moved along a similar line, only keeping my focus on the people inside, not outside, the company. With the IPO, the company's general manager would get the largest number of shares. The high-level executives, too, would gain tremendously. What made the situation complicated was the restructuring plan to be put in place prior to the IPO. Liu was able to do anything, including fire anyone, in the name of restructuring. Those that were fired under the restructuring plan would suffer a huge loss—they would get no shares whatsoever.

"I should have seen it much sooner, but I wasn't paying attention to it until I stumbled upon the date issue in Mi's statement, which I then realized was confirmed by none other than Fu. Now, it's possible for one person to make a mistake, but not for two to make the same mistake. What's more, according to my source, Jiang didn't ever come to the company offices in the month of March."

"So both Mi and Fu lied about Jiang in their statements!"

"Exactly. And they also supported each other's alibi for the night of Liu's murder. That was when the various pieces began to come together: the alibi, the statement, and then, of course, Fu's effort to keep secret his fiancée in Shanghai. He had reason to do so."

"Yes, again it's like those stories you translate. The clues are all there, but it takes a master to connect them," Huang said, rubbing his hands in undisguised excitement. "Why wait any longer, Chief? Let's arrest her. It will be easy to crack a woman like her."

"Let's wait a little longer. There's no hurry, Huang. As the old proverb says, we'll flush out the snake by striking at the weeds around—"

Chen's cell phone rang. Flipping it open, he listened intently, saying only a few words now and then in response.

Huang waited beside him, watching the dazzling white villa that stood on the hill like a castle in a fairy tale, wondering whether he himself was also in a story. The windows shimmered in the light.

"That was about the phone call Mi has just made to Fu from the villa," Chen said, closing the phone. "It's all recorded."

"You had her cell phone bugged?"

"Yes. I didn't have time to discuss it with you. Sorry about that, Huang. It wasn't until yesterday afternoon that I pieced it all together, and I had to act at once. I had her cell phone tapped through a connection of mine—or a connection of a connection, you might say. Also, I had to have those pictures developed in a rush."

"You've moved fast, Chief."

It was true that Chen didn't have the time. But more importantly, Chen didn't say, he knew how Internal Security would have reacted if they had learned about his secret maneuvering.

"Well, to briefly summarize her hysterical phone conversation, she accused Fu of deceiving her, of using her to get rid of Liu, and of landing her in trouble. She was shouting, cursing, and weeping at the same time. It was pretty much as I had guessed."

"What did he say?"

"Not much. First he said she's crazy, then he wanted her to calm down and not blabber anymore."

"But we should be able to tie things up now. That phone call, along with the perjury, is undeniable evidence." Huang added, "I have just one question—how did the two of them get together?"

"The phone call only proves their relationship; it doesn't establish that they collaborated in murder. As for the two getting together, here's what I've gathered from various sources, with some guesswork here and there to fill in the blank spots."

Chen lit a cigarette before going on.

"They joined forces for a variety of reasons, each out of their own self-interest.

"For her, it came out of her disappointment with Liu. She'd hoped to get more out of the affair than just the position of a little secretary. Another girl in her shoes might have been content, as you said, but she dreamed of becoming Mrs. Liu and living happily ever after. At one point, Liu might have made her some promises, which she later found he had no intention of carrying out. When she learned that his son Wenliang would be joining the company as his eventual successor, it was the last straw for her.

"For Fu, it was another story. To begin with, he had always been an outsider in the company. Assigned to the job as a Youth League cadre, he failed to develop enough connections to become a rival to Liu. With the reform in the state-ownership system, Liu began to contemplate the prospect of turning the state-run company into a privately held one for himself and for his family. His son, rather than an outsider like Fu, would succeed him as general manager. It didn't take long for Fu to find out, and the pressure was mounting.

"So Fu and Mi got together. For her, Fu was not only younger, but single too. In other words, he could make her Mrs. Fu eventually. In return, she provided information crucial to his power struggle against Liu. Such an important ally didn't come without a price. He had to convince her that he was serious about pursuing a relationship. Consequently, it was out of the question for Mi to know anything about his fiancée in Shanghai. That accounts for his stealthy behavior at the hourly hotel last Saturday. With the restructuring plan looming over him, his counterplan had to develop fast—"

"You mean the murder plot?" Huang asked. "Was she aware of it all along?"

"She might have guessed something was up. Liu was working on the restructuring plan, but without letting Mi in on the details, which bespoke his lack of trust in her. According to some people who worked there, Liu didn't even keep a copy of the confidential document at the company office. The only copy was in the home office, in a safe-deposit box to which he alone had the key. That night, however, Mi found out that he was going to work on the restructuring plan at his home office. She must have told Fu, thinking that it might be an opportunity for her to steal a look at the document. For Fu, a quick look wouldn't be enough. Fu wanted to find out the details of the plan, and to do that, he had to go there himself. The two conspirators didn't have to poke through the window paper, so to speak. They knew what they had to do. Anyway, Mi was there with Liu that evening and made sure that he had taken the document out of the safe deposit box before she drugged him with a handful of sleeping pills. Fu's original plan might have been what he had told her, but once he was at Liu's home office, he changed his mind. After all, it was in his best interest to get rid of Liu once and for all. With Liu gone, the restructuring plan would disappear as well. If anything, it would then become Fu's company, and he could write his own restructuring plan.

"When Liu was found dead the next morning, Mi knew what had happened the night before. But she was already an accomplice to murder and in no position to say anything against Fu. In fact, to protect herself, she had to cooperate further with Fu. She was totally trapped. Each providing an alibi for the other was the only way out for both of them.

"Jiang happened to be a politically convenient target for Internal Security, so they naturally played along, providing the 'information' that Internal Security was eager to snatch up."

"What a master stroke, Chief Inspector Chen! Because of the pending IPO, it was common for people to work late on a Sunday evening, so it didn't seem unusual for both Fu and Mi to claim to have been there. Your analysis puts everything into a new perspective."

"It's more a stroke of luck," Chen said, "considering all the false clues I've pursued. Besides, if she hadn't made that phone call, we would have had nothing more than circumstantial evidence, not enough to convince Internal Security or the local police."

"Just one more question, Chief. How did you get those pictures of Fu in Shanghai? They absolutely crushed her."

"I asked Detective Yu to look into Mrs. Liu's Shanghai background and in passing, I mentioned Fu as well. I didn't really suspect something, not at the time. Perhaps subconsciously, but not consciously. I was just curious because, like Mrs. Liu, Fu made frequent trips back to Shanghai. Remember what Fu said to us? 'I went back last Saturday, and I'm going there again this weekend.' The last few weeks have been a hectic period for the company, so why was he taking the time to go back to Shanghai? That morning, I also had a feeling that Fu was trying to cut short our conversation with Mi. Anyway, Yu and Peiqin went out of their way to follow Fu around Shanghai for hours. And it was truly a random harvest. But for their help, and of course your help as well, the various pieces wouldn't have been connected.

"Now, time for action, Huang," Chen concluded, getting to his feet. "I am going back in to Mi, and you are going to see Fu. Like the old proverb says, there may be too many dreams for a long night."

"Yes, we have to act before Internal Security can put up more hurdles, interfering with the investigation in the name of the Party's interests. I'll get the search warrants for both of them—"

"Yes, have Fu's place searched thoroughly, and quickly, before he can do anything there."

"I know what to do, Chief. His apartment isn't large, and I'll dig three meters deep into the ground." He added in mounting excitement, "You've mentioned the restructuring plan Liu was working on that night. Indeed, Liu wouldn't have been sitting at the desk without something in front of him. But we have never found it. Nor has Mi mentioned it as something possibly missing. Now I see why."

"The restructuring plan, among the other things—"

Huang's cell phone suddenly rang with a different tone. It was a text message from the head of the special team. Huang showed the message to Chen.

"Jiang will be sent to prison tomorrow, officially charged as the murderer in Liu's case. Who's the man interviewing at the chemical company with you? Internal Security asked."

"Good timing," Huang said with a grin. He didn't write a response to the text. "Don't worry, Chief. We'll beat them this time. I'll bring my notebook along with me and follow all the points you raised at the crime scene."

"When you're there with your team, try to leave me out of the picture. It's your investigation, not mine."

"But how can I do that?" Huang said, shaking his head. "They've already raised the question."

"Try your best, Huang."

TWENTY-THREE

CHIEF INSPECTOR CHEN WOKE up with a lingering hangover.

He sat up, pressing a finger to his temple as he looked out the window. The lake appeared to be still enveloped in mist. Occasionally, a lonely bird could be heard chirping among the trees.

Instead of waiting for breakfast to be delivered to his room, Chen got up and brewed himself a pot of strong black coffee. The previous day had been very hectic, he recalled as he took a slow sip at the fresh coffee.

Shortly after their parting at the bamboo groove, Huang returned to the villa with a couple of local police officers to get Mi off his hands. Instead of rushing straight to the chemical company, Huang phoned his team and had them hold Fu at the office. With Fu unable to return to his apartment, Huang searched it thoroughly even before he obtained a warrant. Huang's surprise move really helped Chen, as Mi had been wailing, crying, and screaming there, her face streaked with tears and mucus, but not saying anything useful. Chen heaved a sigh of relief when she was lead away in handcuffs.

But his peace was short-lived. The chief inspector was soon swamped by phone calls from the Wuxi Police Bureau, Internal Security, the Wuxi city government, and the local journalists. Not all of them seeemed pleased at the surprising turn of the investigation.

There was only one thing the calls had in common. Everyone complained that Chief Inspector Chen should have contacted them earlier, despite his assurances that all he wanted was a quiet vacation in Wuxi.

Chen's assurances didn't sound convincing, not even to himself. After all, the arrest was made at his villa, so he felt obliged to provide some explanations here and there. And that was turning into a terrible headache.

To his surprise, Wanyi, one of the top Party cadres in Wuxi, called him at the center. Wanyi was effusive about Chen's connection to Comrade Secretary Zhao and outlined a plan to entertain Chen in two days on behalf of the city government. Chen had to stall him by claiming to be waiting on some instructions from Comrade Secretary Zhao.

He had hardly finished speaking with Wanyi when Director Qiao burst in. His host insisted on dragging him to a celebration dinner, despite knowing little about the latest developments. Chen agreed readily, taking it as an acceptable excuse to turn off his cell phone. The people at the center had been so helpful that it was the least he could do to acknowledge it. Besides, there was nothing else for him to do. The Wuxi police took over the work, and while he was inundated with official phone calls, the one call he really wanted was the one he didn't expect to get. Shanshan had kept her phone turned off.

It turned out to be an enjoyable meal. For once, he let himself go and behaved like a tourist—eating, drinking, and relishing the moment. He realized it was probably the tail end of his vacation here. Qiao and his colleagues vied with one another as they toasted him at the banquet. Once again, the center was in the headlines, at least locally, for which they were grateful.

As a result, it was quite late at night when he returned to his room, with unsteady steps and the unmistakable onslaught of a coming headache. There was still no message from Shanshan when he checked the phone for the last time before going to bed.

Now, suffering a terrible hangover the next morning, squinting his eyes in the glaring light, he thought there wasn't anything he could really complain about. He reminded himself, gulping strong black coffee, that it would be another busy day. He couldn't afford to relax and recuperate like a real high-ranking cadre.

He turned on his cell phone and checked his messages. Still nothing from Shanshan, though plenty from local cadres and several from Huang. But he decided not to return Huang's call just yet. The sergeant was busy working on the remaining details of the case with his colleagues, and Chen, as he had said to so many, was on vacation.

He had just finished his first cup of coffee when the doorbell rang. The unexpected visitor standing in the doorway was Tian Zhonghua, a heavily built man in his early fifties with gray eyebrows and a sturdy jaw. He was the head of the Wuxi Police Bureau, and Chen had met him before at conferences.

"You should have told us about your vacation here, Chen," Tian said, stepping in to the foyer without waiting for an invitation. "How could you have come here and investigated a case with Sergeant Huang in secret?"

"Oh no, don't be upset with me, Superintendent Tian. Huang is a friend of Detective Yu's. That's why we got together. I came here on a vacation that was pushed onto me, and I had nothing to do here. So I couldn't help talking to him about the case. The credit for bringing it to a successful conclusion is really all his."

Huang might not have been able to take all the credit himself, so Chen decided not to say anything unnecessary.

"I understand, Chief Inspector Chen, but Internal Security doesn't. They are certain that I was aware of your investigation all along."

"Sorry, Tian. I apologize for that. But please tell me about the latest developments in the case."

"We've arrested them. It's only a matter of time before Fu and Mi make a full confession."

"What about Jiang?"

"He's been cleared of the murder charge, but the blackmail charge is going to stick—it has to. Internal Security has made a point of it. He hadn't been officially charged in the murder case, but it was known to a lot of people that he had been taken into custody. If we let him get away scot-free, he'll surely blab to the Western media about being persecuted because of his fight for the environment," Tian said, then added, as if in afterthought, "Of course, he did blackmail some people, and he should be punished for it."

"Frankly, I don't think the statements made against him are that reliable. They were made by people looking to protect their own business interests. That should be taken into consideration."

"As the head of the Wuxi police, I looked into it. Yes, it's his word against theirs. However, some of them did pay him a large amount as a consulting fee. We have evidence of those payments, which he doesn't deny. So we are justified in drawing the conclusion that these were acts of blackmail. Remember, apart from the money he got for the articles he sold to the Western media, he had no other income for several years. A monetary motive is often the most common, compelling motive.

"Besides, there's no denying that Jiang is an inveterate troublemaker. Chinese people should be able to tell the difference between what's appropriate to discuss with the proper insiders and what one can discuss with outsiders. But not so with him. With no real qualifications as an environmentalist, he hues and cries in an irresponsible way, all for the benefit of the Western media and for himself. What's the point of all that muckraking? According to one American newspaper, some politicians have even mentioned him as a possible candidate for a Nobel prize. For what? The answer is self-evident, you see. This all comes at the expense of our government's image. This will be a necessary lesson for him."

"But the problems he exposed are nonetheless real problems that we can't afford to ignore, Superintendent Tian."

"We're taking care of the problems, Comrade Chief Inspector Chen. China's economic reform is achieving unprecedented success, but it may take some time to solve the problems that arise in its wake. Ask people here in Wuxi whether their lives have improved in the last twenty years, and I don't think you'll have to wait long for an answer."

It would be useless to argue further with Tian. Tian had a much higher cadre rank than his and Chen had just claimed he was only here on vacation. He had no right whatsoever to question the way the local police were handling the case. They then steered the conversation away from the political factors behind the murder case, as if having reached a tacit understanding. *What cannot be said must pass over in silence.*

Not long after Tian left, Chen received a phone call from Sergeant Huang.

"I've called you many times since yesterday, Chief, but your cell phone was turned off."

"Sorry, I was overwhelmed by official phone calls so I turned it off. Anyway, the investigation is now up to you and your colleagues." He went on in spite of himself, "How are things going with Fu and Mi?"

"Mi remains hysterical, but she's slowly giving in. Don't worry about it," Huang said with a reassuring chuckle. "My colleagues are working on Fu, and I'm at his apartment again, this time with an official search warrant. I did a thorough job yesterday, but I didn't find a copy of the restructuring plan."

"He might have destroyed it," Chen said after a pause, "But I think there may be something else there."

"What?"

"For what happened at Liu's place that night, there're two possible explanations. One is that Fu had planned to murder Liu all along. But the other is that he made up his mind when he got there. If the murder was unpremeditated, then the perpetrator picked up something at the apartment to use as the murder weapon and took it with him afterward."

"The missing murder weapon? Yes, you talked about some possible items when we were at the crime scene. Let me check my notebook—"

246

"After our discussion at the crime scene," Chen went on without waiting for him to check, "I examined the picture of Liu and his son that was taken last summer. There are nine statuettes in the background. That statuette is an annual award given at the end of the year, but in the pictures taken by your colleagues last week, there are still only nine statuettes. It might mean that Liu didn't get one for the last year. But I talked to his son Wenliang the day before yesterday, and he mentioned that there should be ten statuettes because the company had won the award ten years in a row. Several months after their picture was taken, Liu told Wenliang specifically about winning another statuette."

"Ah, it's in the notebook. Nine of them," Huang said, checking through his notes. "So one statuette is definitely missing, and they are really heavy—"

"But Fu could have dumped it somewhere else. We can't rule out that possibility, Huang."

"I'll start all over again. The statuette is taller than a beer bottle. His room isn't large, practically a dorm room—" said Huang, then he paused and suddenly switched topics. "Oh, I almost forgot. Shanshan contacted me for help, Chief. She asked for permission to see Jiang before he is sent to prison. It is against regulations, but she says that she knows you."

"She does and of course, you may help her. What harm would it cause? You can make arrangements for her, can't you?"

"So you think it would be okay?" Huang asked, not even trying to conceal the surprise in his voice.

"It's not really my concern. It's up to the Wuxi Police Bureau, but I don't see any reason why she shouldn't be allowed to visit him."

"I've thought about it, Chief. He's being transferred tomorrow. I may have the police car pull up outside the bureau briefly while I go to buy a pack of cigarettes at a grocery nearby. She can walk over to the car and talk to him through the window for a couple of minutes. I think that's about all I can do."

"That's good," Chen said. He knew why Huang tried to ask permission, and he could picture the puzzled look on the young cop's face.

"Well—"

"When, Huang?"

"What?

"Her meeting with him?"

"Around noon, that's the time the police car will leave the bureau."

"Help her, Huang. Do it as a favor to me—"

The cell phone then indicated another call coming in. "Sorry, I've got another phone call. I'll call you back," he said before he found out the call was from Comrade Secretary Zhao in Beijing.

"You haven't really relaxed during your vacation, Comrade Chief Inspector Chen."

"You know me, Comrade Secretary Zhao. Being a cop may be my lot in life, but I have truly enjoyed this vacation at the center."

"Some people have complained to me about your having conducted a secret investigation while in Wuxi. I told them that you don't have to let everybody know what you're doing, and in fact, that you were doing some research there, per my instructions."

Once again, Zhao was being supportive, for which Chen was grateful. It might be a good opportunity, he thought, to speak to the influential Party leader about the environmental issues.

"Yes, I wanted to talk to you about something. I've followed your instructions, and kept my eyes open for any problems in China's great reform. The cadre center is located by the celebrated Tai Lake, which is now terribly polluted. I focused my research on issues of the environment. It seems to me that the problem isn't just about one particular lake, or one specific company. Pollution is so widespread that it's a problem all over China. To some extent, it's affecting the core of China's development with GDP-centered economic growth coming at the expense of the environment. It can't go on like this, Comrade Secretary Zhao. Our economy should have a sustainable development."

He then launched into a detailed account of his research, making good use of what he had learned—mainly from Shanshan—in the last few days. Zhao listened without interruption. Toward the end of his report, Chen added cautiously, "In the course of my research, I happened to look into a case related to environmental issues—"

"I knew you would come to that, Comrade Chief Inspector Chen. Go ahead, but you don't have to give me all the details. I'm not a cop."

Chen briefed Zhao about the facts of the case before he made his plea.

"Jiang has been cleared of the murder charge, but he'll still be convicted. Now, I've witnessed firsthand the disastrous damage caused by pollution. An environmental activist should not be punished for his efforts to solve this problem."

"I'm pleased to learn that you are concerned about environmental issues, Comrade Chief Inspector Chen," Zhao said, his voice distinct over the line from Beijing. "We aren't going to leave a polluted lake to our children. And our economy should definitely follow a pattern of sustainable development. I cannot agree more with all of this. There will be a politburo meeting here next week. I'm retired, but I'm still going to attend the meeting and raise this issue. Turn your report in to me as soon as possible. I may use some of the figures in it.

"As for Jiang, it's not up to me to look into a specific case, as you know. For an emerging cadre like you, it's necessary to keep a larger picture in mind—it's not just about one case, or about one person. You've done a good job as a capable police inspector, and as a conscientious Party member too, but you also have to keep the perspective of the local authorities in mind. Their worries may not be totally unjustified."

"But—"

"No *but,* Comrade Chief Inspector Chen. You have a lot of work waiting for you back in Shanghai. A retired old Party member, I, too, have my responsibilities."

That was an unmistakable signal that their talk had ended. And also that Chen's vacation in Wuxi was at an end.

In the distance, he heard the cries of a wild goose flying alone across the lake.

There was no point in his staying at the center any longer. He had done what he could, and he now had to finish the report for Comrade Secretary Zhao. Still, there were things for him to wrap up here.

He had to see Shanshan before leaving. She'd been avoiding him since that night, but he was going to say good-bye to her and tell her that he would come back. What else he could say? He didn't know. He hadn't yet revealed that he was a cop—one that worked in the system and for the system—but she probably had guessed as much.

He went back to the bedroom, where he stood with his hand on the frame of the window overlooking the lake. There was a lone sail drifting across the lake, moving past an islet enclosed in something like white duckweed. He looked at his watch and made up his mind.

There wasn't much for him to pack, and in less than fifteen minutes, he was ready. He then took another look at the empty room, finished the herbal medicine in the tiny thermos bottle, and left carrying his small piece of luggage.

At the front desk, he returned the key to the same receptionist who had greeted him on the day he arrived. Now she was smiling up at him with admiration in her eyes, when Director Qiao hurried over.

"No, you can't leave so soon, Chief Inspector Chen," Qiao said, with sincerity etched on his face. "It's only been a week."

"I really appreciate all that you've done for me here, Director Qiao. But I have to leave and—between you and me—I'll tell you why. I have to finish a report that Comrade Secretary Zhao needs for an important meeting in Beijing. The center is a fantastic place, but with all the buzz about the murder, I can't concentrate on my report anymore."

"I understand, but at least let's have a farewell banquet—"

They were interrupted by a young boy approaching them nervously, holding an envelope in his hands.

"Are you Mr. Chen?"

"Yes, I am."

"Here's a letter for you. Confidential. You need to sign the special delivery receipt for me."

It was a new sort of business in Chinese cities. Instead of sending things through the post office, people used a service for intra-city delivery. With one phone call, a letter or package would be delivered in a couple of hours. The only equipment the business needed was a bicycle or a motorcycle. Chen had no idea who would have arranged for such a special delivery to him.

"Thank you." He signed his name on a form and took the letter, then turned back to Qiao without opening it. "I'll come back as soon as I can, Director Qiao. Let me take a rain check on your invitation."

"Then let the center's car take you to the station."

"That I gratefully accept, Director Qiao."

He walked out of the center's office and a shiny black limousine was waiting for him outside. The limousine driver, a short, middle-aged man with a receding hairline, said in a respectful tone, "Railway station, sir?"

"No, let's go to the Wuxi Police Station."

TWENTY-FOUR

TWENTY MINUTES LATER, THE limousine drove up to the Wuxi
Police Bureau, which was located at the center of the city. It was a
sprawling concrete complex with a shining vertical sign in the front of
the main building and a gray iron gate on the side. Two armed cops
guarded the entrance.

"Do you want to drive in?" the driver asked, glancing first at the
gate and then over his shoulder.

"No, I'll get out here. Right here—not in front of the bureau,
please."

"Whatever you say," the driver said without trying to conceal the
puzzled look on his face.

"You may go back to the center," Chen said. "I'll take a taxi to the
railway station when I'm done here."

"There're several trains to Shanghai today," the driver said good-
naturedly. "Don't worry about getting a ticket. You can buy one at the
train station easily—even just five minutes before the train leaves."

"Thanks, I'll do that."

It wasn't yet noon. Chen looked around for a place to sit. Across the street, he caught sight of a teahouse, which didn't exactly face the bureau but did command a good view of it. It was one of the new fashionable Hong Kong–style establishments, serving tea, as well as other drinks and snacks, with several plastic tables outside and a large pink umbrella sporting a Budweiser logo. It almost looked like an open café. He chose a table behind a willow tree.

Thinking that the local cops might frequent the place, Chen put on a pair of sunglasses. Hopefully no one would recognize him except perhaps Huang.

For a change, he had black tea, with a wedge of lemon placed on the edge of the cup. Sipping at the tea, he noticed a grocery store not far from the bureau. It was a mid-sized store that supposedly stayed open for twenty hours, where customers were constantly moving in and out, around a flowering pear tree standing near the entrance. Chen leaned back in the chair, crossing his legs.

He had made the decision to come here on the spur of the moment. With Comrade Secretary Zhao pushing for Chen's report and Shanshan refusing to accept his calls, this would probably be the only opportunity for him to see her before he left for Shanghai that afternoon.

She wanted to say good-bye to Jiang, a natural gesture to someone in trouble given her generous personality. Chen thought he understood, and if anything, it made him think even more highly of her.

Looking around, he prayed that he could get hold of her before she met with Jiang. Chief Inspector Chen wasn't going to do anything to prevent the meeting. He simply wanted to tell her that he had to leave, and that he would come back.

His cell phone vibrated. He snatched it out and answered it. It was from Sergeant Huang.

"I've called you a couple of times, Chief, but you were always on your phone."

"Sorry, I had a call from Beijing," he said, realizing that he must have been too engrossed in his talk with Zhang to notice the incoming call.

"We had a real breakthrough after I spoke with you, Chief, and it's all due to our conversation. The moment I put down the phone, I started searching Fu's place all over again. You know what? The missing statuette was there, sitting on the top shelf in the midst of some other awards and statuettes, staring me right in the eyes."

"Exactly, like in 'The Purloined Letter.' It speaks of a devilish mind."

"What?"

"That's the title of a short story by Poe."

"Then I have to read it, Chief. Still, working a case under you, I could learn far more than from ten years of reading Conan Doyle or Poe," Huang said, paraphrasing an old proverb. "Anyway, after I bagged the statuette, which was covered with his fingerprints, as well as some tiny black stains—which are Liu's blood, I bet—I went to join my team at the chemical company. They were still working on Fu, who denied everything except for his clandestine affair with Mi, saying that he had just broken it off with her, so she must be out of her mind and reacting to that. With Mi still hysterical and Fu continuing to deny everything, Internal Security actually tried to call into question the investigation's shift from Jiang. Fu might still have had a chance to get away with it, but the sight of the statuette finished him. He collapsed right then and there, and confessed everything."

"What did he say about that night?"

"He said it wasn't premeditated. Shortly after Mi went back to the company, he sneaked into Liu's apartment. Sure enough, he saw the draft of the restructuring plan on the desk, and began to copy it with a scanning pen. According to him, he wanted to get the details of the plan, so he could file a report accusing Liu of plotting to turn a state-run enterprise into a private one run by his family. But Liu unexpectedly stirred, his arm stretching out—"

"Mi might have fed him a handful of pills," Chen cut in, "but not enough to knock him totally out."

"Panic-stricken, Fu snatched a statuette up from the desk and cracked Liu's head with the heavy marble base—"

"Hold on, Huang. The statuette was on the desk, not on the shelf?"

"That's what Fu said."

"It's possible, I suppose. Liu could have had it to the desk for some reason, but it's also possible that Fu said that to make his actions seem less premeditated."

"Afterward, Fu wiped away his fingerprints from the apartment and brought the statuette back home, along with the copy of the restructuring plan and the cup with the sleeping pills from Liu's desk. He burned the document, splintered the cup and threw the pieces away, but he didn't get rid of the statuette. Apparently, he didn't think anyone would notice it in his place, or if they did, would suspect it was the murder weapon. After all, the statuette was now rightfully his, since he was going to be the new head of the company."

"What cruel karma!"

"What do you mean, Chief?"

"The award for the chemical company's success under Liu turned out to be the weapon that killed him. Now, with the company falling into Fu's hands, the statuette became the irrefutable evidence that will convict him. All from an award for increasing production and profit at the expense of the environment. Bad karma indeed."

"You always see things from a different angle, Chief."

"What about Mi?"

"Once she leaned that Fu had made a full confession, she also spilled everything. However, she insisted that she knew nothing about Fu's real plan, and that she didn't give Liu a lethal dose—just a large enough dose of sleeping pills so he would sleep heavily. She also confessed to arranging those threatening calls to Shanshan. That was Liu's idea—to use the hint of triad enforcers to silence her at the critical juncture before the IPO. He asked Mi to make the arrangements, so she paid a thug to call Shanshan from a public phone booth. When Liu died, there was no need to continue."

"No wonder Shanshan stopped receiving those phone calls," he said. "Though that's pretty much what I guessed."

"But you must have realized it was an important clue. I should have followed it all the way back."

It would be useless for Chen to explain. He'd asked Huang to check on the calls simply because of his interest in Shanshan. But to the young cop, the chief inspector must be like Sherlock Holmes, with his every move full of insight.

"Oh, I am calling from my car," Huang continued. "I'm very close to the bureau now. I'll be taking Jiang to prison from there, you know. I have to end this call, but I'll keep you updated one way or another."

"Thanks, Huang. If there's anything new, let me know."

Setting his cell phone down on the table, and then taking another sip at the tea, Chen remembered the special delivery letter he had stuffed in his jacket pocket back at the center. Wondering who could have sent it, he tapped the cigarette ash slowly into a black shell-shaped ashtray.

He took the envelope out, opened it, and upon reading it, sat up in spite of himself.

Dear Chen:

I'm writing this letter because I don't think I can bring myself to say good-bye to you. It is an ending that you and I both should have known was inevitable.

Now looking back, I think it was during the night at your place I began to make up my mind—subconsciously, as you might say. Even at our first meeting at Uncle Wang's eatery, I was aware of something different in you—that you were a man of resources and connections, but at the same time, of integrity and idealistic passion. No, I'm not saying so just for the sake of this letter. What you have done for me, especially after learning that there was something between Jiang and me, speaks volumes for you.

You've never asked any questions about it. With so many things happening around us, and so quickly, I didn't even have an opportunity to tell you more about myself. Yes, I have known Jiang for a long while. We shared a lot of common interests, as you know, and our relationship developed. You must have read the files on him—a man obsessed with his vocation as an environmentalist, to such an extent that he landed me in a mess. I was so upset, I broke up with him. That was before I met you.

Then he got into serious trouble—more serious than he bargained for. It was beyond me to do anything to help. Not for one moment, however, have I suspected him of committing the crimes he was accused of.

For the last few days, I've also been thinking a lot about him. Perhaps I was wrong about him. He must have been aware of the risks, but having made his choice, he has accepted the consequences for what he believes in. That, too, happens to be what I believe in. If I left him in the lurch, I would never be able to have any peace of mind.

Besides, he's not strong, not like you. He needs me—more than ever.

I hope you understand why I'm making this decision. Believe me, it's not an easy one. Can you do me the favor of not making it more difficult for me?

I still don't know what work you are really engaged in. No, I am not complaining. You must have your reasons. But far from being the bookish schoolteacher as you have claimed to be, you are a man with great potential in our society. You can go a long way, I'm sure, within the system.

In contrast, I'm on a political blacklist for what I have done.

You believe you can get me out of trouble, and perhaps you can. This time. If we're together, however, I may bring you no end of trouble, for which I'll never be able to forgive myself. You are "in a position"—as you sometimes say—to make a difference in today's society. You've already demonstrated as much. For your career, you don't really need me—except as a temporary companion during one of your vacations, for a short moment.

Still, the memory of that moment will go a long way for me. One of these days, I may come to pride myself on having been once close with you, being nearly the one for you, even though a voice in the back of my mind said: No, I'm not the one for you.

There's also something that may sound absurd, but it's important to me, so let me say it: even at our closest moment, I had a curious feeling that you were still thinking of something related to your work, something essential to you, but about which I know nothing.

Early that morning, I read the lines you'd written in the dark, as I lay beside you. It is a great poem, and you have to complete it—for me. You see, I'm already taking pride in being the one in your poem.

It reminded me of a favorite poem of mine. So let these lines say what I cannot say. After all, you have your destination, and I have mine, like in the poem.

A cloud in the sky, inadvertent, I cast
a shadow in the wave of your heart.
Don't be so surprised,
nor be so overjoyed—
In an instant everything is gone.

We meet on the night-covered sea;
You have your destination, and I, mine,
If you remember, that's fine,
But you'd better forget
The light produced in the meeting.

Because of the light produced in our meeting, however transitory, over the night-covered lake, can you forgive me for this upset and stay friends?

Shanshan

The poem quoted at the end of the letter was one entitled "Inadvertent," written by Xu Zhimo, a celebrated modern Chinese poet. She, too, had liked poetry in college.

To his surprise, the letter didn't surprise him that much.

She said what she could say. It explained, at least partially, her unexpected visit to him that night, and her sudden decision this morning. Also, she touched upon things he himself had been contemplating. For one, the position that enabled him to make a difference in today's society. He didn't care enormously for the "position" per se, but when looking at the situation closely, he realized that there was a responsibility in being a chief inspector. As long as he held the position, he could strive for justice and security—however small, however limited—for the people.

Was there any point in pushing for a meeting now?

Better to hold on to the image of her in that unfinished poem, in the fragmented memory of the cloud turning into the rain, and the rain into the cloud, with the lake water lapping against the night.

It was time for him to leave, he thought. He folded up the letter.

An occasional siren reverberated in the distance. It began drizzling, just a little. Still, he remained sitting at the table, an empty cup beside him, staring at the gray iron gate in spite of himself.

You're leaving, a cloud drifting away / across the river, the memories / falling like a willow catkin / to the ground, clinging, after the rain.

But was he going to give up so easily?

No, he didn't set that much store by his so-called position or career. Not if he couldn't make a difference in his own life by being with the woman he cared for.

Nor did he think that she made her decision simply because she cared for Jiang more than for him. Rather, it was in the best interests of Chief Inspector Chen, at least so she might have believed. That was why she came to his room that night, and why she let him go this morning.

The gray iron gate began to open with a loud scraping across the street.

She appeared, her face pale, her black hair streaming disheveled over a white dress, holding a plastic bag full of newly purchased food, striding hastily out of the grocery store.

It had been arranged by Huang. How long she had been in there, Chen had no idea. He didn't think she'd seen him sitting behind the tree, waiting. She was waiting as well, but not for him.

A black police van rolled out. It had barely turned to the right which it slowed to a stop close to the grocery store. Huang got out of the vehicle, waved to his colleague in the driver's seat, said something inaudible there, and headed into the store.

A window in the back of the vehicle rolled down and Shanshan hastened over in unsteady steps.

From where Chen stood, he couldn't see clearly. But she was leaning into the car, her face drawn, infinitely touching, and her bare shoulder dazzlingly white against the blaze of the transparent pear blossoms . . .

For a split second, Chen felt as if he were watching a movie, spellbound and from a distance, and the realization hit that she still cared deeply for Jiang, a fighter for a worthy cause.

The moment belonged to the two of them.

It was unthinkable for Chief Inspector Chen, who was but a spectator here, to step out from behind the scenes.

He wondered if he was worthy of this moment. It was Jiang—together with Shanshan—who was fighting, suffering, and sacrificing for the cause of the environment. Chen might have unknowingly taken advantage of the situation—sweeping her off her feet when she was lonely and vulnerable, all by herself.

It was a battle, however hard and difficult, that she wouldn't give up and in which Jiang, with the common language and interest between them, might be the ideal comrade. If she could forgive Jiang for the upset and reach out to him again in his time of need, what was Chen supposed to do?

Questions stretched on like those side streets, turning and twisting, leading him to an overwhelming question: would she ever be able to really forget about Jiang?

For the sake of argument, what was it about her being eventually won over for the chief inspector? If they were together, she'd have to change herself for his sake. A rising political star couldn't afford to have a dissident wife at his back. However "successful" he might prove to be in China's one-party system, would it be fair to expect her to be a good wife and give up the fight that meant so much to her?

Of course, Chief Inspector Chen could change himself for her sake—throwing to the wind all considerations about his career or position. But would he be a good companion for her? At the beginning of his vacation, he'd composed a couple of stanzas, playing with the idea of one's identity existing in others' interpretations. It was true, but not the whole truth. To Sergeant Huang and others, Chen was a capable cop; for all his idiosyncrasies Chen knew that he did make a difference, as he had in the present case, even if it wasn't as much as he would have liked.

In her letter, Shanshan was right about one thing. Chief Inspector Chen was in a position to do something, but probably not if he was by her side, not if he was engaged in something beyond his experience or expertise.

Huang poked his head out of the store for a couple of seconds.

"One more minute," he shouted to the van driver before he disappeared from the scene again, perhaps disinclined to break the two lovers apart that soon.

Chen thought about waiting around until the end of their meeting, but he was changing his mind. After all, what could he say after *their* meeting?

For that matter, what could she say, while still gazing after the police van receding into the dust?

He had no clue. It was too much for him to think about at the moment.

His Wuxi vacation had started abruptly, and in the same manner, it ended. *Forgetting I'm away from home, / in a dream, I was carried away / in a moment of pleasure.*

He was attempting to put the vacation behind him, recalling some lines he'd read long ago, anxious to use the ancient fragments to shore himself up against the present waste and to let the curtain fall over his conflicting impulses of struggle and flight.

Nothing can avert the final curtain's fall. A line from another poem came to him. It sounded like a far-off echo. He wondered if it could yield a clue, or a cue, to the acts being schemed around him.

Then he remembered. It was from a Russian poem about Hamlet standing alone on the stage, praying that he might be released from the cast: *To play the role to the end is not a childish task.*

The drama for the others would go on, of course.

Fu would be punished, and so would Mi, for what they had respectively done.

Mrs. Liu would continue playing mahjong, and Wenliang, studying Beijing opera with the money left to them by Liu.

But what about the lake—the polluted lake?

Whoever succeeded Liu and Fu would manage and manufacture as before—in order to keep the business competitive, profitable, and his position secure, all at the expense of the environment. The Wuxi Number One Chemical Company wouldn't be the only one doing this. Many other companies around the lake, and all over the country, would be doing the same.

The government officials at various levels, well aware of the disastrous consequences, must have acquiesced to all of this in the best interests of the Party.

As a member of the Party, and as an emerging cadre, Chief Inspector Chen could make a number of convenient points in his own defense, but for the moment, he had to quit this scene.

Chen took one step out from his cover, trying to gain another look at Shanshan, who was looking at Jiang in the police van, when he was reminded of the ending of a movie he had seen years earlier.

Toward the end, the lonely protagonist found himself, though successful in his efforts made for a just cause, letting go of his personal desire, watching his love leave with another man.

But Chief Inspector Chen wasn't the man in the movie. Not even close. He hadn't exactly succeeded at any of it, he concluded broodingly, before heading off in the direction of the train station.

He wondered whether he would be able to take a nap on the train, feeling the onslaught of a splitting headache.